"Did you fill your dan

It took the space of two secon___ ___ ___om his past to his present, and Lo___ ___w the moment he did. The lines of his face softened and his arm relaxed. "Still got some openings. Do you want me to put your name in one?" He flashed a teasing smile at her.

Or was it genuine?

Not that it mattered. She chuckled somewhat regretfully. "I think I will have my hands full with the triplets."

"You're missing all the fun." He sounded truly disappointed on her behalf, which triggered a sting of tears in her eyes.

She ducked her head lest he see how his words affected her. "I'm doing what needs to be done."

He made a musing sound that drew her gaze back to him. "I'm going to make a wild guess here and say that's the story of your life…doing what needs to be done."

* * *

Lone Star Cowboy League: Multiple Blessings

Linda Ford lives on a ranch in Alberta, Canada, near enough to the Rocky Mountains that she can enjoy them on a daily basis. She and her husband raised fourteen children—four homemade, ten adopted. She currently shares her home and life with her husband, a grown son, a live-in paraplegic client and a continual (and welcome) stream of kids, kids-in-law, grandkids and assorted friends and relatives.

Books by Linda Ford

Love Inspired Historical

Lone Star Cowboy League: Multiple Blessings

The Rancher's Surprise Triplets

Big Sky Country

Montana Cowboy Daddy
Montana Cowboy Family

Montana Cowboys

The Cowboy's Ready-Made Family
The Cowboy's Baby Bond
The Cowboy's City Girl

Christmas in Eden Valley

A Daddy for Christmas
A Baby for Christmas
A Home for Christmas

Journey West

Wagon Train Reunion

Visit the Author Profile page at Harlequin.com for more titles.

LINDA FORD

The Rancher's
Surprise Triplets

HARLEQUIN® LOVE INSPIRED® HISTORICAL

Special thanks and acknowledgment are given to Linda Ford for her contribution to the Lone Star Cowboy League: Multiple Blessings miniseries.

Recycling programs
for this product may
not exist in your area.

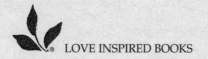

LOVE INSPIRED BOOKS

ISBN-13: 978-0-373-42518-1

The Rancher's Surprise Triplets

Copyright © 2017 by Harlequin Books S.A.

www.Harlequin.com

Printed in U.S.A.

He rescued me because he delighted in me...
It is God who arms me with strength
and keeps my way secure.
—*Psalms* 18:19, 32

To Marie. I see your struggles. I see your strength and courage. I pray God's love into your life.

Chapter One

June 1896
Little Horn, Texas

Louisa Clark pushed through the half-dozen young women to get to the counter of the store. They peered at a sign on top of the oak counter.

"A dime a dance, you say?" One of the pretty women spoke. So young and fresh looking it made Louisa, at twenty-seven, realize she was well past her prime... old enough to earn the title of "spinster." Not that it mattered to her. She was content with her life...found it immensely satisfying.

She edged between two of the young women and glanced at the sign. Dances were being sold at a dime a piece to raise money to help out the many needy families in the area. The ongoing drought left so many struggling to survive. Her heart went out to them. To be unable to care for one's family must surely be the worst feeling in the world.

"There will be a dance Saturday night to wind up

our three-day fair. Every man who wants a dance will have to pay a dime. Won't that be fun?"

She glanced toward the speaker who answered the young lady's question.

Bo Stillwater leaned back on the heels of his well-worn cowboy boots and pushed his equally well-worn cowboy hat back on his head, revealing sandy-brown hair and silvery eyes that seemed to be perpetually laughing at life. She'd met him shortly after her arrival in town and had barely been able to look directly at those eyes. He was a rancher and his twin brother was the preacher at the church next to the doctor's house.

The young ladies turned as one to cluster around the cowboy.

"What about you, Mr. Stillwater? Are you going to pay a dime to dance with each of us?" The young miss blossomed rosy pink.

Louisa felt sorry for her. Had she ever been so young and innocent? Oh, yes, there was a time she'd fancied herself in love. At eighteen she had been naive and full of dreams. She'd loved Wes and trusted that he loved her. But when things got serious enough for them to talk marriage, she had warned him they'd have to wait until Amy and Mother no longer needed her. He had responded that it sounded like she meant for him to wait most of his life. Said he wasn't willing to wait. She wasn't worth waiting for. Nine years later she sometimes wondered if she was finally worth waiting for or if she was meant to always be alone.

Enough dwelling on the past. It offered nothing but painful memories. She glanced at her work-worn hands and the dusty skirts of her dress. She had no time for fussing about her looks. What mattered the most was helping her father with his doctoring and caring for her mother.

In the three weeks they'd been in Little Horn, Texas, she'd helped Father clean the office area and examining room. He'd been seeing patients from the beginning but could now receive them in his office. Getting the rest of the house ready for Mother's arrival was next.

"I've come up with a better idea," Bo said. "I'm going to sell dances with me for a dime. That way anyone who wants to be my partner can be and it's a fine way to raise more money." He held up a piece of paper. "I have slots to fill. Anyone interested?"

The young ladies rivaled each other for the chance to pay money to dance with Mr. Bo Stillwater.

The storekeeper finally turned his attention to Louisa and she ordered the supplies she needed. She wanted more cleaning compound to get the grime off the walls of the kitchen.

"You must be scrubbing that house within an inch of its life," he commented.

"Simply doing what I can to make it ready for my mother." The house Father purchased to set up his medical practice and a home for the family was adequate for the most part. But not for an invalid like her mother. Mother needed things to be extremely clean or she'd catch something and get ill. Her weak heart put her life in jeopardy. Besides utmost cleanliness, she needed the furniture arranged in such a way she could navigate the rooms in her wheelchair. Louisa was anxious to see her mother again and smiled as she thought of how welcoming she would make the house for her and how appreciative Mother would be.

"She'll be along soon, will she?"

"I expect so. She's traveling with my sister and her husband at a more leisurely pace than my father and I took." Plus she'd be sleeping in the best accommodations available and eating in the best restaurants on their journey from Cleveland, Ohio. Father and Louisa had taken the cheapest and fastest transportation and eaten food they'd packed before leaving home. Not that she minded. It had been like a holiday to be traveling alone with her father.

"The doc seems to be doing a brisk business."

"He's been busy," she agreed. "Busy enough that on occasion we've gotten young Annie Hill to help." Annie had assisted Louisa on some of her calls to deliver babies—there'd been four since they'd come. Once the women of the community learned that Louisa was somewhat of a midwife, they had taken to calling her for help rather than bother the doctor. Annie was efficient as an assistant to Louisa when she attended a birthing. She was kind and helpful in other ways, too…such as helping to clean the house.

"Bo's doing a brisk business too." The storekeeper nodded toward the rancher, who took a dime and jotted down a name. "He's determined to bring in enough money to help all those in need, and by the looks of it, he could well succeed. Industrious young man. He'd make someone a good husband." The man's black-shoe-button eyes bored into Louisa. "Say, you aren't married, are you?"

Louisa chuckled. "I really don't see how I'd fit a husband into my already busy life."

"That a fact?" He sounded less than convinced.

"How much for the supplies?" Before she could withdraw the few coins for the storekeeper, the room grew silent and the walls sucked inward, like everyone drew in a deep breath at the same time. A footfall sounded behind her and her neck muscles twitched.

She knew without looking that Bo moved closer and she quickly gathered together her purchases and turned. He stood squarely in front of her, blocking her escape. His odd-colored eyes sent shivers through her. Her gaze darted past his shoulder to the doorway.

"What about you, Miss Clark?" His smile teased.

Six young ladies stared at her. She would not look directly at them, certain she'd see resentment that the handsome bachelor would pay her attention.

"I'm sorry." Her tongue barely functioned. "I don't understand your question."

His grin widened. "About the dance. Can I sign you up to offer dances? And would you care to pay a dime for the privilege of a dance with me?" He lifted his sheet of paper toward her. Already several lines were filled in.

No doubt her cheeks were unattractively red. She felt everyone waiting. Knew she had to say something but his question left her speechless.

She said the first thing that sprang to her mind. "I would not want to take a dance away from any of your admirers." Her purchases pressed hard to her chest, she pushed past Bo and rushed out the door. Why had she said that? She understood the dance was not without its benefits as a way to raise funds. Her answer made her sound as though she didn't care about helping the town. She did care. But between preparing for her mother's arrival and helping her father with his work, there was no time in her life for anything else.

Her life was satisfyingly full. She'd found joy in caring for her mother and making sure her younger sister, Amy, enjoyed a happy and full life despite being frail because of her too early birth. She knew it wasn't her fault Amy was born early but still she carried a burden of guilt. She'd visited a friend and brought home an infection that made Mother ill, made her deliver Amy much too early and permanently damaged Mother's already weak heart.

Bo called after her. "Surely you are going to support the—"

The door clicked shut, closing off the rest of his words.

Of course she would support the county fair. She'd contribute what she could toward the fund-raising because her heart went out to those struggling through hard times.

She would love to help the cause with just one dance with the silver-eyed Bo, but it wasn't to be.

Bo adjusted his hat as the girls around him gasped or giggled as suited their personalities. What was wrong with Miss Clark that she refused to take part in the festivities? Yes, she was a newcomer so perhaps unaware of the needs in the community. The drought affected so many of the ranchers, leaving them near destitute. There were needy widows with children in the area.

And orphans that needed care. He would like to see the young men who worked on the ranches be taught some basic schooling so they could handle their affairs better. Some could not even write their names or do more than basic counting, which left them vulnerable to being taken advantage of.

His final words to Miss Clark died before he could spit them out. *Surely you are going to support the Lone Star Cowboy League.* He was one of the founding members and deeply committed to the causes it sponsored by offering many forms of assistance to fellow ranchers. Lately, it had grown to include anyone in the community in need of aid.

Pretty little Suzanne Bachmeier, whose father owned the shoe-making business, edged closer. "I'll buy her dance." She giggled behind her hand, batting her blue eyes at him. Her blond ringlets danced with her merriment.

Her equally pretty and equally blonde sister, Nora, delicately edged her aside. "No, I will. After all, I'm older than you."

The girls elbowed each other while the rest of the young ladies protested loudly.

He held up his hands. "Now, now. Let's be fair. One dance only until Saturday night. Then if I have any spaces left, I'll…" He hadn't thought of how he'd handle the possibility but now saw what an opportunity it would be. "I'll auction off whatever dances I have left." Pleased with his solution, he tipped his hat at the young ladies and hurried from the store.

Was that Miss Clark turning the corner ahead? He'd catch up to her and explain why the league was so important to the community. He lengthened his stride, easily gaining on her.

She turned to the right. Her pace increased as she turned right again down the next street. He followed, steadily gaining on her. He had most of the block to overtake her before she reached the doctor's quarters.

But his steps slowed as he drew abreast of the black-smith shop. The two boys—Butch, fifteen, and Brady, twelve—huddled in the shadows of the building. Butch spoke low and hard. Brady's shoulders shook. The boys had lost their mother last year.

Bo remembered how that felt. He and his twin, Brandon, were sixteen when their gentle mother had died, leaving the boys under the guardianship of their cruel father. His words still rang in Bo's head. *You'll never amount to a row of beans. Too much like your mother, the both of you.*

Bo sucked in a deep breath. He would not let his father's words hurt him any longer, though they had achieved one good thing…they'd made Bo determined to prove the old man wrong and he was well on his way to doing it by becoming a successful rancher.

"Howdy," he called.

Both lads jerked toward him. Brady scrubbed at his cheeks, wiping away the evidence of a cry.

Bo's gut clenched. His fists curled. He'd never known James Forester to be a hard man, but nevertheless, these boys were having a difficult time. Their situation was different from his and Brandon's. Yet it was much the same. The loss and aloneness of death. What could he do to help them? He remembered the candy sticks he'd purchased at the store. Although he had a genuine fondness for sweets, he would gladly share them if it helped these boys forget their pain if only for a few minutes.

He pulled the little package from his pocket. "I think I bought more of these than I should have. You two care to help me reduce the number?" He took two steps toward them and showed them the array of candy.

Brady moved first and selected a red-and-white stick—peppermint. One of Bo's favorites.

Butch hung back momentarily, then grabbed the cinnamon stick. Two of Bo's favorites gone, but he selected the root-beer-flavored one and the three of them sucked at the candy.

"You boys will be coming to the fair tomorrow, won't you?" he asked.

Butch shrugged. "Pa says we're too busy." The ringing thunder of hammer against anvil bore witness to the truth of those words.

Brady scuffed the toe of his boot against a lump of dirt and said nothing.

Bo straightened. "Maybe he'll change his mind." He glanced down the street. Miss Clark had disappeared into the doctor's house. He was about to again follow after her when David McKay rode up on horseback and called to him. David, one of the three McKay brothers, had a little girl, Maggie. Bo glanced around, wondering what mischief she was up to at the moment. He didn't see the child and tried to relax.

"Bo, we're having trouble getting some of the tents to stay upright. Could you come and give a hand?"

He should have been at the fairgrounds long ago, had been headed that direction when he got sidetracked with his good idea of selling dances and then of convincing Miss Clark to join the activities. All for a good cause. "I'll be right there." He'd talk to Miss Clark later. Perhaps to James Forester, as well. Every bit of money would help, be it admission to the grounds, entry fee for the many contests to be judged, payment for a chance to participate in the many games or a dime for a dance.

He made his way to the fairgrounds, where his intentions were soon shoved aside as he confronted the many demands. He wanted this event to be successful in every way and rushed from one need to the next—helping drive in tent pegs, setting up sawhorse tables for the displays, checking to make sure the judges had everything they needed, pointing out the need to keep the area clear around the horseshoe pits. As dusk descended, people drifted away. The air filled with the gentle sounds of night—a distant owl, even more distant coyotes with their mournful song, a woman calling to a child, a fretful baby crying and the slam of doors as people returned to their homes for the night.

He wandered through the grounds and, satisfied with the setup, he retrieved his horse where it waited patiently and rode to his ranch. Dusk gave way to darkness but he didn't need light to recognize the familiar sounds of his home. The gentle lowing of cattle settling down for the night, the rustle of leaves in the breeze, the call of a duck on the nearby pond. He entered the barn, lit the lantern and took care of his horse before he made his way to the house.

His housekeeper, Mrs. Jamieson, greeted him in the kitchen. "Supper's on the stove."

"Cake for dessert, I see."

She waved him away. "That's for the cake competition tomorrow."

"You'll win the blue ribbon for sure."

She fluttered a towel at him. "I'm just an ordinary cook. You eat up. I've already eaten so I could finish the apron I'm entering in the fair." She disappeared into the sitting room to tend to her sewing.

He eyed the cake with a degree of disappointment but it was good to know Mrs. Jamieson was doing her part to support the fair. He had yet to speak to Miss Clark and persuade her to do the same.

The next morning, he left early for town. People would be coming to set up their wares, to put out their baked goods and sewing for judging. He needed to be there to make sure it all went well. He'd check on things at the fairgrounds, then go over to the doctor's house and speak to Miss Clark. The fair was going to raise a lot of money and be a great deal of fun. She ought not to miss it.

The sound of many people reached him even before he arrived at the site. Not an unpleasant sound. He sat on his horse, grinning widely. It was going to be a success. He turned aside to the spot where animals and wagons were parked for the day and left his horse there. The grounds were alive with people rushing in and out of the tents and booths, preparing for the opening. He began his tour of the grounds, checking every tent, greeting each contestant and wishing them the best. He toured the livestock area, admiring the array of horses, sheep and pigs.

A little later, satisfied that things were ready for the

opening at noon, Bo made his final stop. He stepped into the pie tent, where he would serve as one of the judges. He'd agreed to judge this competition in honor of his mother. She'd made the best peach pie. As the aroma of many pies assailed him, a flood of memories washed through him. Ma, her smile welcoming them, serving him and Brandon generous slices of pie. Father was away, so they could relax and enjoy their time around the table without fear of him coming in and turning the meal into some kind of confrontation. Father took joy in making life miserable for his wife and two sons. He criticized with cruel comments, mocked his wife and sons, and didn't hesitate to use his hands to convey his hateful attitude. Because of his father, Bo, at twenty-nine, had not married and would never do so. Only once had he come close to forgetting his vow and he would not make that mistake again. He had courted a young lady back in Boston. But it didn't work out. He'd watched Valerie berate a child who splashed mud on her and was so angry at her unkindness to the poor little boy that Bo's rage threatened to overtake him. He knew then he had too much of his father in him to ever marry and have children. Like Father had mockingly said. *Don't forget half the blood flowing through your veins is from me.*

Bo would never forget the cruel laughter following those words as if his father was happy to think of his sons living the same sort of unhappy life the elder Stillwater lived.

Instead, Bo would do what he could to make life better for others. He would judge the pies and think sweet thoughts of his ma while he did.

He turned, about to leave, when a sound caught his attention. A cry? A baby? He looked again into the interior of the tent. Row after row of pies upon long tables arranged in a U shape. He was alone in the tent. The sound must have come from a woman walking by with a baby in her arms. But the cry came again. Then a second. And the sound came from nearby. From inside the tent. How odd. His imagination must be playing tricks on him.

He shook his head and took another step toward the doorway. A third cry joined the others. His imagination had gotten very loud. Loud enough to require further investigation. Were some mischievous boys trying to trick him? If so, they were very good at imitating babies.

He went around the top of the U and down the side. The sound grew louder, more insistent. With a sudden rush forward, he rounded the corner, intending to catch the teasing culprits before they could race away. At what he saw, he ground to a halt and stared. A pushcart with deep sides and a broad bottom stood at the end of the table. Three angry little faces screwed up and wailed a protest. Three babies? Who? Where? What? He couldn't bring a single rational thought to his mind. Three pairs of feet kicked a beat to accompany their cries. The worn blue blanket covering them tangled around the chubby feet. A piece of paper lay tucked in beside the thin mattress. He pulled it out, opened it and read the words.

To the Lone Star Cowboy League: Please take care of my triplets. I'm widowed and penniless.

The ranch is dried out. I can't stay there and provide for my babies. I'm also very sick and am going to where I was born to meet my maker. One day, if you could make sure the boys knew I loved them, I'd be obliged. They were born September 30. Was the happiest day of my life.

Surely this was a mistake. A trick. He ducked down to look under the cloths covering the tables. No one. Nothing but trampled grass.

He straightened and glanced into every corner of the tent, hoping to discover someone hiding there. Nothing. What was he to do? He couldn't think over the sobbing babies.

He looked at them again, his heart breaking into three at their misery.

Jasper, Eli and *Theo*, he read on the front of their tiny shirts.

Their noses ran. The one with *Theo* on his shirt pulled at his ears. Little Eli had bright red cheeks. He touched those cheeks. Hot. He touched the cheeks of the other two. Hot, as well. He was no expert on babies but he guessed they were sick. He'd take them to the doctor and then find the mother. *Please, God, keep her safe until we locate her.*

The Lone Star Cowboy League could help this poor mother and her babies.

Chapter Two

Louisa brushed her flyaway brown hair back and braided it. Hopefully it would stay secure for a few hours. She glanced about the rooms of their new abode. The front room was spacious with windows providing a view of the street. She'd arranged the furniture so Mother could sit with her reading and handiwork close at hand and be able to watch the activity out the window. Seeing people scurrying about their business would help her hours to pass swiftly.

Louisa pressed back a rush of guilt. This room was ready, but the bedroom to the right needed more work before Mother came, and the kitchen needed even more cleaning. She should stay home and tend to her work, but all morning she'd watched people rushing down the street all in the same direction…toward the fairgrounds west of town in an open field. The June day was sunny and warm, the windows open to let in the air and sounds carried from the fairgrounds—the hum of voices, the moo, baa or whinny of animals, the occasional discordant musical note as if someone tuned up a violin. Too early for the dance but the billboard said there would be musical entertainment throughout the day.

She might have let Bo Stillwater believe she wasn't interested in the activities but that wasn't true. Her heart stirred with excitement. She would attend, pay her admission fee, throw a few coins at some games, even buy a treat. She'd enjoy herself for a few hours then hurry home. She hadn't decided if she could spare the time to go to the dance but it did sound appealing. Even if she only watched one dance before she left.

With a final look in the mirror to make sure her hair remained neat, she donned her bonnet, grabbed her pocketbook and reached for the door handle as a knock sounded.

"Doc? I need to see the doctor."

Her hand suspended inches from the door, she wondered if there had been an accident. Father had been called away to tend a sick family. Whatever the need, she would have to take care of it. She opened the door and stared at Bo. Her gaze riveted to his face in surprise, and then crying drew her attention to the cart beside him.

"Babies? What are you doing with babies?" Three of them all crying and looking purely miserable.

"I think they're sick. They need to see the doctor."

"Bring them in. Father is away but I'll look at them."

"They need a doctor." He leaned to one side to glance into the house as if to make sure she wasn't hiding her father. "When will he be back?"

"I'll look at them," she repeated.

"But they're sick."

Her spine stiffened. Seemed he shared the opinion of many of his gender: a woman couldn't be a doctor. She'd once dreamed of becoming one but it was impossible with Mother and Amy to take care of. "I've been my father's assistant for years. I'm perfectly capable of checking a baby." Unless they had something other than the normal illnesses that little ones got. Like the time six-year-old Amy had come down with the grippe so severe they feared for her life. Louisa was only eleven but stayed at Father's side helping to care for her sister while Father insisted Mother must stay away for fear she'd get the illness and her heart would not withstand the stress.

"I didn't mean otherwise. It's just…" He trailed off as if he couldn't explain what he meant.

"Bring them in." She threw back the door so he could push the cart inside. She bent over to look more closely at the babies. "We don't see triplets often." She read their names on their shirts and touched each of them as she greeted them. "Hello, Jasper, Eli and Theo."

They were fevered and fussy. Theo reached his arms toward her. She lifted him and cradled him to her shoulder. "There, there, little man. We'll fix you up in no time."

Jasper, seeing his brother getting comfort, reached out his arms too.

Louisa grabbed a kitchen chair she'd placed by the window and sat down, putting Theo on one knee and lifting Jasper to the other. The babies were an armload. At first glance they appeared to be in good health. But they were fevered. She needed to speak to the mother about their age and how long they'd been sick.

Eli's wails increased at being left alone.

"Can you pick him up?" she asked Bo, hiding a smile at his hesitation. Had he never held a baby? After all, if she were to believe the talk around town, he was twenty-nine years old. Plenty old enough to have married. She knew he did not now have a wife. Could he have loved and lost his wife and even a child? So many died in the last epidemic of grippe. Suddenly, and most unwelcomingly, she wondered about the man who took up the third baby. At first he seemed uncertain what to do but Eli knew and leaned his head against Bo's chest. Bo relaxed and held the baby comfortably enough.

Louisa grinned openly as the baby's cries softened. "He's glad for someone to hold him. Where are the parents?" She glanced toward the open door, wondering if the parents had been delayed momentarily.

"Well, that's the thing." He seemed distracted by the tickle of the fine brown hair against his chin. "I don't know."

"You don't know where the parents are?"

He shook his head. "I don't even know *who* they are."

"Then why do you have the babies?"

For answer, he handed her a note and she read it. "They're abandoned?" She pulled each baby close as waves of shock shuddered through her. Not yet nine months old and left to survive on their own. It was beyond comprehension.

He explained how he'd found them in the pie tent.

"I must find their mother before she disappears." He

leaned forward as if to put Eli back in the cart but Eli clung to him, sobbing his protest. Bo looked at Louisa, his eyes wide with appeal, the silvery color darkened with concern for these little ones. "I need to go but how are you going to manage?"

She wondered the same thing. But she would not let him think she couldn't do it. "I'll be okay. Put Eli down. I'll take care of them." Although she hated the idea, she would have to let two of them cry while she took care of the third.

Bo backed toward the door. He seemed to remember he wore his hat indoors and snatched it off.

She deemed Theo to be the most miserable baby and put Jasper into the cart so she could deal with Theo. He rubbed his ears and rolled his head back and forth. Earache. She could offer comfort measures for that. She realized Bo remained at the door and looked at him.

"I meant to come see you earlier." Bo rubbed at his ear much like Theo did. Did he have an earache, as well?

"For what reason?"

"To ask you to reconsider and attend the fair. Perhaps you're not aware of all the needs, but the money we raise is to provide funds for the Lone Star Cowboy League. I'm sure your father has seen how badly many of the people around here need help."

Of course he had. She had, as well. The desperation of so many people pulled at her heart. Like the poor mother of these babies. He continued before she could think how to answer his assumption. "Perhaps it's working out for the best that you weren't planning to go. At least you won't mind if I leave the babies with you until I locate the mother."

She would have liked to refute him but the babies needed her attention and he needed to find their mother. "Things have a way of working out, don't they?" She waved a hand to shoo him away. "You run along now. We'll be fine."

The door closed behind him and she sprang into action. Warm oil for Theo's ears. Cool sponging for all three babies. A drink of water. Thankfully they drank well from a cup. A smile encircled her heart as she tended the babies. They were adorable...three look-alikes...tousled brown hair and brown eyes that followed her every move. She bent over each little boy and kissed the top of each head. Hopefully their mother would be found soon.

She picked up Eli and held him close, swaying and singing to him. The other two watched and listened, seeming to enjoy her sad little tune.

Bo stood stock-still in the middle of the street. She'd waved him away, dismissed him like he was a nuisance. It felt strangely unusual. Mostly the young ladies flocked after him, willingly paid for the privilege of a dance with him. Mothers vied for him to share a meal with their families so he could admire their marriageable-aged daughter. He was not interested in marriage, but to have someone turn down every opportunity to have his attention did tweak his interest. He shook his head, unable to decide if he should be offended or relieved.

He rubbed his chin. The baby's hair had tickled

him right there. Tender feelings had rushed to the top of his heart. A wee one in his arms stirred up a longing as deep as forever…a longing for a child and family of his own.

He shook his head to drive away the errant idea and silently renewed his vow. He would never have children. They deserved better than he could promise them. A shudder snaked across his shoulders at the fear, uncertainty and loathing that came with remembering his father. *God, help me be true to my decision. No one deserves to endure what Brandon and I did.*

There was one certain way to ensure that.

He would not marry.

More used to using the four feet of a horse to cover distance in a hurry than his own two, he broke into an awkward run and returned to the fairgrounds. The position of the sun informed him little time remained before he must judge the pies and even less time to find the missing mother.

He slowed measurably when he reached the grounds. The gates wouldn't open for another hour and yet people crowded the area. Satisfaction warmed his heart. If everyone supported the fair like this, they would make a good deal of money. Enough? Only time would tell. What difference would it make if Louisa did not attend? She was but one woman. The price of one admission.

Yet it rankled that she showed so little interest in the affairs of the community.

He saw the sheriff, Jeb Fuller, just past the gate and called to him. Jeb needed to be notified about the babies and could help look for the mother.

Jeb jogged over and bent close to hear Bo's story. "That's sad. I'll begin a search, but with people from all over the county, it will be difficult to find one woman, especially as you have no idea what she looks like." He moved away slowly, pausing to look carefully at and speak to each woman he passed, clearly asking about the triplets. When they shook their heads, he moved on.

Bo continued on his way to the pie tent. He saw a familiar figure to his right and veered that direction. "Brandon," he called to his twin. His look-alike waved and waited for Bo to join him.

"I thought you'd be judging the pies," Brandon said.

"I'm on my way there now. But first…" He again related the story of the triplets. "If we can find the mother before she disappears, we can help her look after the babies."

"I'll start asking around. Where are they now?"

"At the doctor's. His daughter is taking care of them."

"Good. She seems a capable, no-nonsense person."

"She refused to pay to dance with me."

Brandon blinked. "I never thought you'd have to pay someone to dance with you."

Laughing at his brother's misunderstanding, he explained his idea for raising more money. "But Miss Clark refused to take part."

Brandon's eyes flashed amusement. "Sounds like someone's pride is hurt." He gave Bo a playful punch on his shoulder. "You'll get over it."

Bo grabbed his arm in fake pain. "Ma told you not to hit me."

The two laughed at the memory of their childhood

then parted ways—Brandon to look for a missing mother and Bo to the pie tent.

The two other judges waited impatiently. The church pianist, Constance Hickey, her red hair pulled back so tightly into her bun that her eyes could barely blink, had volunteered for the job. Except *volunteered* was too mild a word. She insisted that she knew pies like no one else and no contest would be fairly judged without her help. Standing beside her was banker George Henley, who had put up a cash prize for the winner.

One by one, they circled the entries, savoring each sample and rating it according to a complicated system Mrs. Hickey had come up with. Bo forced himself to concentrate on the task. Too many things vied for his thoughts—wondering how Louisa was managing with the babies, hoping that Brandon or Jeb found the missing mother, and overall the sad-happy memories of his mother, who made a pie for the three of them every time Father was away…an occurrence that happened far too seldom.

They narrowed the entries down to six possibilities. Both George and Bo made up their minds but Mrs. Hickey insisted the selection couldn't be rushed.

"My reputation depends on being one hundred percent sure."

Bo stuffed back the thought that her reputation stemmed from her propensity for gossip.

Finally she made her decision and the blue, red and yellow ribbons were attached.

Bo raced from the tent before they were done and hurried through the grounds. He found Brandon and Jeb near the front gate. "Find her?" he asked.

"We've asked throughout the crowd. No one saw a woman pushing a cart—or rather, many women were seen pushing some kind of conveyance. No one knows of triplets," Jeb said. "We'd have heard if they were from the community."

"What are you going to do?" Brandon asked as if finding the babies made them Bo's responsibility.

"First thing we need to do is get this fair opened and then we need to call an emergency meeting of the league." He went to the gate and held up his hand to signal he wanted people's attention. It took a few minutes for the crowd to quiet.

"Welcome to the County Fair. As you all know, it's to raise funds for the Lone Star Cowboy League, which was originally formed to bring ranchers together to help each other through troubled times. Since then our concerns have grown to include other families struggling to survive the drought. So open your purses wide and spend freely, but most of all, have a good time." He stepped aside and let the gatekeepers take admission as the crowd filed in.

Bo remained close by, and as the members of the league passed, he informed them of the emergency meeting. "At the office tent in half an hour."

Having informed all of them, Bo hurried about the grounds. If the mother was sick, where would she go? Somewhere she could rest. Maybe a place she could keep an eye on the babies. He squeezed his hands into fists. Imagine being so desperate you left three babies alone, not knowing when they'd be discovered or by whom. This was one of the reasons they'd started the Lone Star Cowboy League—to prevent people from doing desperate things because of desperate circumstances.

He passed women he didn't know but they were always accompanied by family. Nowhere he looked did he find a woman alone and ill, and with no more time to search, he hurried to the meeting.

"Fight. Fight."

Bo heard the chant and groaned. The fair had only begun and already a situation he didn't care to deal with. He jogged around the corner of the livestock tent housing prize goats and pushed his way through the crowd of young people. He saw the combatants circling each other, fists up and scowls marring their faces. Peter Hill and Jamie Coleman. He should have guessed. The two families had been feuding long before he and Brandon arrived in the area four years ago. He wasn't sure what the disagreement was about. Wasn't even sure they knew, though he'd heard muttered words about some valuable family heirloom.

He stepped between the two young men and pressed his hands to the heaving chests. Twenty-year-old Peter Hill likely outweighed his opponent by fifty pounds of grit, muscle and raging anger. Jamie Coleman, a year younger, fair as autumn grass, bounced on the balls of his feet as he waited to get in a jab.

Bo didn't even bother to ask about the disagreement. This pair found a hundred different reasons to start a fight. Or if not them, a couple of the younger boys. With three Coleman boys and three Hill boys, it seemed there was always a fight. Thankfully the girls resorted to insults and snubs. If there was a way to force the two widowed parents to work out their differences, perhaps the children would stop sparring, as well.

"I don't want the fair ruined by the lot of you fighting. I want people to have fun and feel safe." Bo waited until the two eased back before he lowered his hands. "Peter, why don't you go over to the garden tent and see how your ma fared with her carrots. They looked mighty fine to me."

Peter scowled at Jamie. "Don't think this is over." But he left.

Bo faced Jamie. "Find something else to do besides fight."

"I didn't start it."

"Next time walk away."

Jamie spun on his heel and did exactly that.

Bo sighed and rubbed the back of his neck. He could do without all these problems. And if he didn't hurry he was going to be late for the meeting he'd called.

He returned to the main pathway between booths. People came from all over the county to display and sell their wares. He eyed the fine saddles in one booth and promised himself he'd come back for a closer look. Booth after booth revealed the abilities of the Texas people—fancy tooled leather harnesses, fine linen embroidered tablecloths. For a flash he thought of his mother. Wouldn't she have liked one of those? Across from that booth Mrs. Longfeather showed her turquoise and silver jewelry and other Native crafts.

"The young bucks are restless," she said in her soft voice.

He understood she referred to Jamie and Peter.

"I should have given them a hard task to do so they wouldn't have time for getting into trouble."

"Some are born for trouble as the sparks fly upward. Others need the strike of the flint to start a fire." She paused and studied him with her bottomless black eyes. "Still others turn from the fire, afraid of its burn, at the same time depriving themselves of its warmth." Her study of him continued. Was she trying to tell him something? But she turned away and arranged a display of jewelry.

Bo hesitated. He wanted to know where she saw the Hills and the Colemans. Where she saw him. Except he didn't. Like she'd pointed out, some men would deprive themselves of warmth in order to avoid the burn. And why he saw his father in the flames, he could not say. Shaking his head, he hurried on.

Before he arrived at the meeting tent, he stopped to speak to one of the boys he spent time with through the Young Ranchers program they'd started last year. "Would you run to the doctor's house and ask Miss Clark to bring the babies here?"

The boy looked a little startled, then took off like a shot.

Bo ducked into the tent that served as a temporary office—meant mainly for lost and found children and items, a first-aid station, and to provide information. The members of the league were all there. Abe Sawyer and Gabe Dooley, both ranchers, had joined the original members. Bo glanced about, making eye contact with each of them before he began to speak.

"We have a situation." He explained about the triplets. "We haven't been able to find the mother, so in the meantime, we must make arrangements for these babies."

Every one of them stared at him. He couldn't say if they were shocked more by the fact of triplets in their midst, that the babies had been abandoned or the thought of asking someone to take on the care of three babies.

Lula May McKay, wife of Edmund, one of the three McKay brothers, and the only woman on the league, was the first to speak. "My heart goes out to this woman. I know what it's like to feel so desperate." She'd been a widow with five children to care for when Edmund found her and fell in love with her. He wrapped an arm about her shoulders and pulled her tight to his side. "I was fortunate enough to have Edmund come alongside me. We need to find her and let her know that we will help her."

There came a murmur of agreement.

Bo nodded. This was what the league stood for... helping those in need.

Brandon had joined the meeting at Bo's invitation and Brandon stepped forward. "If I may speak?"

The others grew quiet.

"Jeb and I have been asking around to no avail. The mother seems to have disappeared."

Jeb stepped to Brandon's side. "It can prove mighty hard to find someone who doesn't want to be found in a crowd like what's out there." He tipped his head and they all nodded, the sounds from outside plenty loud enough to let them know the crowd's large size.

Blustery Casper Magnuson spoke. "People don't vanish into thin air. You're the sheriff. You should be able to find her. Isn't that what we pay you to do?"

Lula May waited for the protests at Casper's remark to die down. "Where are the babies now?"

"I left them at the doctor's to have them checked out."

David McKay stepped forward to speak. "Are you telling us the babies have something wrong with them? Is that why the mother left them? Three sick babies is a lot of work."

His sister-in-law chuckled. "Sometimes one child is a lot of work." That brought gentle laughter from everyone at the reference to eight-year-old Maggie, who kept her father on his toes as he tried to keep her out of mischief.

Casper waved them to silence. "Three sick babies who aren't even part of our community. I don't see that we have any responsibility toward them. Send them to the orphanage at New Braunfels."

All three of the McKay brothers spoke at once, protesting that idea.

The discussion grew louder and more discordant.

Bo tried to get control of the meeting but Casper was not about to be silenced.

The tent flap parted and Louisa pushed the cart full of babies into their midst. Her father followed.

Bo released his pent-up breath, relieved that the doctor had seen the babies. As quickly as it escaped, his breath rushed in and stalled. What if the doctor had bad news about the three little ones?

No one spoke. Even Casper stopped yelling as they all stared at the matching babies.

Whatever Louisa and the doctor had done for them, the babies were no longer crying and sat up in the cart, looking around the circle of strangers. Theo's bottom lip quivered and tears pooled in his bottom eyelids. Eli stared unblinkingly and Jasper lifted a pudgy little hand as if to say hello.

Lula May was the first to recover. "They're darling. Oh, Edmund, can we take them home?"

Edmund's mouth worked but nothing came out. Lula May nudged him. "I'm joshing." Bo thought she looked dead serious. "Of course we can't take them. Our hands are full with our own family."

Doc Clark cleared his throat. "These babies are sick. Nothing serious. Colds and ear infections, but I think it's best if they stay with us until they're healthy. That will give me more opportunity to assess their development, though from what I've seen, they are sturdy babies. Louisa can look after them."

Bo watched Louisa for her reaction but her expression gave away nothing. "Are you okay with that, Miss Clark? I seem to recall you mentioning how busy you were."

She shifted from smiling at the babies to frowning at him. "They need medical attention at the moment."

He took that as her agreement to keep the babies for as long as they needed medical care and turned back to the others in the room. "We need to come up with a plan for when they've recovered."

Casper crossed his arms to consider Louisa. "You should find yourself a husband. Then you could keep the triplets for good." He muttered under his breath, "We should find a way to marry the spinster off." He squinted at Bo. "Seems to me that you and—"

Bo saw the man's intent and held up his hand to stop him from finishing his troublemaking statement about Bo and Louisa.

But if he thought he needed to protest Casper's unkind remark about Louisa being a spinster, she soon proved she didn't need Bo's defense. She faced Casper with a steady gaze. "Mr. Magnuson, you have a wife and a home. You should keep the babies until their mother is found."

Casper sputtered, not used to being brought up short. "I have four children. I can't afford to feed three more mouths."

"Three babies are too much for one family," CJ Thorn said. The local rancher and his wife, Molly, raised his brother's twin daughters as well as their baby son. "It takes a lot of expense and hard work to feed three more mouths, but if we only ask for people to take one baby, it might be manageable."

Bo observed the three McKay brothers squirm and their faces grow hard as the merits of splitting up the babies were discussed.

David McKay leaped forward. "I strongly oppose having them separated." He glanced at his brothers. "I know firsthand how painful it is to grow up knowing you have brothers but they aren't part of your life. It wouldn't be fair to do that to these little ones."

The meeting grew quiet at the intensity of his speech.

"We'll find a way to keep them together," Lula May said, and it seemed she spoke for the others as no one voiced any disagreement.

"The Cowboy League could provide financial support to any family that takes the babies," Bo pointed out, and the others nodded.

"That way we can keep them in the community." CJ Thorn seemed to like the idea.

Bo realized that he and the others had decided the triplets belonged here.

"If Miss Clark can care for them until we find a more permanent arrangement, that would be great," CJ continued.

"Yes, of course."

Lula May sidled up to Louisa. "Won't this mean you'll miss the fair? I know how much you were looking forward to seeing all the displays."

She was? Bo thought she had no interest in the activities.

Louisa shrugged and smiled. "Responsibilities before fun. Isn't that so?"

Lula May lifted one shoulder in resignation. "It often is."

The babies began to fuss. Louisa turned the cart toward the door. "I'll take them home and care for them."

Lula May stopped her. "Do you need help? I could…"

Louisa gave the woman a serene smile. "You stay and enjoy the fair. I can manage them."

Bo watched her depart. She'd wanted to attend the fair. Had willingly given it up to tend the babies. Somehow that did not fit in with how he had judged her. He shook his head. He did not like being wrong and certainly didn't like the feeling that he'd been faulty in his assessment.

He took a step after her, intending to follow and apologize. But for what? A wrong opinion?

Instead, he turned his thought back to the fair. Time to see how things were going.

Maybe he'd think of a way to ease his mind about Louisa Clark before the day was done.

Chapter Three

Louisa rushed home with the babies, her mind whirling as fast and loud as the creaky wheels of the cart. Apart from knowing the triplets were miserable with their colds and sore ears, she savored the idea of three little ones to hold and comfort for a time. It was like having her sister, Amy, back in her care. She smiled. More like three Amys.

The meeting had gone well. She chuckled, causing the babies to look at her in surprise. Jasper grinned and gurgled, his discomfort momentarily forgotten.

She leaned over and whispered, "You want to know why I laughed? Okay, I'll tell you but you must promise not to repeat it to anyone." Jasper gurgled happily. Theo sucked his thumb and regarded her solemnly. Eli leaned against his two brothers, content to be with them.

Louisa's heart expanded with a love so intense that for a moment, she couldn't find room to fill her lungs. This must be how mothers felt when they saw their offspring. Then she remembered her promise to tell them her secret and she glanced about as if to make sure no one spied on them. "I know I surprised Mr. Bo Stillwater and it felt good. Yes indeed, it did." How did he feel knowing he'd mistaken her refusal to sign up to dance with him as meaning she didn't care about the fair? She shrugged. Likely he'd not given it a second thought.

She glanced over her shoulder, a little disappointed she wouldn't get to attend, then turned back to the three chubby boys. "It's worth it to be able to play with you for a few days."

They reached the doctor's residence and she pushed and lifted the cart up the steps and into the house. "I don't know where you're going to sleep. This cart isn't big enough." There was a sturdy metal crib in her father's office but he'd need it if anyone brought in a sick baby. "Are you used to sleeping together?" She looked from one to the other. "You're not going to tell me? Well, fine. I'll figure it out myself."

Theo's bottom lip quivered. Louisa recognized it as the precursor to his crying. Once he started, all three would cry. "I'll have something for you to eat in a moment. But please don't cry. It's hard on the ears." She had left oatmeal simmering on the back of the stove and it was now well cooked, suitable for babies. Father suggested they be introduced to foods slowly until it could be determined if they were used to eating solids yet.

She poured milk into a cup. Eyed the two other cups she'd pulled from the cupboard. But she only had two hands and it took one to steady the baby and the other to hold the cup. She ignored the remaining cups. She'd go from baby to baby letting them drink. She started with Theo as he seemed the one who cried the easiest.

Jasper bounced up and down, eager for his turn. Eli watched placidly, so she gave him the cup last.

She prepared the oatmeal, then sat them up in the cart and went from one mouth to the other feeding them. Before she made the round, the first mouth popped open, waiting. She laughed softly. "I feel like a mother bird."

Theo's cheeks grew flushed and he refused more food.

"Poor baby. Your fever has returned. And your ears are sore."

All three of them grew flushed. How was she to sponge them at the same time? "You wait here. Don't go anywhere."

They sobbed and pulled at their ears. She dashed out the back door and grabbed the washtub off the nail on the wall. Thankfully the water pails were full. Otherwise how was she to get water and watch the babies at the same time? Her respect and sympathy for the ill mother grew by leaps and bounds.

She poured a few inches of tepid water into the square washtub and then stripped the boys of their cute little shirts. For a moment she hesitated. How was she to tell them apart without the shirts with their names on them? She studied them hard. They looked as alike as three peas but they acted differently. Theo was the shiest, cried the easiest and sucked his thumb. Eli was the most watchful of the three and seemed to react to what he saw around him. He liked being close to his brothers. Jasper was the friendliest. But just to be sure, she tied a different colored bit of yarn around each ankle.

Satisfied she could tell them apart, she sat them

side by side in the tub, supported against the sides so they couldn't fall, and as she splashed water over the babies to cool their fevered bodies, she sang a lullaby she'd once sung to Amy to soothe her.

Jasper laughed and batted at the water. Eli's eyelids drooped and Theo sucked his thumb.

"Nap time." But where were they to sleep? The cart was too small. They weren't safe on a bed. They'd roll off or crawl off. That left the floor as the safest place. She dressed the babies and put them in the cart, then spread a thick quilt in the middle of the living room floor.

Eli was almost asleep and she put him down first. He opened his eyes, but as she laid Theo beside him, he snuggled close to his brother and closed his eyes again. She laid Jasper on the other side of Eli and soon the three of them slept.

She wandered to the open window to listen to the sound of music, cattle and many voices blended together. Seemed the fair was going well. The league would be able to add to their coffers. Disappointment stained her thoughts. She had been looking forward to seeing the many booths, listening to the fiddlers, buying a treat from one of the concessions. Truth was, she'd anticipated a few hours of fun. Squaring her shoulders, she turned from the window and watched the three little boys. A smile filled her heart and warmed her eyes. These three were every bit as much fun as a fair.

How long would they sleep? She had no idea. But she wasn't prepared to leave them unattended and slipped to her room to get her Bible. She sat in the big armchair where she could keep an eye on the babies and opened the Bible. She stroked her fingers over the pages. Only eight years old when her mother presented it to her, she'd read it so often that it was now well-worn and much loved. The gold gilt had worn off the edges; a couple of pages were loose. Eventually she would have to get a new one, but giving up this one would be like losing a dear friend.

The book fell open to one of her favorite passages. Psalm eighteen. She read a couple of the verses that meant the most to her. "He delivered me because he delighted in me. It is God that girdeth me with strength and maketh my way perfect." Sweet calming peace filled her soul. The way laid out before her required sacrifices but none that God couldn't satisfy in other ways. Making sure Mother was happy and well cared for provided her with joy. Her glance went from the babies to the door of the room where Mother would sleep. Would taking care of the triplets mean she wouldn't have the room ready for Mother's arrival?

The details were in God's almighty hands, so Louisa need not fret.

A footfall sounded on the outside step and she rushed to the door before anyone could knock or call out and wake her charges.

If they were looking for Father, she would send them to the fairgrounds, where he had stayed to take care of any injuries that might occur. She eased open the door, her finger pressed to her lips to signal the caller to quiet. Her hand dropped to her side as she looked into the silvery eyes of Bo Stillwater. "Is something wrong?" Why else would he come? She glanced over her shoulder. If Father needed her, who would stay with the babies?

He lifted a towel off the plate in his hand. "I brought you a piece of pie." There were four slices. "I didn't know which was your favorite, so you have a selection. Apple, raisin, blackberry or, my favorite, peach."

"Oh, my." Was that the best she could come up with? But his thoughtfulness left her practically speechless. Somehow she expected him to be enjoying the adulation of the many young ladies at the fair. Perhaps she'd misjudged him. "That's very thoughtful of you. Will you come in and join me? We'll have to be quiet." She tipped her head to indicate the sleeping babies.

For answer, he tiptoed in and closed the door quietly behind him.

She crooked her finger to indicate he should follow her to the kitchen. They eased past the baby-covered quilt. She pointed to a chair and he sat while she took two small plates and two forks from the cupboard. "I love raisin." She took that slice and pushed the peach one to a plate and handed it to him.

He thanked her. "I judged the pie contest."

"Really? Who won?"

"A Mrs. Rawlings with her apple pie. She isn't from this area." He savored a bite of the peach pie. "Good but not as good as my ma used to make."

"Your mother is dead?"

"She died when I was sixteen." He ate his pie slowly, thoughtfully as if lost in memories.

"I'm sorry." She meant to do everything in her power to keep her own mother alive for a good many more years.

"Me too."

"And your father?"

"He passed away almost five years ago."

She wondered at the harshness of his voice. "You must miss him a lot."

"Not as much as you'd expect." Seeing the surprise and curiosity in her study of him, he added, "He wasn't a nice man."

"I'm truly sorry to hear that."

His hand paused halfway to his mouth with another bite of pie on his fork. "Not half as sorry as Brandon and I were to live with it." He lowered his fork to his plate with the pie still there. "I'm sorry. I don't usually grouse about my past. Forget I said anything." A beat of regret, and then he tipped his head toward her plate. "You haven't tasted it yet."

She took a bite, chewed slowly and let the flavors lie on her tongue a moment before she swallowed.

"How is it?" he asked.

"A little too sweet for my taste, but then, I'm somewhat of a pie judge myself."

He leaned forward. "How's that?"

She chuckled softly. "I've taken care of my mother and sister, who is five years younger than me, and run the house since I was twelve years old. Of course, we had a part-time housekeeper, as well." Father had insisted she attend classes. Not that Louisa objected. At that point she'd still harbored her dream to become a doctor. "Her name was Mrs. Keaton and she taught me how to bake all sorts of things. Year after year, her pies won the blue ribbon at the local fair, so you might say I had an excellent teacher."

"You would have liked my ma, then. She was an excellent pie baker." He cleaned his plate. "Not that we had pie very often."

That seemed a curious remark. "Why is that?"

"Ma saved it for special occasions."

A note of sadness in his voice made her ask, "What constituted a special occasion?"

He gave a laugh totally devoid of humor. "Father being away."

She didn't need any more details to understand Bo and Brandon had suffered under their father. How sad. She glanced past him to the sleeping babies. She couldn't imagine treating them poorly or standing by while someone else did. Though they might well grow up to be mischievous and need a firm hand. Who would provide it for them?

"Sorry. Didn't I just say I wasn't going to bemoan my past?"

"Seems one's past is a building block of one's present and perhaps one's future." When had she grown so philosophical? She expected him to laugh but he only raised his eyebrows.

"That makes me curious. What shape does your past building block take?"

"Well, I have always had a loving family, so I count myself fortunate."

"No suitors?"

This conversation was getting far too personal. After Wes she had no time or inclination for courting. His painful rejection had taught her a valuable lesson. His words still echoed in her head. *Look in the mirror, honey. You aren't worth waiting for.* "Care for another piece of pie?"

"No, thanks. Save them for yourself to eat later."

She felt the steady watchfulness of his unusually colored eyes and looked everywhere but at him. He did not need to know the details of her personal life. She was about to ask him how the fair was going…hoping he would understand it as a gentle hint to return to the grounds, when one of the babies fussed. Before she could get to her feet, all three cried.

She rushed into the room to rescue them. Bo followed on her heels but stood back, looking both lost and afraid. Afraid? Bo Stillwater? How could that be? But she didn't have time to think of anything but crying babies. She scooped up Theo first, realizing he would become upset faster than his brothers. But how could she comfort him and tend to the other two?

Bo was there. She'd take advantage of another set of arms. "Could you hold him?"

He stepped back. "You saw me earlier. I don't know anything about babies."

"No time like the present to correct that. Sit there." She indicated the armchair.

He sat, or rather, he perched on the edge of the cushion. The volume of the crying intensified.

"Sit back." He barely got himself pushed to the back of the chair before she put Theo on his lap. He looked uncomfortable, but she needed his help so ignored it. She grabbed his hand and pulled his arm around the baby.

Theo shuddered a sob and then gave Bo a crooked, watery-eyed grin.

Bo grinned back.

Louisa hurried to the other two. Eli wriggled away and she caught him halfway across the floor, scooped him up and perched him on Bo's other knee. Eli ducked his head, shy before this big man, but Theo jabbered at his brother and they smiled at each other.

Now to take care of Jasper. She picked him up, crooning a comforting tune, but he continued to fuss, rubbing his ears. "Time to put some drops in there, isn't it?" She headed for the kitchen to prepare the oil but stopped in the doorway. "Can you take care of those two while I tend Jasper's ears?"

"It seems I have no choice."

She couldn't tell if it was regret or something else that deepened his voice. Nor did she have time to dwell on it. She rushed about putting warm oil in Jasper's ears, then returned to the other room. Took Theo and left Jasper in his place. She tended his ears as well, then gave him back to Bo and tended Theo. None of them seemed fevered at the moment. Perhaps they were over the worst.

She was happy about that, except once they were better, the babies would go to a home. As they should. It was purely selfish on her part to want to keep them longer. "No sign of the mother?"

"We're still looking."

"Have you arranged a home for them until you find her?" she asked as she returned to the living room. With Jasper perched on her hip, she gathered up the quilt and draped it over the sofa.

"Not yet. As everyone says, three babies is a lot."

She looked at the two sitting on his knee, touching each other's fingers and smiling. Jasper sat happily enough on her hip. "I don't know. At the moment, it looks like exactly the right amount." She studied him openly. "For a man with no experience, you seem to have a knack for this. You'll make a good father."

He shook his head vehemently. "No. Fatherhood is not for me."

"Why ever not?" He was tall, broad shouldered, good-looking, had the attention of all the young ladies in the community. Seemed he had everything needed to find a perfect mate and raise a bunch of sweet little Stillwater offspring. Heat raced up her throat at the wayward trail her thoughts had taken.

"I fear I would turn out to be like my father."

She blinked twice. Thankfully he wasn't looking at her so wouldn't have cause to think she looked like a startled rabbit. "I've only been here a short time but I have certainly not seen or heard anything to that effect."

"Good. Then what I'm doing is working." He sat the babies on the floor and strode to the door. "I must get back to the fair." He paused as if realizing that he left her to manage three babies on her own.

Not that she couldn't do it. But it had been nice to not feel so alone and overwhelmed. The poor mother. How had she coped? "I hope you can find their mother."

"I'll do my best." Still he hesitated. "Will you be able to manage them?"

Her throat tightened. No one ever asked if she could handle her responsibilities. And she'd never suggested to anyone that she couldn't. Her opinion of him shifted a little more to the right as she waved him goodbye.

Words and images battered the inside of Bo's head as he hurried away. Eating pie. All safe and homey. Like it had been with Ma. Watching Louisa jostle a baby on her hip. Were women born knowing how to comfort infants, how to carry them? How to dole out gentle touches? He looked at the hand she had drawn around little Theo.

She didn't look like Ma. She didn't sound like her and yet something about her reminded him of his mother. And not only because she knew how to bake a pie, though he had no reason to believe it so except her own words.

You'll make a good father. If only he could believe it possible. Holding those babies had him wishing for things beyond his reach.

His long, hurried strides took him to the fairgrounds and he welcomed the diversion from his tangled thoughts.

He had but one goal in mind—make this fair as successful as possible. And thus raise enough funds to meet the needs. And with three babies to care for until they found their mother, the needs had grown.

What if they never found the mother? The sheriff didn't seem to be overly optimistic that they would.

If they didn't, then someone would have to take them on permanently. He smiled as he thought of how much fun it would be to see those three babies grow into little boys and then young men. But it wouldn't be him doing that job.

He paused to speak to the gatekeeper. "How is attendance?"

"Beyond expectations, I'd say. Jeb took away a bag of cash an hour ago."

"Great to hear." The sheriff had been delegated to take the money to the bank to have it kept in the safe.

He continued on his way, and as he rounded the

corner of a tent, stepping over the rope fastened to the tent peg, he noticed a young boy of six or seven huddled next to the canvas, sobbing his heart out. "What's wrong?"

"I—I losted my mama and papa."

Being careful not to make the boy feel threatened, he squatted down. "Do you want me to help you find them?"

The boy scrubbed away the tears and nodded.

Bo held out his hand and led him toward the office tent, expecting the parents would go there to report their missing child. Indeed, as he led the boy inside, a woman let out a cry and raced over to enfold her son. The father, although less demonstrative, wrapped his arms around them both. "Thank you," he said to Bo.

"I was scared," the boy sobbed. "I thought I'd never see you again."

The man turned the boy to face him. "If you are ever lost I will find you. I promise."

The boy leaned into his father's shoulder.

Bo stepped outside the tent. That was how a child should feel with his father—safe and certain. Unfortunately, that was the ideal but not the reality for many.

He heard raucous laughter and hooting toward the livestock tents and hustled through the crowd toward the sound. He soon saw what amused everyone and stood back to watch a boy not yet man trying to control a goat. Seemed it would be easy to pull the lead rope and drag the animal back inside, but if the animal thought she was going to be dragged, she raced toward the young fella and he jumped out of the way to keep from being bunted.

Bo was about to step in and lend a hand when an older man emerged from the tent and strode toward the struggling pair. He grabbed the goat around the neck and led her bleating and protesting inside while the relieved younger man hurried after him.

Another example of a good father. Was God sending them as reminders that he hadn't known that kind of fathering? That he had his father's blood flowing through his veins and would most certainly fail to be the kind of father a child deserved?

"Thief. Thief. Stop that man." He jerked around in time to see a figure dart out of sight and like many others, joined in the chase. Jeb came around the corner, alerted by the call. He reached out and caught the culprit.

It was but a young boy…maybe twelve or thirteen.

"Pa?" He looked around for his father.

Bo watched a man duck back, prepared to let his boy stand on his own. Perhaps even had sent the boy to snatch the money, knowing it would go easier with a youngster. In fact, Jeb dragged him back to the leathersmith display and had him return the money, then let him go with a warning.

If Bo needed any evidence to prove the evil of bad fathering, this was it and he strode away. The rest of the afternoon sped away quickly as he spoke to each vendor and visited with his friends and neighbors. It was especially heartening to see Molly and CJ Thorn with their baby son, Isaac. They had married recently, brought together by the matchmaking efforts of CJ's twin nieces, who giggled as they chased after a bit of red bunting. He wished them nothing but happiness in their life together.

Several times young ladies came up to him and gave a dime in exchange for a dance with him on Saturday night. There was one woman who did not offer him a dime. Louisa. Of course, she was too busy, but still, he wished it otherwise.

He paused to order coffee and two cookies at a booth and deposit the required coins. "How are sales?" he asked Mrs. Carson, who was taking her turn running the booth.

"Brisk." She seemed pleased.

Finished with his coffee, he returned his cup and turned in time to see eighteen-year-old Annie Hill and nineteen-year-old Jamie Coleman slip behind a tent. So that was the way it was. Perhaps it would be the means to ending the feud between their families. His jaw tightened. More than likely it would simply increase the tension in the feud.

The shadows lengthened and people began to drift away except for those who would stay and watch the animals. The fair was over for the first day.

Jeb called him over and together they went from booth to booth collecting the money that would go to the league. Bo's grin widened with every stop. "We've done much better than I could have hoped and two more days to go."

As they left the grounds with the heavy money bag, Bo noticed a man watching them from the protection of the trees and pointed him out to Jeb. "He's the father of the lad you caught stealing."

Jeb studied the man carefully. "I'll be keeping an eye on him."

"Let's get this money into the safe." They hurried to the bank, where George Henley waited to lock it up for the night.

Bo let out a relieved sigh when the safe closed and George locked it. His tension eased marginally as George double-checked the locks on the front door and the windows then let them out the back and locked it securely.

The worst thing Bo could imagine was having that money stolen.

"It's safe," George assured him.

"I'll post a guard to make sure," Jeb said.

"I'll stay here until you get someone." Bo had no intention of letting anyone try to get into the bank even if they weren't able to crack the safe.

"You don't have a gun."

George pulled a derringer from his side pocket and handed it to Bo. "It's not much but it's all I have."

"I'll be back shortly." Jeb trotted away.

George paused a moment then leisurely walked away…as if to communicate to anyone watching that he had no concerns.

Bo wished he felt half as confident. He palmed the little gun and remained alert to every sound and movement. There was no sign of the man he believed to be a danger, but still he did not relax until Jeb returned with two men carrying rifles and wearing sidearms. One stood at the front door, the other at the back. Even then Bo hesitated to leave them.

Jeb gave him a little push. "Trust us to do our job."

"Put that way…" He made his way around to the front of the building and stared up and down Main Street. Lights glowed in some of the businesses as if the owners had last-minute things to do. He followed the same path he had yesterday in his desire to catch up to Louisa and convince her to be involved in the fair.

His steps slowed. Was that only yesterday? It seemed much longer ago.

He reached the doctor's house and stood on the sidewalk studying it. How was Louisa doing with the triplets? Were the babies feeling any better? Was it too late to go to the door and ask?

A lamp burned inside. He crossed the street and hesitated in front of the house.

A demanding cry reached his ears and he made up his mind. She might well need someone to help her. He rapped on the door and waited. His toe nudged something and he bent to pick up three worn toys—a stuffed bear, a stuffed rabbit and a stuffed cat. How odd. Who would have dropped the toys there?

He glanced up and down the street but saw no one. At that moment, Louisa opened the door holding one squalling baby. Another cried from behind her.

He handed her the toys. "Could you use an extra pair of arms?" He might not be the sort of man to be a good father, but he could at least help Louisa care for the babies until further arrangements were made.

Chapter Four

Louisa couldn't remember ever being so relieved to see someone come to the door. Father had been home a couple of hours ago but was called away again almost immediately. She struggled alone trying to cope with the babies growing increasingly fussy. Now Bo was here and she meant to take advantage of another pair of hands. She grabbed his arm and dragged him inside. "They're all crying at once." She handed him Theo. "Sit in the big chair and hold Jasper too." Thankfully he obeyed her request without comment. Likely he took in her ruffled appearance, her hair in untidy strands, and decided she needed rescuing. She hurried to explain her desperation. "They've napped. They've eaten and consumed their milk. I've treated their earaches and sponged them to take down their fevers, but they are more and more unhappy. I don't know what I'm doing wrong." She'd wiped noses and changed diapers. She'd sung. Most of all, she felt like joining them in a good cry.

He jostled the two babies on his knees as she put more warm oil in Eli's ears. He wailed a protest.

"What makes babies unhappy?"

"Being sick. Having earaches."

"What else? Maybe missing their mama?"

She stared at him. How had he seen the problem so clearly? "Of course. The poor little mites." Every bit of fatigue and frustration ended. "Maybe these little toys you brought will comfort them." She handed one to each of them. Only Jasper took the offered toy.

"I didn't bring them. They were on the step. I thought maybe you dropped them or—" He bolted to his feet, a baby in each arm. "Their mother? I must look. You sit and hold them while I try and find her." They traded places and she sat with the three babies squirming and sobbing in her lap.

As he dashed out the door, she sang to the babies. "Safe in the arms of Jesus."

A little later, he tapped on the door and reentered. Eli slept but the other two continued to fuss. Seeing that Louisa had made a bed for them on the floor again, he took Eli from her arms, laid him down and covered him with a light sheet. Then he took Jasper and left Theo with Louisa.

"They seem to like my singing," Louisa said somewhat apologetically.

"Then sing."

She cleared her throat and began the song again. "'Safe in the arms of Jesus.'"

"Good choice." He grinned at her then joined his voice to hers, his deep and rich, like finest chocolate, and even the fussing boys grew quiet as if they wanted to hear him better.

Soon the two babies slept in their arms.

Louisa didn't want to put Theo down. Didn't want to end this moment of sweet harmony. Bo made no move toward putting Jasper down. Perhaps he too felt the stir of something peaceful between them.

"How was the fair?" she asked, her voice low so she wouldn't disturb the sleeping baby in her arms.

"A good turnout. We brought in more than I expected. That's a good thing. Seems we'll need more money than we originally thought." He inclined his head toward the babies.

"How sad that a woman feels she has to give up on her offspring." Though her note suggested she expected to die. If they could find her, perhaps they could aid her so she would live.

He nodded. "But an unselfish act, wouldn't you say. I'm sure it was extremely hard for her but she loved them enough to do what she thought was best for them."

Louisa understood about sacrifices for the sake of love. "Love is a powerful compeller."

"I saw it in action today." He told her about a lost boy being reunited with his parents and an older boy helped by his kind father. "Then to keep things in balance there was this other man." A man who appeared to send his son to commit a crime then to abandon him when he was caught. "It reminded me so much of my father. Not that my father was involved in crime. Oh, no. He was an upright citizen with a successful business. All I can say is he must have treated his employ-

ees and customers better than he treated his family."
He shifted Jasper. "I find that odd. Shouldn't those in
your family deserve the best you have to give?"

"I certainly believe that."

He studied her across the room, his pale eyes catching the lamplight and holding it.

She wanted to say more. Wanted to learn more about
him. Tell him about her family. But again, she couldn't
find the words.

The door eased open and Father entered the house,
smiling when he saw the triplets all asleep. "Bo, it's
good to see you helping." He smiled at the baby sleeping on Bo's lap then turned to Louisa. "Has their fever
stayed down?"

"It's been two hours since it last spiked."

"Good. Good. Let's pray it lasts."

Louisa's conscience stung. She'd been so preoccu-
pied she hadn't thought to pray for the babies since
earlier in the day.

A quiet knock came on the door. Father opened it
to Brandon Stillwater.

"I thought I would check on the triplets and see if
there is anything they need." He glanced about the
room at one curled up on the floor, another in Louisa's
lap and the third sleeping in Bo's arms and chuckled.
"Looks real good on you, brother."

"Don't be thinking I'll do something foolish. You
know how I feel about this." His glance included the
babies and Louisa.

Oh, yes, he included her. Not that he needed to. She
was no more interested in marriage and family and *him*
than he was in her and domesticity. She eased to her

feet and lowered Theo to the quilt beside Eli, then lifted
Jasper from Bo's arms, doing her best not to touch the
man but failing. Her hand slid across his chest, feeling
the strength and warmth. Her arm brushed his shoulder. And her heart reacted with a kick against her ribs.
She ignored her reactions and put Jasper down beside his brothers. She stood over them, smiling at how
peaceful and sweet they were.

Bo and Brandon stood on either side of her, fenc-
ing her in so she couldn't escape. Escape? From what?
She knew what she was—her mother's caregiver—and
who—the doctor's spinster daughter. The plain one.
But she was at peace with her role in life. The role
God assigned for her. Except looking after the babies
and sharing their care, even for a few minutes with Bo,
triggered a deep maternal longing.

"I've heard there is nothing more peaceful than a
sleeping baby," Brandon said. "And here we have it
in threes."

Father stood to one side. "I hope they stay that
peaceful throughout the night and their fevers don't
return."

"Why don't we pray for that?" Brandon had his hat
in hand and held it to his chest. "Father God, You see
here these three little ones. We trust You have sent
them to us for a reason. Help them get well. Help them
sleep well."

Bo didn't wait for his brother to finish. "Help us
find their mother and be able to help her. And may the
fair be a success."

"And may Your name be honored. Amen."

Louisa realized the two men finished each other's

speech and likely their thoughts. Wouldn't it be fun to see the same thing, only with three little boys? Even now they interacted among themselves with a unity she found endearing.

Bo and Brandon stepped toward the door in unison. "We bid you good-night," they said as one. And in matching movements placed their hats upon their heads as they left the house.

Louisa grinned. "Do you suppose they know their actions are like mirrors of each other?"

Father chuckled. "I don't suppose they do." He looked at her temporary arrangement for the triplets' bed. "Will they be okay here on their own for the night?"

"I plan to sleep on the sofa so I can keep a watch on them." They were able to scoot around a bit but hadn't moved much so far because they weren't feeling well. No doubt once they felt better that would change. It would be a challenge to keep them safely corralled.

That was a problem she'd deal with when the time came and count herself blessed for the little time they were with her. She covered a huge yawn.

Father chuckled. "I can see you're tired. I'm off to bed. I hope they sleep for you. Good night, daughter." He kissed her on her cheek and retired to his room closest to the clinic area off the kitchen.

She didn't move for a moment as she looked toward the room not yet ready for Mother. Somehow she must manage to tend to that job as well as care for the triplets. A smile lifted the corners of her mouth. The room could wait. For now she would enjoy having some babies to care for.

She prepared for bed, careful not to make any noise

and disturb the peaceful babies. With a pillow for her head and quilt for cover, she got as comfortable as she could on the sofa. It had been a busy day and her muscles welcomed the chance to relax.

Sleep came softly, filled with dreams of three little boys toddling about, laughing at each other and running to her for comfort. Even in her dream she knew it wasn't possible but the dream was sweet, nevertheless.

A sharp cry wakened her and she looked about, disoriented. Then remembrance flooded back and she bolted upright. One of the triplets was crying. If she could get to him in time, she might prevent him from waking the others.

Even as she struggled to her feet, a second voice joined the first. By the time she lit the lamp, all three fussed.

One sounded hoarse. She bent close. Theo struggled to breathe. The other two coughed. They had grown worse. She gathered Theo into her arms. "Poor little boy." She rubbed his back and spoke comfortingly to him.

The other two lay at her feet, coughing and miserable.

She sat on the floor, her back to the sofa, cradling the babies around her. She propped them up on pillows so they could breathe easier but Theo's air whistled in and out. He needed steam, but when she tried to push to her feet, they all protested and she sank back.

Father slept through it all, for which she was grateful. His nights were often disturbed and cut short by calls.

The sound of Theo's lungs working so hard grew

more intense. She needed to boil water but she didn't have enough hands. If she went out of their sight, they would panic, making it even more difficult for them to breathe.

Lord, help me. She should have sent for Annie but the girl was so excited about going to the fair that Louisa didn't want to spoil her fun. In fact, she hated to ask anyone to give up time at the fair.

Theo coughed and gagged. He struggled to suck in air.

A dark wave rushed through Louisa. *Don't die. Don't die. Please, God, help me.*

Relying solely on instinct and experience as the doctor's daughter, she flipped him over and patted his back. He coughed and coughed until she thought he would surely cough out his lungs. And then he sucked in a whistling breath and her own lungs gasped in air.

She could not delay any longer. She must steam Theo—all of them—and ignoring the tortured cries of Jasper and Eli, she perched Theo on her hip as she hurried to the kitchen, built up the fire and filled the kettle.

How would she get steam to each of them? Normally she would have built a tent out of sheets, but if she disappeared from sight to fetch them, the babies would get even more upset. She grabbed the nearest thing that would work—a linen tablecloth. Placing a pot of steaming water on a chair where she could make sure the triplets couldn't touch it, she sat on the floor, gathered them to her knees and draped the cloth over them all, her head forming one tent pole, the back of the chair, another. Steam filled the small area. The moisture dampened her pores, and within minutes, the babies' breathing eased.

She remained there, closeting them into a cocoon of moisture. The water cooled but inside the tent the air continued to be warm. The babies coughed, but they didn't choke.

Theo began to whistle again with each breath. Knowing she couldn't leave it so long this time, she folded back the cloth and did her best to slip away from the babies. They fussed at being disturbed but she had no choice and repeated the procedure.

Even when the triplets slept, she dare not let herself fall asleep for fear she wouldn't hear a change in their breathing soon enough.

Oh, for morning. Maybe some good soul would appear to help her. Finally the first pink rays of sunrise colored the eastern sky. Father rose, but at the sound of someone in the waiting room, he immediately left. "I'll see who it is." A moment later, he stuck his head back in the room. "A man has been seriously injured in a fall. I must attend him. Will you be okay?"

She'd managed the babies all night. "I'll be fine." But as he left she realized how alone she was.

Who would help her? She pictured Bo with babies on his knee. They had settled for him. But he would assume they were in her capable hands and turn his feet toward the fair. Already she could hear sounds of the animals coming to life and the people who had camped nearby awakening and calling to each other. The scent of their campfires teased her nose.

The babies stirred. Theo breathed easier but Eli did not.

She abandoned them long enough to get dressed and boil more water. They protested at her departure but she had no choice even though their crying further compromised their ability to get in enough air.

She desperately needed another pair of hands. *Lord, please put it on someone's heart to stop by and offer help.* Maybe Brandon would check on the babies and she could ask him to send Annie.

It wasn't Annie she wanted to show up or Brandon she wanted to knock on the door and offer to help. It was his brother. But she understood that Bo had no reason to call. He had other things on his mind that precluded Louisa. Too late, she reminded herself she should have thought the triplets not herself.

Leaving his capable foreman Clint in charge of the ranch, Bo left early for town, anxious to supervise day two of the fair. His heart overflowed with gratitude for the success of day one. Peaceful with the knowledge of how well the day had gone, he'd expected to sleep soundly, but a riot of images troubled his rest. A man sneaking into the bank and finding the safe left open. The money gone. Another scene of wind blowing away the tents and leaving nothing but the shivering figure of a lone woman. Mixed feelings as he realized it was the mother of the triplets. Three babies struggling to climb into his lap. Memory of the latter dream brought a smile to his lips.

There was something mighty appealing about the idea.

A hard frown quickly replaced the smile. He would

never be a father. He couldn't trust himself to be what a child deserved.

He leaned forward in anticipation as he approached Little Horn. Families and groups of people camped along the side of the river and in the shelter of the trees, staying the entire three days of the fair. Everyone moved about, preparing breakfast and visiting with those around them.

Bo waved a greeting to those he passed, happy to see how many stayed for the second and, hopefully, the third day. He didn't stop even though several invited him to join them for coffee or breakfast.

Something urgent pressed to his mind and he rode directly to the bank. Two men—different than the two from last night—held their positions, one at the back and one at the front of the building. Both waved to him. The man at the front called, "Everything is as it should be."

Those words sang a refrain in his head as he continued on his way to the fairgrounds. Again, people were up and about, feeding their animals and taking care of business. No tents had blown away. None had fallen down. Edmund McKay rode over to his side. He was a responsible rancher, a founding member of the Lone Star Cowboy League. He'd recently married Lula May, a widow with several children. It appeared the man had found happiness with the newly-acquired family. Bo wished him all the best but wouldn't allow himself to think he'd like the same things.

"See you're checking on things," the man said.

"See you are too." They grinned at each other.

Edmund's brother David joined them in time to

overhear their remarks. "How are the babies?" he asked.

"I'm headed that way to check on them now," Bo answered. "No one has heard anything about the mother?"

The sheriff sauntered over. "I asked around. She had to arrive by some means, so I asked Mr. Crenshaw at the train station if he'd noticed anything unusual. He chuckled and said with so many people coming and going about, all he took note of was whether or not they had a ticket." Jeb shook his head. "He wasn't any help."

Bo thought of how much he and Brandon had relied on their mother's love and care. It had gone a long way to balancing out the way their father treated them. He wished the same steady presence for the triplets. "I sure wish we could find her."

"We'll keep looking," Jeb reassured him before he patted Bo's horse and moved on.

Bo moved on as well, heading down the street toward the doctor's house. *Everything as it should be.* The words sang through his head again. When he realized he thought of Louisa and the babies in the same song, he silenced it. He would check on the triplets. Only out of concern for their well-being. Not because he enjoyed the warmth of their little bodies against his chest or because he liked the way they accepted him. And most definitely not because watching Louisa with them soothed his soul. No, it was simply his duty to make sure they were okay. When people asked him about them he wanted to be able to answer them with the latest information.

He arrived and took his time draping the reins over

the post and looking about as if taking stock of the early morning activities. Anyone observing would come to the conclusion he wasn't in a hurry to see the occupants of the house before him. He wanted to convince himself of the same.

He sauntered casually up the steps and rapped on the door.

Louisa threw back the door, grabbed him and pulled him in. She held Eli, the baby's eyes glassy, his nose running.

The other two wailed at being left. He took in the rumpled quilt and white sheet on the floor. The scattering of pillows. The wooden-back chair in the middle of the room. A very marked contrast to the peaceful scene of last night.

"You need some help?" He didn't wait for her answer but went to the big chair and pulled the pair from the floor to his knees.

Louisa stood in the middle of the room. Dark shadows curled below her brown eyes. Eyes that had a hollowed-out look to them.

"A rough night?"

She scraped a hand over her brown hair. "I know I look a mess."

She certainly looked worn-out and frazzled but a mess? No. There was something appealing about her looks…like a woman who put the needs of the triplets ahead of her own. "You look like a woman who spent a difficult night with three babies." How would she react to that observation? It didn't sound complimentary though in his mind, it was.

Her chuckle made him blink.

"If you intended that to make me feel better then thank you, but I have to tell you it missed the mark."

He grinned at her. "Believe me, it was meant as a compliment."

Her gaze searched his. "How is that?"

No reasonable explanation came to mind but he did the best he could. "To see you willing to give of yourself for these little fellows...well, it reminds me of my own mother."

A sweet expression smoothed her face. "That's a very nice thing to say." She sat in the chair facing him and lifted Eli to her shoulder, patting his back.

On his knee, Jasper and Theo seemed content to lean listlessly against him. "I thought they were on the mend."

"All three of them developed coughs in the night. They took turns having a croup attack." She leaned her head against the back of the chair. "I think they're improving this morning." Slowly her gaze came to his, full of warmth. "Now that you've compared me to your mother, I think I deserve to hear more about her."

He shifted to accommodate the restless babies. "She was the most patient woman. She tried to protect us from our father by sending us to the nurse as soon as he came home, but Father knew that's what she did, so when we turned seven he said we no longer needed a nurse. That's when we really got to see him for what he was. Before that whenever we saw him and Mother together she smiled and looked happy. But we soon learned it wasn't real. She tried her best to hide how hurt she was but she couldn't all the time. He would tell her she was useless. Nothing but a pretty useless ornament. She'd never be able to survive without him. So often she was reduced to tears." He stopped speaking as his throat tightened. He'd never before told anyone how he'd felt but now the words poured forth. "I wanted to protect her but soon learned if I intervened it only made things worse for her. I can't tell you how often I was ashamed because I couldn't help her." His insides grew brittle as he recalled the cruel words and taunts. "He tried to turn Brandon and me against each other but he couldn't succeed."

She shifted Eli to her other shoulder. "I'm so sorry. No one should have to endure such treatment." Her eyes softened around the edges so that she looked like she smiled although her mouth did not curve. There was something soft about the way she held her lips. As if comfort came naturally to her. Perhaps it was the product of being a doctor's daughter.

Something about that look, whether it be sympathy or pity, he couldn't say, but it dripped into his heart like honey. He didn't even try to reason why he should think such a thing, though perhaps it was because she didn't judge or condemn or offer solutions. Merely said it shouldn't have happened. "I couldn't agree more," he said after a moment of consideration.

"You said she died when you and your brother were sixteen. What happened after that? Did you boys leave home?"

"We both thought of it and discussed plans. But one thing stopped us."

"Tell me what it was."

"Our mother."

She blinked. "But... I don't understand."

"We stayed to honor her and the sacrifices she'd made for us." He could see the confusion in Louisa's eyes and continued with an explanation. "I remember early on when we first realized how cruel Father was. I thought she should leave. She told me she would never do so because he would not let her have her boys. She would suffer any kind of agony to be with us. Brandon cried at her answer. I squished my fists into balls and told her I would never stay if it wasn't for her. She held me and told me to remember I was responsible for my actions, not his. And God said we should honor our parents. She eventually convinced me that I would be happier doing things God's way rather than my own. It's why we stayed."

"That's very decent of you."

He shrugged. "We both knew it was what both God and Mother would want."

"Did it get easier?"

His snort of humorless laughter jerked Jasper's attention to him. The baby's nose ran and Bo pulled out his hankie and wiped it clean. "Poor little man. You aren't feeling well, are you?"

Tears welled up in Jasper's eyes and then he burrowed his face into Bo's shirt.

Bo patted the little back. Theo watched without moving. Bo rubbed his back too and earned himself a sad smile.

He returned his attention to Louisa. "To answer your question, no, things didn't get better. Father suffered a stroke a little more than two years after Mother's passing. Frustrated at his limitations, he got even meaner. We took care of his affairs, hired a big strong man to help with his needs and took care of him until his death four years ago." He let out a long gust of air. "There are still days I feel the burden on him across my shoulders."

"And then you came to Texas?"

"Lots of opportunities here."

"And a chance to forget the past?"

"I suppose that's part of it but I'll never forget what my father was like. I don't ever want to forget how he was." He would not be lulled into thinking he could make plans, live dreams, enjoy the things his heart yearned for at times…like a child of his own, a wife to share life with. He was his father's son and he would never forget it.

Her gaze bolted to his, searching, seeing. He wasn't sure how much he wanted her to see. Did he want her to know the depth of his pain at the ugly things Father had said? The fear of his raised hand? The horribleness of his temper tantrums after his stroke? But he couldn't tear himself from her look, and at the way her lips gently smiled he wondered how much she'd understood.

A faint whistling sound pulled his attention to Jasper. "Is that him?"

Louisa sprang to her feet. "He's getting croupy again." She jostled Eli on her hip. "I need to steam him." She rushed to the kitchen and returned with a kettle. "I've kept the water ready all night." She filled the basin on the chair and grabbed the white cloth. "I make a little tent for them and we stay under it until their lungs release."

"Them?"

"The three of them seem to keep in step with each other."

She lifted Jasper from his arms and gave him Eli

before she sank to the floor, settling the baby on her lap. She pulled the cloth to her chin. "Unless you care to join us?"

He saw her intent. The babies getting steamed to ease their airways. "This is what you did all night?"

"For much of it." She touched her hair.

He looked at the two babies he held. Theo looked at him solemnly. Eli looked at Louisa. Bo cocked his head toward Eli. "I hear him whistling." That provided reason enough for his decision and he sat shoulder to shoulder with Louisa, the babies on his knees, and pulled the cloth over them. "This reminds me of some of the games Brandon and I played."

"It must have been nice to have a brother the same age."

"Not to mention with the same face." He grinned at her. "It was nice. Still is."

Louisa rubbed Jasper's back, helping him relax. It eased her tension, as well. To think of a woman—Bo's mother—enduring such a marriage and doing it willingly for the sake of her boys left her shaken. But it appeared to have made Bo a thoughtful, kind person. The truth hit her like a sledgehammer. "You were on your way to the fair, weren't you?" She reached for Theo. "I can manage. You go on about your business."

He shifted to look at her, his odd-colored eyes bright even under the white tablecloth. Maybe even brighter than normal because of it. "I don't know how you managed three sick babies on your own last night. Or did your father help?"

She gave barely a shake of her head. "No need to

judge him for that. He often misses his sleep while he takes care of his patients."

"I have no opinion one way or the other but one woman and three babies. There simply aren't enough arms to go around. When we find their mother I will make sure she has someone to help. The poor woman."

"She has my sympathy, indeed," Louisa said with heartfelt agreement, then recalled her prior comment. "I took care of them last night. I can do it again. Don't feel obliged to stay."

He continued to study her until she had to look away. It wasn't like Jasper didn't need her attention, she thought by way of providing herself an excuse other than being far too aware of a man sitting beside her under the privacy of a cloth. If anyone should enter… She gave a mental shrug. They'd have to take but one look at her, see the way her hair drooped about her face, take note of her soiled apron and rumpled dress to realize it meant nothing but caring for the triplets.

"I do feel obliged," he said after some seconds when the only sound was the harsh breathing of the babies. "I feel obliged to make sure these babies are okay and I don't have to be overly bright to understand it's too much for one person."

Her heart lifted to know she'd have help. "What about the fair? You could ask Annie to come and help."

"I saw Annie and she was enjoying herself. No reason to rob her of this occasion. There are lots of people there to take care of things at the fair. I expect Brandon will come looking for me and I'll explain the situation to him. That is unless…"

She turned at the question in his voice and their

gazes caught and held, taking her into places she'd long ago boarded over…places of sharing and caring with a man. She tried to pull herself away from that forbidden place. Hadn't Wes taught her that she couldn't expect a man to understand her home duties? That and the passing of time that had brought no interested suitor into her life. She was content it should be so and jerked her thoughts back to the conversation. "Unless what?"

His voice lowered. "Unless you don't want me to stay?"

Not want him to stay? If only he knew the truth. That she found herself liking his company just fine. Maybe a little too fine. She pulled her gaze away to look at the babies. All this silly thinking came from spending a sleepless night with them. Swallowing down her errant longings and pushing her thoughts back into hiding, she faced him, smiling at the foolishness of not wanting help. "I accept your offer."

"Good thing." His voice lowered several degrees. "Because I wouldn't have taken no for an answer."

She laughed at the way he said it. As if he truly meant to stay whether she had been brave enough or not to say it was okay.

Content to accept his help and his company in order to tend the babies, she sat back. Jasper's breathing eased and he fell asleep in her arms. Eli's chest still drew in hard as he fought to get his air in. Steam filled the small tent. Moisture pooled on her cheeks. She grabbed a towel she'd used before and wiped her face, then offered it to Bo. She almost giggled at the water dripping from his nose and chin.

He wiped his face dry and patted Theo's dry, as

well. Theo looked unblinkingly at Bo, his eyes wide and focused.

"Did you ever see such a look of trust?" she asked.

Beside her, Bo stiffened. "If you mean me, he'd soon learn his trust was misplaced."

What had he said about fearing he would be like his father? She couldn't recall the exact words, but from what she'd observed of him even before he helped with the triplets, it seemed unlikely he was at all like his patriarch and she told him so.

"I once told my father I vowed I would never be like him. He laughed in my face. 'Don't ever forget half the blood flowing through your veins comes from me.' I vowed I'd never forget."

"But surely you can see—"

"I know what I know. I will never take the chance."

She sank back to the edge of the sofa, pressing her body into its rough texture. Her elbow brushed Bo's and she felt his tension. What could she say to ease it? "Did you get your dance card full?"

It took the space of two seconds for him to shift from his past to his present and she knew the moment he did. The lines of his face softened and his arm relaxed. "Still got some openings. Do you want me to put your name in one?" He flashed a teasing smile at her.

Or was it genuine?

Not that it mattered. She chuckled somewhat regretfully. "I think I will have my hands full with the triplets."

"You're missing all the fun." He sounded truly disappointed on her behalf, which triggered a sting of tears in her eyes.

She ducked her head lest he see how his words affected her. "I'm doing what needs to be done."

He made a musing sound that drew her gaze back to him. "I'm going to make a wild guess here and say that's the story of your life...doing what needs to be done."

She tried to read his meaning. Did he think as Wes had that she was overly responsible? Or did he admire the quality? Or was it nothing more than an observation...a comment meant to pass time?

He'd said she reminded him of his mother, who had endured so much for the sake of her boys. Perhaps it meant he understood, even appreciated, the choices she made to serve her family. "My mother is an invalid. She needs someone to take care of her." She sat back, a happy smile on her face and in her heart. "Mother will always need help but I am so pleased that Amy has grown from a weak baby and a sickly child to a woman who is well enough to live a full life. One of the happiest days of my life was when she got married. And Lawrence is a fine man. I have no qualms about turning the care of my little sister over to him."

The water in the basin had cooled but all three babies drowsed, breathing easier for the moment, so she hesitated to shift any of them to fetch more hot water.

A gentle tap came to the door and both Louisa and Bo jerked the covering off their heads.

"Come in," Louisa whispered, hoping whoever was there would consider the fact that three babies might be sleeping.

The door eased open and Brandon stuck his head through the door. Seeing Bo and Louisa with the babies huddled in their arms and a third across their knees, he grinned widely and his eyebrows arched upward. "I came to see how the babies were doing and then I meant to go looking for Bo." He kept his voice to a whisper. "Everyone is a little concerned that he hasn't shown up at the fair. Some even wondered if he'd run into some kind of trouble."

Louisa had heard stories of rustlers and arsonists and other nasty deeds before their arrival. Was there real concern for Bo's safety? If so, she might try to find a compelling reason for him to stay there and help with the babies until the danger passed.

"What sort of trouble?" she asked Brandon.

He grinned. "Seems Bo interfered with a robbery yesterday. Could be the man whose plans he thwarted might be a little angry." He took in the chair and the pan of cooling water. "Looks like the babies have been needing a lot of attention. Could I do something?"

Louisa considered the offer. Both Stillwater men willing to stay and help with the babies? She wasn't about to turn down that offer.

Chapter Five

Bo could see that Louisa welcomed Brandon's offer of help. He tried not to wish his brother would find it necessary to leave. "Shouldn't you let the league know that you found me safe and sound?"

"They can wait." He touched the water in the basin. "I'll get some more boiling water." And he headed for the kitchen. Bo sighed. He loved his brother. They enjoyed each other's company. But whereas Bo had decided he wasn't interested in marriage and a family, Brandon believed God had set him free from the chains of his upbringing. It wasn't that Bo didn't trust God as he said to Brandon on many an occasion, but some things weren't worth the risk. He preferred to trust God to help him be true to his conviction that no woman, nor child, deserved to discover what it meant to carry his father's blood.

We are cleansed by the blood of Jesus, Brandon replied every time the conversation came up.

Unaware of where Bo's thoughts had gone, his brother

boiled water and refilled the basin. The babies started to fuss. Jasper again struggled to breathe.

"Time to make a tent," Bo said and pulled the cloth over his head, enclosing Louisa, as well.

Brandon sank down next to Bo and pressed him hard over to Louisa's side. "I'll take that one." He checked the name on the shirt. "Theo. Hi." He settled the little guy on his lap. He nudged Bo. "This reminds me of the tents you and I used to build." He leaned forward to look at Louisa. "We went from building tents from sheets to making forts out of anything we could find." He laughed. "We were fortunate to live on the edge of the city, so we would escape to the woods and build our forts."

A sense of peace replaced Bo's tension. "That's how I met Russell Maynard. He was like a father to me. Taught me all about farming." It was because of Russell that Bo became a rancher.

Brandon nudged him again. "He could have punished you for going into the pen with his horses—" He directed his remarks at Louisa. "Bo thought he could ride one of the horses but he'd never ridden anything but a gentle old mare. It wasn't that kind of horse. Right, Bo?"

Bo chuckled. "A horse was a horse, as far as I was concerned, but I knew those animals were a lot better-looking animals than the one we rode." No need for Louisa to think he had utterly failed. "I did manage to get on the back of one."

"Only to be tossed off on your face."

"But I got on again."

"And got tossed off again. I think you would have

done it all day if Russell hadn't intervened. He grabbed Bo by the back of his shirt and held him with his feet barely touching the ground. Told him that interfering with a man's livestock could get him into serious trouble."

Bo shuddered. "I thought for sure he'd take us to Father. Father would have made sure I learned my lesson." He had quaked inside at what form the wrath might take. "Instead he said he expected me to show up every day after school and on Saturday mornings to help with chores." A smile pulling at his lips, he turned to Louisa. "Little did he know how happy I was to agree. It was no punishment for me." He gave a low laugh. "I realized later that he knew exactly what he was doing. And I have been forever grateful."

"God never overlooks the needs of one of His children," Brandon said.

"He provides what we need to live the life He has assigned us." Louisa spoke softly.

Bo wondered at the tone of her voice. It sounded like she needed God's provision in unusual amounts. He longed to know what she meant.

The water again cooled as he and Brandon entertained Louisa with stories of growing up and learning about life on the farm. She laughed often and he discovered he thoroughly enjoyed hearing her amusement and being at least partly responsible for it.

The babies breathed easier. Louisa shifted the cloth off them and the air dried the beads of water on Bo's forehead.

She glanced at the clock. "Oh, my. Look at the time.

I'll make us lunch." She eased Jasper to Bo's arms and hurried to the kitchen.

Bo and Brandon sat side by side, watching her prepare food. Bo knew Brandon thought the same as he… it was nice to watch a woman cook for them. It brought back pleasant memories. Yes, Mrs. Jamieson prepared his meals on a regular basis but this was different.

A little later, she lifted the babies out of their arms and settled them on the quilt. They shuffled and sighed but stayed asleep. Bo, Brandon and Louisa sat down to enjoy creamy vegetable soup and sandwiches made with homemade bread and thick slices of cheese.

They'd barely finished when the triplets stirred.

"They'll be hungry," Louisa said and set out a bowl of soup. She looked about at the two men. "Do you want to help feed them?" She wrapped towels around each chubby little neck.

"Sure," Bo said, not giving Brandon a chance to voice an opinion.

Louisa put a baby on each of his knees and Theo on Brandon's, then sat in front of them and spooned soup from one to the other.

He looked at Brandon and saw his amusement reflected in his brother's eyes. They both laughed.

Without missing a beat in the continual feeding process, Louisa glanced at them, her eyes asking what was so funny.

"They're like little birds in the nest," Bo said.

She chuckled. "I thought the same thing. But at least they eat well and drink from a cup." She offered the triplets milk in a cup and they each dipped their heads forward to take it.

Tummies full and breathing easier, the boys sighed.

Louisa lifted Jasper and put him on the quilt. "They'll either sleep or play together. I notice they're happiest when they have each other." She took Theo and put him next to his brother. She handed out the toys that had been left at the door.

The two little boys looked at each other and made happy sounds.

Bo sat Eli in between them. He leaned forward to touch his brothers and chuckled.

Brandon stood watching them. "We must find their mother."

Bo knew Brandon shared his thought. These babies needed their mother. In their experience, no one loved like a mother. But then he thought of the people in the community who had married a spouse with children or taken in orphaned children. For the most part those children were well loved and taken care of with maybe one or two exceptions. He thought of two orphans—Jo Satler and her little brother, Gil. He thought the pair to be about ten and six. Their widowed mother died a few months ago and the two children stayed with friends. But mostly they seemed to be on their own. Bo often spotted them hanging about town unsupervised.

There was a sound at the door. Louisa hurried to open it before knocking could waken the babies. "There's no one here."

She was about to close the door when Bo noticed something on the step. "Brandon, did you drop something on your way in?"

"No. Not me."

"It looks like—" Louisa picked up the pile of material and lifted one then a second and then a third. "Like well-worn baby blankets."

The three adults rushed to the door to look either way up and down the street. Bo was sure he'd spot a frail-looking woman—the triplets' mother, who had to be the one leaving the toys and blankets. There were a dozen or more people going about their business, but they were all either locals they recognized or clearly not alone.

Bo grabbed his hat and ran into the street. Brandon followed on his heels.

"You go that way. I'll go this." As Brandon went in the opposite direction, Bo looked around the corner of every building, went into every place of business. He knew Brandon would be doing the same. He headed toward the fairgrounds. No woman alone. He wasn't sure what he looked for but somehow thought he would recognize her by a furtive manner or with some indication she was ill.

He saw nothing of the sort and was delayed several times as people stopped him to ask regarding one detail or another about the fair. Two young ladies asked to be put down for the dime dance with him. He wrote their names and took their dimes but hurried away. Perhaps Brandon had tracked down the missing woman.

Brandon met him in front of Mercy Green's Café, which was doing a brisk business. He hoped her patrons were also spending money at the fair.

"I didn't locate anyone who might be the triplets' mother," Brandon said.

"Nor I." Bo scrubbed at his chin, realized Brandon

did the same thing at the same time. Brandon noticed Bo's actions and they laughed.

"I'll inform Miss Clark of our failure to find the mother." Bo looked up and down the street. "I suppose it's possible that the woman has left town."

Brandon squeezed Bo's shoulder. "Until we find her, the babies are being well cared for. They're very sweet babies." Brother considered brother solemnly.

Bo shook his head. "No, they aren't going to make me change my mind about a family."

Brandon shifted to consider the doctor's house. "But perhaps Miss Louisa Clark will." And before Bo could disabuse him of such a notion, Brandon adjusted his hat and strode away.

Bo lifted a hand to stop him, then dropped it. Brandon knew how he felt and why. He watched until Brandon turned the corner then went to the door. Not hearing any crying and thinking the babies were still sleeping, he tapped lightly.

Louisa opened and held her fingers to her lips. She led him past the sleeping babies to the kitchen. "Did you find her?"

"'Fraid not."

"I'm sorry." They stood side by side watching the triplets sleep.

They moved away to the back door so as not to disturb the babies and looked out the window. Three boys ran up the alley in a game of tag. In the yard behind the doctor's residence, Mrs. Martin took three drying towels off the line. The orphaned Satler children moseyed by hand in hand.

"Jo has not spoken since her mother's death. It's such a shame," Louisa said. "What will become of them?"

"I wish I could assure you everything will work out for Jo and her little brother. And for them," he added, indicating the babies in the other room. "And I hope it does. It takes family and a good community to raise good children. They have the latter in Little Horn. But they must have a family. We need to find their mother." He'd said it to himself and aloud so many times as if by repeating it often, he could make himself find the woman.

Louisa squeezed his hand. "We will continue to pray and trust God to answer in His time."

"And His way?" Bo's question was scarcely more than a whisper. "I confess that Brandon finds it easier to stand back and trust God's way than I do. I prefer to—" He'd been about to say "be in charge." That did not convey the real meaning of his feelings. "Do what I can to make sure things work out. Like supervising the fair."

She had only touched his hand for a moment and now shifted to give him a rueful glance. "I feel bad that I'm keeping you from that task."

He chuckled. "You aren't. They are." He tipped his head toward the triplets. "No, that's not exactly honest. I expect you could manage fine without my help and yet it makes me feel like I'm doing my part by staying."

She nodded, her look thoughtful. "I won't deny that I've appreciated your help." She chuckled, a sound as soft as spring rain. "And I enjoyed hearing of your adventures on Mr. Maynard's farm. Happy stories." With a gentle sigh, she moved back to watch out the window. "You and Brandon really enjoy each other's company."

"So we do. I can't imagine life without him. But I expect you have the same thing with your sister. What did you say—she's five years younger than you? Did that create too great a distance?"

"It wasn't so much the age difference." Did he detect a note of regret in her voice?

"Then what?"

She leaned against the window frame and shifted her gaze back to him, seeking something from him… something he wished he could give. But he had nothing to offer her. Nothing but a few minutes of his time.

"I suppose it was our roles. She was a frail baby who needed lots of extra care, and because my mother wasn't well, I provided it as much as I could." A faraway look came to her eyes as if reliving those days with her sister.

"So looking after these babies is familiar to you?"

A smile brightened her expression. "Except Amy was the only one. I don't know how I would have coped with twins or triplets. But yes, I've dealt with croup and colds, scrapes and bruises, fevers and rashes before, though not necessarily because of Amy. We did our best to keep her from such things. But I've helped Father on many occasions. In fact—" her smile grew rueful "—I once thought I might like to be a doctor when I grew up."

She seemed the sort of woman who wouldn't let an obstacle stand in her way. Why, look how she bravely took on the care of the triplets. And how she tackled cleaning the house. Several people had mentioned how hard she worked at it and he had only to look around to see the place was spotlessly clean. "Why didn't you pursue that?"

"I was needed at home."

Such a simple statement but one which carried a world of responsibility and spoken without a hint of regret. He nodded. "A person does what a person knows they must do." It seemed they each had their own expectations to live up to. His curiosity about her grew.

"I suppose you have a suitor back east waiting for you."

She developed a keen interest in the view out the window, practically pressing her nose to the glass. "I don't have much time for such socializing."

A day or two ago he would have taken those words as meaning she wasn't interested in courting, was perhaps a bit too full of her own importance, but after spending a few hours in her company, he caught the regret in her tone that she likely meant to disguise. He sensed a deep pain behind the words.

"Louisa— May I call you that?"

She lifted one shoulder. "Seems sharing the care of three babies gives us the right to address each other by our Christian names."

"Thank you. Louisa, have you never had a beau?"

She dipped her forehead to the window glass. Her shoulders rose and fell.

He longed to rub her back as he had the babies'. More than that, he had an urge to pull her into his arms and hold her tight, offering comfort and—

He had nothing of consequence to offer her or any other woman.

"I did once." The sadness in her voice made him ache. "What happened?"

She rolled her head back and forth. "I had my family to take care of and he wasn't willing to wait."

Those few words provided him with a glimpse into her life. A life of sacrifice on behalf of those she loved. Again he was reminded of his mother, though he struggled to convince himself that was all he saw...all he felt.

A footstep sounded at the front door and Louisa hurried away to stop the caller before he knocked.

Bo followed more slowly, his thoughts warring one with another.

One of the ranchers, David McKay, stood in the doorway. He glanced at the sleeping babies and without speaking signaled to Bo that they needed to talk.

Bo eased past the triplets without disturbing them.

"We have a problem," David whispered. "There's money missing from one of the booths. The seller claims he's been robbed but Casper is accusing him of pocketing the money. I can't find Jeb or Brandon. You better come and see what you can do."

Casper Magnuson was an arrogant loudmouth known for stirring up trouble with his aggressiveness. Bo had often wondered how his wife, Celia, endured his behavior. But like his own mother, she put up with it for the sake of her children.

"I'll be right along." He glanced back at the babies, then met Louisa's determined gaze. "Will you be okay on your own?"

"I can manage."

He admired her for her singleness of purpose.

* * *

Louisa closed the door and leaned against it. Why had she admitted that Wes wasn't willing to wait for her? Bo had no reason to care and yet…yet. She sighed. For a moment she wished he did…wished it mattered to him.

How silly of her. It no longer mattered to her, so why would it make a difference if it did to him? No reason whatsoever.

His company had been nice. So was having help.

She returned to the kitchen, a smile on her lips. Visiting with the Stillwaters as they worked together to tend the babies had been a pleasant break for her.

Bo and Brandon—identical in looks and yet so different. Bo let no one into his heart. Brandon let everyone in. At first observation, it seemed they responded in opposite fashion to their past, but maybe their reactions weren't so different. Both doing their best to counteract the heritage left by their father's cruelty. At least that was how she saw it. Likely someone else would see it differently. She'd be the first to admit she spent far too much time on her own, thinking on things. Perhaps drawing conclusions that were completely unfounded.

One by one in quick succession, the triplets wakened. Eli coughed but didn't sound croupy. Louisa could only hope and pray they were over the worst. She spared a glance at Mother's bedroom. If the babies were on the mend, could she squeeze in a few minutes of cleaning while they slept? She must not fail to have the room ready when Mother and Amy arrived. And Lawrence, of course. She chuckled at her oversight. Although she trusted him completely with her mother and sister, she still thought of their care as her responsibility. It was hard for her to believe Amy and Lawrence would continue on farther west once they brought Mother to Little Horn. Would she ever get over thinking she needed to guard Amy's health?

A knock sounded and she called, "Come in," rather than try to get to her feet to answer the door in person.

Lula May McKay stepped inside. "I had to come by and see how you are managing." She took in the triplets sleeping around her and smiled. "What a sweet picture. I'd stay and help but I have to work at the food booth today." She asked if there was anything Louisa needed, but when Louisa declined, she departed, in a hurry to take care of her responsibilities.

Her visit wakened the babies and Louisa gave them all a drink of milk.

Again someone knocked at the door.

"Enter," Louisa called.

Mercy Green, owner and operator of the café, stepped inside. "I won't keep you a moment, but I wondered if you had time to prepare any meals. Three babies! My. It is more than I can get my head around." She indicated the covered plate. "I brought you something to eat."

"Thank you." That took care of the need of the moment.

Mercy returned to take care of her café.

The afternoon passed, with no opportunity for her to clean the bedroom. The babies ate and played; they slept and cried. Coughed and needed to be steamed twice more.

Father returned later in the afternoon. "The fair is very busy," he said. "I've dealt with a steady stream of minor injuries." He quickly assessed the three babies. "You'll send for me if you need me?"

"Of course."

"I have no doubt they are in good hands."

Her father's praise eased through her.

He continued. "I've not seen so many people in one place since we came west. The members of the Lone Star Cowboy League should be very pleased. I imagine they will raise a good deal of money."

"That's great. Bo mentioned that they would offer the triplets' mother some financial assistance." Privately she thought they should also offer a mother's helper. "Three babies is a lot of work for one mother. Especially if she's ill."

"I wish they would locate her. Perhaps I could do something to help her health improve."

"I wish it too."

"By the way. I've received a letter from your mother." He pulled an envelope from his breast pocket. "Seems Mother hasn't been able to handle the traveling as well as we hoped. They've decided to spend a few days in Nashville to give her a chance to rest." He handed her the letter.

She skimmed the message. "I wish they would have provided more details about her illness. Perhaps I should go to her."

Father looked a little worried but shook his head. "There are lots of doctors in the city. I'm sure they can provide whatever care she needs. We'll have to trust that Amy and Lawrence can take care of her." And then as an afterthought, he added, "Plus, don't we know she is in God's capable hands?"

"Of course." How was it that she'd had to be reminded so often of her faith in the last few days? She said nothing more about Mother, knowing Father would be as concerned about her weak heart as Louisa. But the delay did provide a small reprieve in getting the bedroom ready.

Father checked the babies and said they were still sick, which she already knew. Then he left to return to the office tent at the fair.

She gathered the babies into her arms to rock them and sing to them as the hours raced by.

The sun's rays slanted through the western window. Through the open sash she listened to the sounds coming from the fairground and the laughter and conversation of those passing on the street. Perhaps Bo would think to stop by. Not that she couldn't manage without him.

She brushed her hair into place and changed into a clean dress in the hopes Bo—or even Brandon—might visit in the evening.

Annie rushed in the door and hunkered down with the babies. "They're adorable. I can stay and help if you want." Her eyes sought the door and Louisa knew she longed to join the festivities out there.

"Thanks for offering but it isn't often there are so many things going on in town. You run along. I'll be fine." Annie hurried away.

Besides, she hoped for help from another source. But neither Bo nor Brandon came.

Louisa was alone except for three babies and she grinned at them.

She gave them a bedtime snack and a drink of warm

milk, washed their faces, changed their diapers and settled them for the night, smiling as they looked around
to make sure their brothers were there. Theo reached
out and took Eli's hand and within minutes they fell
asleep, holding hands. Jasper snuggled close to Theo
and with a sigh, joined his brothers in dreamland.

Louisa slipped away, opening the door and stepping
outside to enjoy the cool of the evening. The two Bachmeier girls hurried by, waving then giggling together.
The blacksmith's two boys darted past, the younger
one checking over his shoulder as if someone chased
them. Louisa glanced down the street but saw no one
who might be after the boys.

She studied the area carefully, wondering if the triplets' mother might be lingering nearby. But she saw
no one who might fit that role, and leaned against the
door frame where she could keep an ear open to the
boys and yet enjoy the sounds of merriment from the
fairgrounds.

Strange how the sounds of laughter and lively music
made her sad.

The sounds grew less and then ended. Flickering
flames of fires indicated where families camped. The
night settled down around her and yet she lingered outside, watching, listening…and waiting?

Of course she wasn't waiting. Who or what would
she wait for? Father returned.

"How are the babies?" he asked.

She gave him a report.

"Do you need any help?" He yawned.

She knew he was tired. "I'll be fine." She could
manage the babies but it was a full-time job.

Not until the campfires died down and only the usual night sounds existed did she close the door to the outdoors and prepare for bed.

An hour later she was still awake, her heart too empty for her to sleep.

She shook herself. Enough of this. She knew what she needed to cure her of the doldrums, and she went to her tiny bedroom to get her Bible and sat at the kitchen table, the lamp turned only high enough to enable her to read.

Be strong and of a good courage, fear not, nor be afraid of them: for the Lord thy God, He it is that doth go with thee; He will not fail thee, nor forsake thee.

She closed the Book. Why did she wish for things she couldn't have when she had all she needed? God's promises were enough for her.

Bo had been busy with so many things at the fair after he left Louisa with the triplets that the afternoon slipped away faster than he could have anticipated.

He'd settled the disagreement between the vendor and Casper Magnuson by reminding the latter of the robbery of the previous day. He'd searched the grounds for the thieving man and his son, but if they were around, they were mighty good at keeping out of Bo's way.

His progress through the grounds had taken hours as people stopped to talk to him.

"The fair is going good," Floyd Farmington said as

he fell in at Bo's side. "'Twas a good idea you had to extend it to three days."

"Thanks. Coming from you, that means a lot." The man supported every fund-raising event in the community. Had auctioned off picnic baskets last year to raise funds for the new church and parsonage where Brandon now lived.

Others had stopped him to congratulate him on the success of the fair. Before he knew it, the crowd had dispersed and the booths closed down.

Jeb and two others of the Lone Star Cowboy League requested he join them as they took the money to the bank, where George Henley waited for their arrival.

Two by two, the four of them rode down the street, Bo and Edmund McKay bringing up the rear.

"Don't move your head." Bo spoke out of the side of his mouth. "But isn't that a man pressed to the side of the café?"

Edmund shifted and adjusted his hat. "Yep. Sure is."

He could think of only one reason for someone hiding in the shadows close to the bank…the thieving man waited for what he thought was an opportunity to relieve them of the funds and what better time to intercept the money than just before the men reached the bank. That would only work if the robber had accomplices. There were so many strangers in town it was impossible to eliminate the possibility. "You ride around on by as if you are still headed for the bank. Give me two minutes to go around the back and then you return. We should be able to corner the man."

He reined around as if returning to the fair and waited until he was out of sight to turn his mount toward Mercy Green's Café. He swung out of the saddle and proceeded as quietly as his boots and the growing darkness allowed. The sound of hoofbeats told him Edmund also returned and he broke into a run and rounded the corner.

He skidded to a stop. Nothing. No one. "He's got to be close by," he called to Edmund, and they searched up and down the street but to no avail.

Acknowledging defeat, they went to the bank, where the money had been safely locked in the safe, and he reported his suspicions. "The man is as slippery as a snake." Which made him even more of a risk.

"I'll have a look around too," Jeb said, and the men disbanded, leaving two armed guards at the bank.

Darkness had fully descended when Bo finally got a chance to go by the doctor's house. Through the window he saw a lamp burning very low. Should he stop? Were the babies sleeping? He'd listened. Not a sound. He'd stared at the house for several minutes, wanting to be inside, where he could assure himself all was well. But he turned away. He could hardly justify a social call that late at night. Instead, he rode home. Even in the dark, he knew when he passed the boulder that had given Big Rock Ranch its name.

Clint stepped out of the shadows at his approach. "Hi, boss. I was beginning to think something happened to you."

"I appreciate your concern. Lots of things to take care of at the fair."

"It doing good?"

"Yep. By the way. You and the boys take tomorrow off and go see for yourself."

"Thanks, boss. I knew you'd say that so I already told the boys."

"Night."

Bo covered a yawn as he entered his house. Mrs. Jamieson had long since retired for the night. But although he was tired, he was too wound up to sleep. Why was that man hanging around the bank?

His thoughts easily left that problem behind and ended up at the doctor's house with Louisa and the babies. Had they had more croup? How would she have managed? Did she miss him? Wish he'd stopped by? He fell asleep with a silent protest on his tongue about those questions.

Eli had gotten croupy. Louisa had steamed him and ended up falling asleep on the quilt beside the babies. She wakened stiff and sore with one of the babies patting her face and she laughed. So what if Bo hadn't come by last night to check on her. The joy of caring for these babies was reward enough. All three stirred and she gathered them into a hug. Jasper giggled, Theo ducked his head against her arm and Eli burrowed closer. "You are little darlings. I wish I could keep you."

Jasper tilted his head and babbled something at her.

"You're feeling better, aren't you?"

He jabbered a response.

She gave each of them a good look. No runny noses. No fevers. Theo sneezed and ended on a cough. Perhaps they weren't completely well yet.

She scrambled to her feet and picked her way around the little bodies to the kitchen. Father came from his room, yawning. Seeing the coffee wasn't started, he ground beans and dumped them into the pot along with water.

Louisa smiled. Father didn't like to talk until he'd had his coffee.

Jasper crawled after her. Eli saw what Jasper had in mind and followed, scooting along in a hip hop fashion on his bottom. Theo sat and watched, considering the other two for a moment, then flopped to his tummy, pushed himself to all fours and followed them. He reached her legs and pulled himself up.

Louisa laughed. "How do you expect me to make you breakfast when you wind about my legs?"

Eli whined as if he understood she didn't have breakfast ready.

The coffee boiled. Father poured himself a cup and sat at the table to drink it. "Did they have a good night?"

"They're much better." Louisa looked at the babies at her feet and then at her father. "Could you keep them by you while I make breakfast?" She didn't wait for his answer but shuffled the babies over to him. Jasper smiled at Father. "If you hold him the other two might stay here too." Again she didn't wait for any sign of agreement but lifted Jasper to Father's knee and, before anyone could protest, hurried to the stove to start preparing breakfast.

Father looked from one to the other. "Nice-looking boys, aren't they?"

"They're sweet." Before she had the potatoes and eggs fried, Theo lay back on the floor and fussed.

She grabbed the heel of the bread and tore it into

three and handed out portions to the boys. They sucked eagerly on it.

As soon as the breakfast was cooked, she dished up portions. How was she to feed them on her own? Father was a good doctor but he had never fed a child. Always turned that sort of thing over to Louisa or the mother of sick children.

How had the triplets' mother managed?

The cart. She retrieved it from the back step, parked the boys in it and fed them. "They're eating well."

"They're much better," Father said. "Good to see." He cleaned his plate. "I best get back to the fairgrounds. There's been a steady stream of minor injuries. Thankfully nothing serious."

He was gone and she was alone with the triplets.

Alone but not alone, because God was always with her and that was enough.

Chapter Six

Bo was on his way back to town as soon as the sky grayed with sunrise. He passed campers preparing their breakfast and waved to each group. He reached the fairgrounds and rode by each tent and booth. All was as it should be.

He rode on to the bank. Two guards alert and watchful. Each waved to him. All was as it should be there too.

All the same, he rode around every building to make certain that scoundrel wasn't hanging about waiting for the doors to open. Not that it meant the safe was open but would a thief realize that?

"Mr. Stillwater." Mercy Green called out from the door of her café. She crooked her finger to indicate she wanted to speak to him.

He turned aside, hoping it wouldn't be another day of constant delays preventing him from returning to the doctor's house and its occupants.

He slipped from his horse and strode over to her.

"We…that is, the ladies of the community…knew

those little babies would need more clothes, so we gathered together a hamper for them." She handed him a laundry basket full of little clothes.

"Thank you. That's very thoughtful." He should have realized the need and taken care of it. His failure to do so provided a much-needed reminder that Bo Stillwater was not cut out to be a father.

Or a husband. He fixed the words firmly in his mind as he continued on to the doctor's residence.

He wrapped the reins around the hitching post and carried the basket to the door and knocked gently.

From inside came the sound of babies. To his inexperienced ear they sounded happy and he smiled. His smile widened when he heard Louisa laugh. He knocked louder, too eager to see what amused her to wait for her to hear a soft rap.

She laughed again and said something but he couldn't make out her words and then she pulled open the door. If he wasn't mistaken, she wore a different dress than yesterday, a dark blue one that made her brown eyes darker. Her brown hair had an attractive untidy look to it. Her amusement wreathed her face in beauty.

He jerked the thought back. No need to be standing in the doorway admiring her even if he found her well worth admiring.

One of the babies perched on her hip. He was shirtless. "Theo?" he guessed.

"Yes, he's needing a little more attention than the other two." She stepped aside to indicate Jasper and Eli sitting on the floor, each with a big wooden spoon. Jasper banged his on the floor and looked to Eli for a reaction. Eli laughed. Pleased at his accomplishment, Jasper banged the floor again and they both laughed.

Louisa chuckled. "They are so good at amusing each other."

Bo grinned at the pair and laughed as Theo reached for his brothers. "He wants to join the fun."

Louisa sat Theo close to the others and handed him a wooden spoon to bang. All three wore only a diaper. She turned back to him. "Come on in, unless you have something else you need to do."

"No, I came to see how you were doing." He wondered at the way her cheeks pinkened but perhaps it was only because of bending over to put Theo down.

"The ladies sent this for the triplets." He handed her the basket.

She fell on it eagerly and started pulling out little shirts and holding them up. "This is great. I had to wash their shirts but they haven't dried, so I've had no choice but to leave them like this. Thankfully the day is warm enough that it doesn't pose any risk to them." She pulled out three matching shirts. "Look at this. These are brand-new. Someone has spent their evenings making outfits for the babies." Her voice caught and she swallowed loudly. With a sniff, she continued. "I wonder if Mrs. Carson and her quilting circle did this." She pressed the shirts to her face.

Bo turned away, the tender gesture pulling a dozen stops from his firmly encased heart.

Louisa set the shirts aside and continued lifting other items, examining and exclaiming over each. "I'm touched to see how much people care for babies they don't know."

"That's the beauty of a small town."

"I'm still discovering how much the community is like family."

"How were they during the night?" He kept back a dozen other questions. Had they slept? Had she been able to sleep? Were they over their colds? Did she miss him? He clamped down on his teeth. That was not a question to even allow himself to think.

"Jasper and Eli seem to be over their colds but Theo is still coughing."

Their gaze went to Theo.

"He doesn't seem as energetic as the other two," Bo observed after a moment. Theo seemed content to watch his brothers.

"I know but I can't say if that's his nature or if he doesn't feel well yet. If only we could find the mother." She gave Bo a sorrow-filled look. "It could be he's missing his mama. Poor little man."

"We've looked. Sheriff Fuller has sent telegrams to all the neighboring towns but so far no one knows of a woman with triplets."

She shook her head. "As the doctor's daughter, I can tell you how rare triplets are. Everyone in her community would know. It makes me wonder how far the poor woman traveled."

He mused on the idea. "I can't imagine how she must feel. Sick and alone. If she truly is dying I hope she finds people to love her and be with her through her final hours."

Her mouth worked as if holding back a cry.

He cupped his hand to her shoulder. "I'm sorry. I

shouldn't have said that. We're all doing our best to find her."

She nodded, her eyes brimming with tears.

He was a man. He wouldn't cry and yet he felt a strange sting at the backs of his eyes.

She leaned into his hand and somehow his arm slipped around her shoulders and he pulled her closer. She shuddered and sucked in air.

Did his closeness bother her? In a nice way or otherwise?

"After spending two nights with the babies, I can't begin to think how a sick woman alone did it. Whether or not we find their mother, the triplets must not be allowed to think their mother was weak in any way."

"I agree." They remained thus, with Louisa looking downward as if to hide from him her worries and concerns, or even her hopes, while he studied the top of her head and breathed in the homey scent of her— some kind of soap from washing the babies' shirts, a yeasty smell of baked bread and something beyond that, a sweetness of fresh mown grass and wild summer roses.

Theo plopped to his tummy and reached for Eli's spoon, his own forgotten at his side. Jasper banged his on the floor, drawing surprised chuckles from the other two.

Louisa stepped back and smoothed her skirt. "I'm sorry. I don't usually let the events of life bother me."

He sensed a whole world of practicality on that statement. "You said something earlier. That a person does what a person knows they must do. Does that mean you accept disappointments and responsibilities and never seek to get what you need or want?"

Her smile was tender, gentle, perhaps slightly chiding. "It simply means that I strive to find what I need in serving others." She glanced at the babies. "Can there be anything more rewarding?"

He wanted to hear her admit there might be more she wanted and yet he couldn't fault her thinking. His own mother had lived under the same philosophy, and because of her choice to endure their father's cruelness, he and Brandon grew up knowing love from her.

He said as much to Louisa. "I pray these little ones will grow up knowing love."

Theo lifted his arms to her and she scooped him and kissed him on his plump little cheek, earning her a pleased—if somewhat shy—smile.

He noticed the cart he'd found the babies in and had an idea. "Are they well enough to be out and about?"

"I think so. In fact, fresh air and a change of scenery might be good for them. Are you suggesting I take them for a walk?"

"Let's take them to the fair." He pulled the cart close. "We'll take them in this."

Her eyes lit with excitement, and then she banked it back. "I don't know if I can handle all of them at once in public."

"Not you," he corrected her. "Us. Between the two of us, we can manage. Just think, perhaps the mother is still around, and if she sees her babies, she won't be able to stay away." It surprised him how much he wanted her to agree to the outing. "And people can see for themselves how they are instead of asking me and wondering if I know what I'm talking about." He grinned widely. "They have every reason to question my knowledge on babies."

She tipped her head and her eyes sparkled as she studied him. "I don't know why they should. You've shown yourself most capable with them."

Even if he had, it meant nothing in the long run.

Perhaps realizing he wasn't about to respond to her statement, she changed the subject. "Yes, let's take them out. I'll get them dressed." She selected the three new, matching shirts and poked what seemed like too many arms into sleeves and buttoned the fronts. From the basket of clothing items, she selected three pairs of little short pants and three pairs of knit bootees. The triplets sat in a row on the floor, Louisa on her knees before them. She sat back on her heels and smiled at the babies.

"Look at you. You're going to steal the hearts of everyone who sees you." She grabbed a nearby brush and combed their dark brown hair to one side, laughing when Theo's insisted on going the opposite direction of his brothers'.

"They are ready." She picked up Eli and parked him in the cart. He lifted Jasper, and before she could get Theo, Bo settled him in the cart.

The three of them smiled and gurgled.

"I think they know they're going out," Louisa said.

When she reached for the handle of the cart, Bo stepped forward. "I'll drive."

"Wait while I get my purse."

He was about to tell her he would pay her way but she'd ducked into the kitchen.

Three pairs of worried eyes followed her departure.

"Don't worry, boys. She'll be back."

They spared him the shortest of glances, then turned to watch for Louisa to return.

She stepped back into sight. "I'm ready." She'd donned a fetching blue bonnet.

The babies all grinned and bounced to see her.

Bo laughed outright.

"What?" Louisa touched her hair where it showed around her bonnet in rich sorrel tones.

He wanted to grab her hand and say he would never laugh at her. And she had no reason to think anyone would criticize her looks. "These three little guys looked like they'd lost their best friend when you were out of sight, and when you came back, they were downright happy."

She bent over them and kissed the top of each head. "We've gotten to be pretty good friends, haven't we?" She darted a glance at Bo.

Did she include him in that statement? Feeling mighty fine at the idea, he pushed the big, clumsy cart from the house and, with Louisa close to his side, they began the trek to the fairgrounds.

It was normally a half hour to the grounds. Allowing for the heavy cart, Bo might have expected it to take a bit longer, but he hadn't accounted for the interest the triplets stirred. They met dozens of people and everyone—man, woman or child—stopped at the sight of three matching babies. The questions and comments ranged from "Are they identical?" to "They are the most adorable babies I've ever seen." Bo found the last one pleasant and the first silly.

It took well over an hour to reach the grounds.

Louisa insisted on paying her own admission. "I want to do my part to contribute to the fund."

He'd misjudged her badly to begin with but there seemed no point in admitting it again. Instead, he turned his efforts into making sure she enjoyed herself.

There was so much to take in that Louisa couldn't decide where to look first. Between the interest the triplets triggered and the many tents and booths, she wasn't sure which direction to turn and gladly let Bo guide her.

Besides, to be perfectly honest with herself, she rather enjoyed having him be in charge.

"Show me where you discovered the babies," she asked.

"Follow me. But first, why don't we look at the flower displays. They're on the way."

Some of the bouquets were past their prime after spending three days in the heat of the tent, but still, Louisa studied each one. The wildflowers caught her attention. "These look like wild daisies." Only not quite. Dark red centers, pink inner portions of petals with a yellow fringe. Some lacked the yellow border. "They're beautiful."

"Texans call them Indian blanket."

"I like that."

There were more and Bo provided the names of each. Mexican hat, bluebonnets and so many others.

There were flowers from gardens as well, but the babies were getting restless, so they moved on, always attracting attention.

The three McKay brothers stopped them.

David McKay spoke gently to the babies, earning him a wide smile from Jasper, a shy smile from Theo and a slow one from Eli.

"I'm relieved that they are together," David said. "It's important."

Edmund looked from one baby to another. "How do you tell them apart?"

"By their personalities." She pointed out how each of them reacted differently to the men greeting them.

Josiah's wife, Betsy, joined him, their three-year-old son, Eddie, at her side and a baby close to the same size as the triplets in her arms. Josiah lifted Eddie up so he could see the triplets.

"Three babies the same." Eddie laughed outright and the triplets gurgled their pleasure at his attention.

Betsy patted Louisa's arm. "You are a brave woman to take on three babies. I have my hands full with one." She leaned close as if she wanted only Louisa to hear her words. "I'm praying for their mother to be found and in the meantime for you to be able to look after the babies. Like David says, it's important that they stay together."

"I can't imagine separating them." She told the McKays how they sometimes held hands and how they looked for each other before they would settle.

David McKay leaned back on his heels. "I keep saying we need a home for orphans so we can keep siblings together and in the community that they are already a part of."

Louisa didn't point out that perhaps the triplets were part of another community, because she didn't want to think they might be spirited away by relatives.

They moved on, headed for the pie tent, but Louisa had already learned how slow progress was with so many interested in the babies.

Bo led them into more tents—to look at displays of garden produce, samples of hay and grains, samples of sewing and handcrafts. They stepped into a tent featuring paintings by people in Grant County and Louisa drew in a sharp breath.

"Who would have guessed there was so much talent in the county?" She circled the displays, filling her senses with color and wonder. Many were paintings or drawings of the Texas Hill Country, portraying it in a way that highlighted its beauty. Some were of people at work. She particularly liked one of a man with his hat pushed back on his head as he paused from forking hay to a wagon and another of a child playing with a colt.

Again, the triplets grew restless wanting to be on the move.

They finally reached the pie tent. Only the three ribbons and the names of the winners remained.

Bo explained why. "We auctioned off the pies last night." She admired how he thought of so many ways to raise money.

He led her around the corner. "The cart was parked right there." A sad note deepened his voice.

Louisa wished she could make things better for everyone. That she could give the triplets back their mother in good health. That a suitable helper and maybe even a husband could be found for the woman. She wished she could erase the pain of Bo's past. A pain that made him certain he could never be a husband or father. From what she'd seen, he'd be a very good father and a considerate, thoughtful husband. Why, look how he helped with the triplets. How he comforted her with but a touch on her shoulder. Her breath wobbled from her.

He reached over and squeezed her hand. Another comforting touch, although he would think her little display of emotion stemmed from the thought of three abandoned babies and nothing more. He'd never know how his touches triggered a lonely ache. They'd both been clear about not being interested in a future that included marriage.

She forced herself to think of nothing but the present. "What will the league do with the money it's raised?"

"We'll have a meeting to decide. Our original goal was to help families struggling to survive. But Dave McKay made us see the need of a home for orphans. And now with the triplets to provide for—" He shook his head. "Even if the fair is successful beyond my imagination, I don't see how we can do all that."

He still held her hand and she turned her palm to his and pressed enough to communicate her caring. "God will provide."

Smiling down on her, he said, "Thank you for the reminder. One of Mother's favorite verses was 'My God shall supply all your need according to His riches in glory by Christ Jesus.' Then she'd quote another verse saying the two of them belonged hand in hand. 'He that spared not His own Son, but delivered Him up for us all, how shall He not with Him also freely give us all things.'"

She watched smile lines fan out from his eyes and

the silvery light of his irises sparkle. "Your mother sounds like a faithful Christian."

"She managed to remain sweet and retain her sense of humor despite our father." Bo grew serious, perhaps even sad.

Five ladies entered the tent, spied the babies and rushed over, oohing and aahing over triplets.

They were strangers to her. Louisa watched the babies, hoping for some indication that they knew one of the women. But although they enjoyed the attention, not one of them lifted their arms to be picked up.

Theo turned away from the ladies and reached for Louisa.

Tucking the joy into her heart to cherish in the future, she picked him up. "I should take them home. They're getting hungry."

"Goodbye." Bo tipped his hat to the womenfolk and pushed the cart from the tent. "No need to go home. There's plenty to eat right here."

The idea appealed far more than it should. Far more than she could allow herself. She should refuse, but as if sensing that she hesitated, Bo sweetened his offer. "You haven't seen half the fair yet. You'll want to have a look at the goods that are for sale."

It proved far too easy to say yes and she let him guide her toward a booth where Molly Thorn and Lula May served a choice of two soups and an array of sandwiches. Molly's baby slept in a nearby basket.

"What will the little boys eat?" Bo asked.

"They'll enjoy the cream of vegetable soup." She let Bo order for all of them and then followed him to the long trestle table with plank benches on either side.

She settled Theo beside his brothers, tested the temperature of the soup on her lip, then fed them. Within minutes a crowd surrounded them. She leaned over to whisper in Bo's ear. "I've been watching to see if the triplets recognize anyone, but so far they haven't."

"I've been doing the same thing." His smile turned her heart upside down and shook out all the locks and keys.

This can't be happening. Not to me. I have no room in my heart or life for anything but my family. I'm allowing the excitement of the fair and the joy of caring for the babies to make me wish things could be different. They can't. My family needs me.

And if they didn't, she would still be a plain woman. Not worth waiting for.

Chapter Seven

Bo found it difficult to take his eyes off Louisa as she fed the babies. Love poured from her in every word, every gesture, every smile. Had he ever seen a woman so full of love? So ready to share it freely?

She'd make someone a good wife. She'd be a wonderful mother to a fortunate child, or children.

He bit off a large mouthful of the roast-beef-and-mustard sandwich. She'd been clear that she didn't have time for marriage and a family. Someone needed to convince her she deserved both.

He chewed rapidly. That someone would not be him and he shifted his attention to the triplets. Between them, they'd eaten all of one and most of a second bowl of soup and he went back to the booth to get another for Louisa.

Molly leaned over the counter to speak to Bo. "It looks like another romance blooming."

Bo knew she meant him and Louisa, but with no desire to fuel speculation, he glanced over his shoulder. Molly's sister, Daisy, and young Calvin Barlow wandered by. "You mean your sister? How do you feel about that?"

Molly gave him narrow-eyed study. "You know that's not who I mean, but very well, if you want to pretend otherwise, I'm pleased for Daisy. She deserves every happiness." And with a little huff, she turned her attention to the two men at Bo's left.

She was right. He intended to pretend otherwise and he took the soup back to Louisa.

Her eyes softened with her thanks.

That look undid whatever bit of resolve he'd been able to muster.

One day, he reasoned. He would enjoy her company for one day. All for the sake of making the fair a success.

He amused the triplets while Louisa ate and then they moved on. She had yet to see the many booths and the various forms of entertainment. The babies fell asleep as they bounced the cart across the ground. A moment of doubt raised its head. He assumed she would enjoy the many wares for sale but perhaps she would see them as inferior to the things she had seen in the city.

The first booth they came to displayed an array of embroidered items.

Leaving Bo with the sleeping babies, Louisa rushed forward. "This is beautiful work." She exclaimed over many items, then chose a pair of pillowcases to purchase. "Mother will love these." Joy glowed from her face and echoed in Bo's heart. He couldn't recall ever seeing a woman take so much pleasure in a simple purchase. Especially when not for herself. Valerie would have scoffed at even attending a fair such as this. He could almost hear her say "Pastoral" in a tone that made it sound anything but pleasant.

Why had he gone out with a girl like that? Of course, she hadn't been that way at first. But as they got to know each other better and she didn't feel she needed to impress him, he'd seen more and more things he didn't like.

Did he need further evidence that people changed? The experience fueled his fears that, given the right circumstances, he would turn into his father. But such dark thoughts could not linger under the clear blue sky, the sound of merriment around him and the company of a young lady who appeared to enjoy everything the fair offered.

She asked the saddle maker about his work, she admired the carved clocks and tooled leather works. Then she saw Mrs. Longfeather's display of jewelry and hurried to the booth.

"I have been waiting for you," Mrs. Longfeather said in her soft voice.

"Me?" Louisa pressed her hand to her chest.

"Yes, I have watched you. You are a sweet mother."

Louisa lifted her hands in protest.

Mrs. Longfeather waved away her words before Louisa could voice them. "I know the little ones are not yours. But they know they are loved and that is what every child needs." She gave both Bo and Louisa a hard look. "The love does not need to come from the father and mother so long as it comes early and comes often." She turned to Bo. "Young or old, all need love."

He couldn't deny it. Even though he knew he should.

Mrs. Longfeather's unblinking study made him want to look away and yet he could not. "You're a man with love to give." Before he could ask for an explanation or argue that sometimes heredity overcame love, she turned her probing look to Louisa. "You too have love to give."

Louisa smiled. "Of course. I love these babies."

Mrs. Longfeather took her hands. "I mean love for a man." She released Louisa. Bo could not bring himself to look at Louisa. Did not want her to look at him and see how Mrs. Longfeather's words sent a spear of longing straight through his heart, leaving a gaping hole.

"Now, for Miss Louisa, I have something special." She held out a beautiful silver-and-turquoise hair comb. "Would you take off your bonnet and let me show you how to wear it?"

Louisa hesitated but Mrs. Longfeather waited with the comb in the palm of her hand. Louisa untied the strings on the blue bonnet and slipped it from her head.

"Lean closer."

Louisa did so and Mrs. Longfeather ran her fingers through Louisa's hair, catching a few hairpins and laying them aside. In a matter of seconds, she scooped Louisa's hair to one side, twisted the long locks into a coil and held it in place with the comb. Louisa's brown hair showed off the comb becomingly.

"How much?" Louisa asked.

"A gift to remind you of how much love you have to give." Mrs. Longfeather caught her chin and turned her head side to side. "It's beautiful. See?" She turned Louisa's head so she faced Bo dead-on, the comb flirting from the side of her head.

Louisa's gaze caught his and held it, her eyes full of dark mysteries as old as mankind.

Bo's mouth went dry. His tongue proved too wooden to work.

"Do you not think so?" Mrs. Longfeather persisted.

Bo swallowed hard and wished for a drink of cold water. "Very becoming," he managed to grate out.

Mrs. Longfeather laughed, a low, throaty sound. "Now put the bonnet in beside the babies and go enjoy yourselves."

"Yes, ma'am." Laughter bubbled up inside Bo. He'd prayed and hoped for a successful fair and for people to have a good time. He wished it for Louisa. Why not include himself?

They moved on. Several times Louisa touched the comb. "Wasn't that a little odd?"

Bo would have wished for her to voice it differently, perhaps with a little more hope in her voice. "Mrs. Longfeather might be able to see things the rest of us can't. Sometimes older people are able to."

"But what she said isn't true."

"You don't have love to give to a man?"

She stopped and looked into his eyes. "Do you have love to give?"

He shrugged. "Maybe love isn't always enough."

She turned back to looking around. "It would seem so."

"Bo Stillwater, come over here and join the competition," Edmund McKay called.

Seeing that they were arm wrestling, Bo shook his head. Edmund was well-known for his strength.

"It's for a good cause," Jeb said.

Bo looked around at the crowd of men, seeing a challenging grin on several faces. He looked at Edmund, who sat at the table, his arm crooked, ready to take on someone. Bo knew he had likely bested everyone around him. Edmund was as strong as an ox.

He sighed. "Do you mind?" he asked Louisa, wishing she would say she did or that the babies would waken and all start crying so he would have an excuse to miss this humiliation.

"Oh, you go right ahead. This looks like fun." Her eyes twinkled as if she meant to enjoy the event.

"Only costs a penny," Edmund said.

Seemed he had no choice and he tossed his penny into the cup, sat down, rolled up his sleeve and prepared to be defeated.

CJ stood by as judge. As Edmund and Bo grasped hands, CJ checked their elbows. "On my count. One, two, three."

Bo leaned all his strength into his arm and pushed at Edmund's hand, edging it backward. Was Edmund exhausted from the many times he'd already done this?

Those clustered around them cheered and clapped, urging on the combatants.

Bo's shoulder muscles bunched as he exerted every ounce of his strength. Would Louisa be impressed if he bested Edmund? He glanced toward her. She smiled, her eyes dancing with the contagious excitement of the crowd.

Their gazes fused. Time stopped. Bo's heart refused to beat.

Edmund slammed Bo's hand to the table and the crowd erupted in a mixture of laughter and cheers. Bo rose and shook hands with Edmund. His eyes staying with Louisa, he hurried back to join her, the cart between them. The shimmer of air around them and the warm beat of his heart drowned out the presence of everyone else. Nothing existed but the two of them.

She shifted away first. "Sorry you lost."

Lost? What had he lost? Nothing. He'd gained… gained a… No. He could not allow himself to think there could be anything sweet and lasting between them. He sucked in air and turned to look at Edmund taking on a man built like a lumberjack. "It was for a good cause." He grabbed the handle of the cart and they moved on.

They passed a merry-go-round ride with live ponies wearing pretty collars and funny hats.

Louisa laughed. "How clever." She seemed content to linger, watching the children ride the ponies.

For his part, Bo was happy to be there watching Louisa.

She must have felt his gaze on her. She turned. "What?" She touched the comb in her hair. "It looks silly, doesn't it?"

He caught her hand before she could remove the comb. "Don't take it out. It looks very nice." He couldn't say if it was the comb, the atmosphere of the fair or something else entirely, but he'd never before noticed how beautiful she was.

Again their gazes blazed a path to each other.

A feeling akin to hunger caught at Bo's innards.

He had already eaten but perhaps a sweet would end this foolish reaction. He tore his gaze to a different direction. Mr. Arundel, owner of the general store, ran a booth nearby with a bright display of candies placed where passersby would see it first off.

"Do you like candy sticks?" His voice crackled.

"I do."

He pushed the cart across the space—the grass trampled by so many feet there remained little but dust.

"My treat," he said, giving the array a good deal of study. He selected two, cinnamon and peppermint, his favorites.

"What's your choice?" He thought he could look at Louisa now without feeling as if he stepped into a chasm.

She requested a green apple flavor.

"Only one?" he asked.

"Yes, thank you."

He handed over his pennies and stuck the red-and-white-striped candy into his mouth.

Helen Carson spotted them and hurried over to take Louisa's elbow. "You're exactly what we need."

Louisa leaned back and refused to move. "For what?"

"For a third woman for the clothes-hanging contest. Come along."

"But I'm not good at such things."

Mrs. Carson exerted a little more pressure setting Louisa's feet into motion. "You don't have to win. Just play. It's for a good cause, after all."

Louisa sent Bo a helpless look.

He shrugged and followed, pushing the cart full of babies. It sounded purely selfish but it would do his ego good to let her feel defeat in a contest as he had done.

Mrs. Carson paused to let Louisa drop her penny

in the waiting cup, then directed her to a clearing be-hind a small booth where three lines were strung. A basket of laundry waited at the end of each. Two other ladies were ready, and seeing Louisa, they rubbed their hands in glee.

"On your marks, get set, go," said Mrs. Carson, and the three ladies bent to get the first item and peg it to the line.

Eli opened his eyes and yawned. He pushed him-self upright.

Bo reached to scoop him out of the cart before he woke the others, but already, Jasper and Theo stirred, so he left Eli with the others and sat them up so they could see out. "There's Louisa." He pointed and the trip-lets watched her, jabbering away as if cheering for her.

Bo leaned back on his heels, his arms crossed over his chest, and watched, as well.

She had one more garment hung than the other two and slowly gained until she had three more, and then four more. She reached the end ahead of the other two ladies, setting up a cheer from the onlookers.

She looked around.

Even from this distance, Bo saw a blush brightened her cheek. She quickly unpegged the items, dropped them back into the basket and rushed over to Bo's side, taking with her the prize—a wooden clothes-peg painted blue.

"Congratulations."

She kept her head lowered.

He dipped his head, trying to see her face. "You won." Shouldn't she feel some kind of joy over the fact?

"I never expected to," she mumbled. "I'm not very good at—" She shrugged and didn't finish.

He guffawed. "You're obviously very good at hanging clothes."

She finally lifted her gaze to his and his heart stuttered at the darkness he saw.

"Louisa, what's wrong?"

She shook her head. "The babies are awake." She bent over them. "Did you have a good nap?"

Three baby boys gurgled their pleasure at her attention.

But Bo wasn't prepared to let it go. This was not the time or place, though, and he moved them toward a table where they could get coffee or cold water. He chose water and brought back cups for all of them. The babies drank eagerly. A passing woman gave the boys each a cookie and they were occupied with eating them.

Louisa sipped her water and looked into the distance.

Bo sat beside her. "Tell me why it upset you to win that contest."

She turned her cup round and round, studying it as if she hoped to find a secret message. "I don't know if I can."

"Try."

"It will sound silly."

"Not to me."

She finally looked at him, searching his eyes for the truth. He'd spoken honestly so had nothing to hide and let her look as long and hard as she wanted. Never breaking the look between them, she answered softly, almost apologetically. "I don't need to tell you

I'm plain. A plain spinster. I've not had many beaus because of that and because—" She looked past him. "Never mind. It doesn't matter."

His teeth ached at the look on her face. "Louisa, you aren't plain. You're beautiful. And you're unmarried because that's how you want it to be."

She rolled her head back and forth, darkness filling her eyes. Before he could ask for an explanation, her gaze lightened. She smiled, though he judged it to be a little uncertain. "I do not mean to complain. I have my family and that's enough for me."

He wondered if she believed what she said.

Louisa grabbed the handle of the cart and pushed it toward the thickest of the crowd. Her cheeks were hot and no doubt, bright pink. She hoped Bo wouldn't notice…or if he did, that he'd put it down to the heat and her hurried pace.

He'd said she was beautiful. Her heart fluttered within her chest. Perhaps because of the comb Mrs. Longfeather had put in her hair.

A trio of young ladies rushed up to them. Strangers to her, but then, she didn't know everyone in the county as Bo seemed to. They ignored her as if she had grown invisible. Their attention focused on Bo as they blushed and tilted their heads, looking up from under their eyelashes.

"You're Mr. Stillwater? The one selling dances?" The little blonde blushed even more furiously and her friends giggled.

"That's me." He took three dimes and wrote three more names on his card.

Louisa glanced at his card and saw it was almost full. She was no good at batting her eyes at a man nor at dancing. It was time for her to go home and back to the reality of her life. She was about to suggest it when a man rang a bell.

"Wild horse bucking in ten minutes. You won't want to miss this." He passed on, repeating his message.

Bo took the cart from her. "Let's hurry and get a good place to watch."

What could she do but follow?

He found a place next to the fence and pulled her to his side, parking the cart at his other side. "You guys will want to see this too," he said to the babies as he lined them up so they had a view.

In minutes, people pressed tight on every side so Louisa was crowded hard against Bo. He put his arm around her, grabbing the fence on her opposite side so that she was protected by his arm, sheltered by his body.

She did her best to convince herself he only did it to keep from being crushed between her and the cart. Or for some other noble reason. Not because he felt anything for her. They had both been clear about that possibility.

CJ Thorn climbed the steps to the top of a platform opposite them. "Folks, the contestants in this competition have paid two bits for the privilege of getting tossed in the dust by a wild horse." The crowd laughed as did Louisa, though her amusement was minor in comparison to the awareness of the weight of Bo's arm across her back, the warmth of his body next to hers, and the scent of the soap used to launder his shirt and something more subtle—a masculine scent that triggered a rapid beating of her heart.

CJ called the first contestant, bringing Louisa's attention back to the arena in front of them.

Two cowboys threw open a gate, and a horse and rider erupted into the larger, dusty pen.

The horse twisted and bucked, sometimes all four feet off the ground and twisting at the same time. Cheering and shouts of advice roared from the crowd.

The cowboy hung on for dear life, often leaning far out to one side or the other, and his head snapping back so she feared he would be injured. And yet he stayed on the back of the horse until the animal ground to a halt.

The crowd grew even louder as they clapped and cheered for the cowboy.

Louisa let out her breath. Only then did she realize she clung desperately to Bo's hand. But she could not force her fingers to relax as the horse was led from the arena and another cowboy prepared to ride.

This one lasted only long enough for the two men at the gate to get it closed before the horse tossed him to the ground. The horse pranced around the fallen man.

Louisa pressed harder to the fence. "He'll be killed."

But the horse raced away and the man got to his feet and waved before he jogged out of the arena amid much clapping and cheering.

This was too intense, the risks too great. She wanted to leave. But even if she could have ducked under Bo's arm and pushed her way through the crowd, she didn't move. The event mesmerized her, she told herself by way of excuse, but she failed to convince herself. The truth was she didn't want to leave the protectiveness of his arm. It meant nothing to either of them. But still, she wanted it, if only for the moment. Being seen as someone worth sheltering. So she stayed, enjoying the notion for the few minutes she'd have it. Soon enough she would return to reality and happily taking care of her family and the triplets.

How long would she be allowed to enjoy the babies? They had recovered from their colds and could go to a more suitable home any time now. She would not ask Bo if alternate arrangements had been made. She'd know soon enough.

As she planned to do with Bo, she would also do with the triplets. She'd allow herself to enjoy the temporary pleasure of their company.

Six more men rode unbroken horses. Three more were bucked off.

CJ called, "That's four for the horses and four for the cowboys. Folks, that's the end of the bucking contest. I hope you enjoyed it."

More clapping and cheering and sharp whistles.

Theo cried. Bo scooped him up, leaving Louisa feeling exposed, abandoned, alone. She sighed. Her time of pretending had ended.

Struggling to pull her emotions back into line, Louisa comforted Eli and Jasper while Bo took care of Theo. The crowd around them dispersed, moving on to the next attraction.

She was about to say she needed to take the babies home when the youngest Coleman boy came running up to her.

"Your father says he needs you. Can you come quickly?"

Chapter Eight

"I'll take you to the tent where he is," Bo said, although he was reluctant to leave this spot. For the short time they'd watched the bucking horses, he'd been able to enjoy holding her close. Having her cling to his hand. Experiencing a sense of providing for her and the babies all the things he'd never know from his father—attention, protection and security.

For a few minutes he'd enjoyed success in that area of his life. A temporary success but it nevertheless made him feel a bigger, better man than he'd ever before experienced.

Young Coleman rushed ahead, turned to see that they were following and signaled them to hurry.

"Can you tell me what's wrong?" Louisa called, but the boy waved his arm to follow. She turned to Bo. "It must be serious for Father to call for me."

Bo could see her mind had gone to the medical emergency. "You go on ahead. I'll bring these little guys." The cart limited how fast he could move.

"You're sure?" She hurried ahead even as she asked the question.

"I'll catch up."

She lifted her skirts and, without breaking into a run, moved at a high rate of speed, catching up to the Coleman boy. The crowd closed behind them and Bo couldn't see them even by craning his neck. He settled back and tried to be content with his slower pace but his heart felt hollow. He might as well get used to the sensation. It would be his for the future.

Tug Coleman grabbed Bo's elbow. "A fine kettle of fish when my family can't come out in public without being attacked by one of them Hills."

Bo almost welcomed the intrusion into his wayward thoughts. Not that he cared for the way the Hills and the Colemans feuded. This was a problem he meant to address at the next Lone Star Cowboy League meeting.

"What's happened now?" he asked, half dreading the accusations Tug would fling at the Hills. He liked the man fine. Tug had spent a lot of time helping fix up the fairgrounds. Mrs. Hill had not lifted a finger, not even sent in her son Peter, a big strong man of twenty.

"That Peter Hill beat up my Jamie and him being older and bigger by far than Jamie."

It did seem unfair. If Bo harbored any hope that the romance between Annie and Jamie would mend the fences between their families, this latest row would make that impossible. A fight between Jamie and Peter was unfair in any sense of the word. He could understand why Tug would be upset.

The older man stuck his head around Bo. "Where's that Miss Clark? She was supposed to help her pa.

He has his hands full what with my Jamie all busted up and two cowboys complaining they was hurt. And some kids throwing up. What do their parents expect if they let them eat until they're sick?"

Bo picked up the pace. It sounded like Louisa would be needing a hand with things. "Miss Clark hurried on ahead." The meeting tent that served as an information center, a lost and found station and also a place for the doctor to treat any injuries came into view with no sign of Louisa or the Coleman boy. "She's already there."

Tug rushed into the tent and Bo followed at a good clip that had the babies bouncing and laughing.

Chaos reigned inside the first-aid area or so it seemed to Bo, but Louisa looked completely in control. Her father tended a cowboy who appeared to have a broken leg. Louisa told the mother with the throwing-up boy to make sure he used the bucket. She bent over Jamie Coleman and lifted his eyelids.

"How long were you out?"

"A long time," said Annie Hill. She hovered nearby, her brother behind her, his bloodied fists still bunched.

"Not long enough," Peter growled.

Annie spun around to face her brother. "You had no right to hit him, you big bully."

Peter scowled at her. "He was making moony eyes at you. He's a Coleman. He can stay away from you."

Mrs. Hill rushed in at that moment and took in the scene. "What's going on?"

Tug stood toe to toe with her. "Your boy hurt my Jamie."

Dorothy Hill snorted. "Not without cause, I venture to say."

"That's right, Ma." Peter stood shoulder to shoulder with his mother. "He was acting lovesick over Annie."

Dorothy flung around to confront her daughter. "He better not be telling it straight. You know how I feel about the Colemans."

Tug planted himself in front of Dorothy again. "There's nothing wrong with the Colemans."

"At least the Hills are honest," she retorted.

Bo looked around the angry bunch and then back to Louisa as she continued to examine Jamie. A nasty cut over one eye bled freely. She wiped up the blood and applied pressure to the wound, then turned to the two families. "Could someone please explain to me what you're fighting about?"

"The Colemans stole a diamond ring from us," Dorothy shouted.

"Your uncle lost it fair and square in a bet," Tug shouted equally loud.

"He was drunk."

"Says a lot for the Hills," Tug said.

Peter stepped forward. "You take that back."

Tug shoved him aside as if he were of no consequence. Dorothy rushed to his aid and shoved back.

Bo could hardly hear himself think over the yelling, and then to make it worse, the babies started to cry.

"Enough!" Louisa's shout silenced them and everyone stared at her in surprise. "Bo, kindly escort these people outside. Annie, you stay and watch the babies while I tend Jamie's wounds."

He knew leaving Annie with Jamie would only fuel the rage burning between the two families. Indeed, both Tug and Dorothy yelled a protest.

"I'll watch the babies and Annie can go too," Bo said in a quiet voice that he hoped would soften the raucousness around him.

Louisa gave him a look of authority that made him draw back. "I need Annie. She's my helper."

He glanced at the girl who saw no one but Jamie. How much help was she going to be? But then she shifted her attention and hurried to the triplets and soon calmed them.

Bo knew he wasn't needed and the knowledge whipstung his thoughts. Shouldn't Louisa have asked for his help? Or did she think he might act like his father, shouting and cursing at everyone? He waved an arm toward the Hills and Colemans. "Come on—everyone out so the doctor and assistant can do their work."

Mrs. Hill looked ready to argue.

"I think that means you," Tug said.

The woman took a step toward Tug, fire in her eyes.

Bo pushed the lot out of the tent before a brawl could erupt. He stood at the tent flap as if guarding the entrance when, in fact, he wanted to go back and ask Louisa if she thought it wise to encourage the attraction between the two young people.

He heard her gentle voice as she talked to those inside, and his ire at being shooed out, at having his opinion disregarded, faded as he recalled the few hours they had shared this day. She was capable, tender, caring, and a tad shy and uncertain of her own attractions. He leaned back on his heels with a pleased smile. He could overlook her decision. After all, she wasn't aware of how long the feud between the Hills and the Colemans had existed.

Jamie came from the tent, a bandage around his head. His eyes were red and already swollen.

Tug grabbed his shoulder and looked him up and down.

Louisa stepped outside. "He'll have a couple of black eyes but nothing more serious." She looked around at the others, including Tug in her study. "Seems to me you could all find something more productive to do than fight. There are booths to help at, animals to clean up after and likely a hundred other jobs that need a little man power or woman power. I'm sure we'd all appreciate it if you'd turn your energies to something more constructive."

Annie pushed the cart out and kept her head down, darting only fleeting glances at Jamie. Her behavior was vastly different from earlier, and Bo wondered if Louisa had cautioned her not to be so blatant about her interest in Jamie. His opinion of Louisa climbed several degrees.

Tug dragged Jamie with him in one direction and Dorothy grabbed Peter and hustled him in the opposite.

Bo glanced from Annie to Louisa. His gaze stalled at her. If he had any words or warning or correction, they fled before her steady look. All he could think was how beautiful she looked with a smudge on her cheek as she stood drying her hands on a towel.

"I'll leave the babies with you," Annie said, her words seeming to come down a long, hollow tunnel. Bo was vaguely aware of her slipping away.

"Father says he doesn't need me anymore. I'll take the babies home and fix their supper." She grabbed the handle of the cart and started toward the exit.

Bo fell in at her side and reached for the handle.

"I'll be okay. You'll need to stay at the fair."

"I won't be needed here for some time." Not until the dance, which he now wished he hadn't signed up for. It was for a good cause, he reminded himself.

Louisa pushed his hands aside and gripped the handle. "You don't need to feel sorry for me."

He yanked the cart to a halt and stared at her. "Why would I feel sorry for you?"

She looked away from him as if keenly interested in the booth selling hand-knit socks for men.

He knew she was only trying to avoid looking at him and caught her elbow, turned her to face him. "I find myself admiring you more and more."

Her eyes widened. "How can that be?"

"You're smart and capable and kind and beautiful." The words tumbled from his mouth.

She pushed the cart through the exit at a rate that made the triplets giggle. "Like your mother, as I recall."

"In good ways, but you aren't my mother."

She darted him a doubtful look. His eyes must have said what his heart felt, for she stopped walking and met his gaze full on. Something shifted inside him at that moment. A longing that he so vehemently denied all his life rose to the surface. This woman made him want to be everything he dreamed of, everything he feared was impossible.

Someone bumped into him, freeing him from his foolish thoughts, and with a regretful smile, he pushed the cart along the dusty trail back to town. Neither of them said anything.

What could he say? The things he wanted were not for him. Nor did she wish for them, either.

Louisa tried to sort out her thoughts. Tried to bring them back into submission. *You aren't my mother. You're smart and capable and kind and giving. You aren't plain. You're beautiful.* Why was she asking for such compliments? And why was she believing them? She needed to get back home and set the perimeters of her life.

It seemed to take forever to reach the house. And another forever to push the cart inside.

She lifted Jasper to the floor so he could move around. She'd half expected Bo to leave immediately. But he put Theo and Eli next to their brother and sat cross-legged on the floor with them.

As if prepared to stay and amuse them.

Louisa knew she should insist he leave. She needed to guard her heart. She needed to remember who and what she was. A spinster with a mother to care for. With a start she realized she had not said *plain* spinster. She closed her eyes as an ache clawed at her insides. Even hearing Bo say those words triggered a long-denied wish. All her life she'd been viewed as the plain and practical sister. Amy was the beautiful one. Oh, to have someone believe she was beautiful.

"I'll amuse them while you make supper for them."

Bo's words jerked her from her troubled musings and she hurried to the kitchen, stirred up the coals and soon had eggs boiling so she could feed the triplets soft-boiled eggs.

When they were ready, she put them in a bowl. How was she to feed them with Bo sitting in front of them?

"Bring me a spoon and I'll help."

Jasper bounced up and down, making eager little sounds when he saw the food.

Eli watched, waiting, and Theo's bottom lip puckered out.

Louisa knew the babies weren't going to wait while she tried to decide how best to handle this situation, so she gave Bo the bowl of food and hurried to the kitchen for another spoon.

Bo shifted over upon her return, and with barely a hesitation, she sat beside him on the floor, their shoulders touching, his knees brushing hers.

Three little mouths popped open. She chuckled. At least the babies gave her nothing but pleasure. No wondering what they thought of her. As long as she fed them and gave them lots of hugs, made sure they had dry bottoms and regular sleep, they accepted her with open hearts.

Except this too was temporary. "What will become of them?"

Bo didn't miss a beat in the feeding. "God willing, we'll find their mother and be able to help her."

"I wonder if the mother trusted God to meet her needs."

"What do you mean?"

"Well, if she did, she must have wondered if God failed her."

He spared her a glance between Theo's and Eli's open mouths. "Isn't it when things look the worst that trust is most important? My mother used to say that if everything went smoothly we wouldn't realize how much we needed God."

"Yes, I know that's true and I've seen it many times in my own life." She told him about worrisome days and nights when Amy seemed so fragile and all they could do was pray. And when Mother suffered infections that strained her weak heart. "God answered our prayers and restored them to health. I sometimes wonder if I would have continued to trust Him if one of them died." Her words caught in her tight throat.

The babies slowed down their eating and Bo shifted to face her. "You might have found that's when you needed God the most."

She nodded. "Is that how it was for you when your mother died?"

"Her love for us lives on." His eyes darkened to a dull pewter. "Trusting God when Father lived was harder."

Sensing the pain of his past, she squeezed his hand. "And yet you stayed with him."

"We didn't feel we had a choice. Someone needed to make sure he was taken care of." Something sweet and powerful filled his expression. "In hindsight, I can see that the hard times were the best times for my faith. They forced the roots of my faith to grow deep in the bedrock of God's love and provision."

"That's a beautiful picture." The sound of a passing group of people drew her attention to the window. The sun slanted toward the western sky. It was getting late. Yet Bo made no move toward leaving.

"Would you care to have supper with me?" Where had those words come from?

"I'd like that." They both pushed to their feet and made their way to the kitchen with the babies. Thankfully there were leftover potatoes, some fresh peas a patient had given them and bread. She fried the potatoes and eggs, and cooked the peas. In a few minutes, she served them each a plate of food. They sat across the table from each other.

"Would you ask the blessing?" she asked.

He reached for her hands and bowed his head to pray.

She barely heard his words but her heart swelled with thanksgiving. How right it felt to share a meal with a good man, to have babies playing contentedly nearby. She forbade herself to steal from the joy of the moment by reminding herself it was only temporary.

As they ate, they talked. He told her about his housekeeper and how she kept his house clean and made his meals. "She won the cake competition with her chocolate cake."

She told him how Mrs. Keaton not only excelled in pies but also taught her to clean house. "She was meticulous. Insisted I must always dust behind every bit of furniture. Keeping the place spotless is necessary for my mother's health." She turned her attention toward Mother's bedroom. "I've left her room until last so there won't be a speck of dust there when she arrives." She would have to get Annie to help with the triplets so she could get back to cleaning. "What will happen to the triplets if their mother isn't located?"

He shook his head. "There's talk of separating them because three babies is a lot of work and money, but

David McKay, who'd been separated from his brothers as a child, spoke vehemently against that. At the moment, I don't know anyone who can take in all three." He searched her gaze. "They're happy here but I know you can't keep them. You already have far too much to do."

Denial sprang to her lips. "I'd like nothing better than to keep them but I am unmarried. And once Mother comes…" No need to point out the obvious.

"In the meantime, I will certainly help you all I can."

With a ranch to run, how much time would he have to help? Yet the promise of his presence made her picture more evenings spent taking care of the babies and sharing a quiet meal.

"That was a lovely meal. Thank you." He glanced at the clock on the wall by the table. "I feel bad at offering my help then leaving you on your own, but my duties call me away."

"You mean the dance?"

He pushed to his feet and found his cowboy hat where he'd dropped it coming into the house. He patted three little heads, then straightened to face Louisa. He lifted a hand. If he meant to pat her head…she took a step backward to put a stop to that.

He caught her hand. "Walk me out."

She allowed him to lead her past the babies, who watched their every move. They stopped at the door. He took both her hands and pulled her close. So close she could feel his breath on her cheek, hear the thud of his heart…or was it the thud of her own?

She lifted her face to him, searching his eyes for what

he meant by this. Did he want to kiss her? She rubbed her lips together. She'd welcome a kiss.

What was wrong with her? They'd both been crystal clear that neither of them were interested in anything more than friendship. Why, if not for the triplets, he would likely never have come to her door. And when the babies left, would he ever come again? She knew the painful truth to that question and slipped her hands from his.

"Enjoy yourself at the dance."

Before she could step away, he caught her hands again. "I wish you could come. It feels wrong to leave you here to take care of these babies, who are no more your responsibility than they are mine or anyone else's in this town."

"But I don't mind." She again pulled free of his hold and this time stepped away. A dance was the last place she wanted to be. There had been more than enough social events forced upon her when she got to play the part of wallflower. "You need to go and dance with every girl." Her words sounded a little harsh even to her own ears. "Raise lots of money for the league. After all, it will be needed to help the babies."

"I could stop by after the dance and tell you how it went."

For a moment she considered saying she'd wait up. But it would be inappropriate to ask a man to stop by so late at night. Even if not for that reason, she would have forced herself to say no. Pretending would only make it more difficult to deal with reality when it hit.

Perhaps she could allow herself to believe more was possible.

But how could it be? She had to care for Mother. She *wanted* to care for Mother. She had to help Father. Had to accept her life held its limitations.

Chapter Nine

Bo left the house and stood on the step, staring at the closed door. He'd wanted to kiss Louisa. Still wanted to. Just as he wanted to take her to the dance and dance every number with her. At least she'd had the good sense to pull away before either of them could do something foolish like kiss.

He spun around and made his way back to the fairgrounds as fast as he could and went right to the big tent, the sides lifted to let in the evening air. A wooden platform for the dancers sat in the center with tables and chairs circling it. Sawdust on the ground would keep the dust down.

The musicians made their way to the tent. "Bo, did you bring your guitar?"

Before he could answer, Brandon called out. "He's too busy dancing to play tonight." His brother fell in step beside him. "Seems to me you're spending an awful lot of time with the doctor's daughter for someone who has vowed to avoid women. Oh, wait, you only mean to avoid any sort of commitment."

"Last time I checked, we were the same age, and unless you have a secret wife somewhere, you're no more married than I am."

Brandon shrugged. "Waiting for the right woman to come into my life."

"Yeah, me too."

Brandon chortled. "From what I saw today and all the reports I've heard, I think you might have found her."

Bo had enough of teasing. "If you're referring to Miss Clark, you can forget it. She's no more interested in marriage than I am. I was merely helping with the triplets. By the by, anyone heard anything about the missing mother?"

Brandon sobered. "Not a word from anyone. How can a woman have triplets without anyone being aware of the fact?"

"And how can she get into town without anyone noticing? We couldn't go two feet without someone rushing up to us to comment on the triplets."

"It's certainly odd." They circled the tent. Assured that all was ready, Bo went to the gate. A fence surrounded the dance tent. It would do nothing to stop people from sneaking in without paying admission but they wouldn't be dancing without paying for the privilege.

People began to trickle in. The trickle turned into a flood. Brandon clapped Bo on the back. "Looks like there's a fine crowd." The band began to play a tune. The ladies lined up, ready to receive money in exchange for a dance.

Bo checked his card. The Bachmeier girls were first. He hoped they wouldn't giggle the whole time.

Harold Hickey took his place by the band and called out for the squares to form for the first dance.

Bo always found it hard to believe that the man who joked and called such fine dances was married to Constance Hickey, whose gossip hurt so many people.

He took Suzanne's hand and away they went, swinging and do-si-doing. As he feared, Suzanne giggled every time their hands touched. Nora took her sister's place with more giggling.

Bo danced every dance. He knew the local girls, but the ones from farther afield he knew only by the name they provided when they paid their dime. Some giggled. Some refused to look directly at him. A couple of them chattered nonstop even when he was out of earshot. Long before the evening was out his feet hurt, his head spun and he wearied of the young ladies.

Floyd Farmington stepped into Harold's place and called for attention. "Folks, we have a very special, once-in-a-lifetime opportunity here. We are going to auction off the last dance with Bo."

Bo's feet cried out a protest and he longed to be able to slip through the cracks in the dance floor and disappear. Asking Floyd to auction off Bo's last dance seemed a great idea when he'd arranged it. His only thought being the possibility of adding more money to the fund.

"Come on up, Bo."

Doing his best to look happy about the prospect before him, Bo stood at Floyd's side.

Floyd circled Bo while grinning widely, then faced

the crowd. "How is it that Bo remains unmarried?" He tilted his hand toward Bo. "He's a good catch. Tall, strong and handsome…or so I'm told."

That earned him a burst of laughter from the crowd.

"Bo owns his own ranch. Shucks, gals. He even has a twin brother waiting to perform the wedding ceremony."

Brandon waved, his grin informing Bo how much he enjoyed seeing his brother in this situation.

Floyd continued. "Ladies, come on up and have a good look. Single ladies only." More laughter as the young ladies rushed to stand before Bo.

Bo understood Floyd only wanted to drum up interest but Bo wished he'd get on with auctioning off the dance.

Floyd leaned over to speak in a conspiratorial way to the gals. "There must be someone among you who sees the potential in this fellow. And who can say whether or not this final dance might be when he falls head over heels in love with you."

Bo's ears burned and likely flashed like hot lanterns.

Floyd straightened. "So what am I bid? A dime? Who will give me a dime?"

A dozen hands shot up.

"Eleven cents?" Not one hand went down. "Twelve, thirteen." As Bo endured being auctioned off like so much livestock, the bids grew. Twenty-five cents. Fifty.

A young woman he'd danced with earlier in the evening pushed to the front. Bo was fairly certain her name was Irene, and if he recalled what she'd told him about herself, she lived in the far northwest corner of the Grant County. He remembered nothing else.

Irene stood directly before Floyd. "I got me a farm that needs a strong man. I'll give you a dollar to dance with him."

Floyd rubbed his hands together. "A dollar! Do I hear more?" No one else offered another bid. "Going once, going twice. Sold to this hopeful young lady."

Bo nodded, smiled and waved as the crowd clapped.

But Floyd wasn't done. "I've done my job, young lady. Now you do yours and make him fall in love."

Irene blushed like the brightest of sunsets.

Bo's ears grew hotter.

The band struck up a slow waltz and Bo led Irene to the dance floor. No one else joined them. Oh, great. Did everyone think they could watch him fall in love… lose his good sense…right here in view of them all? "Last dance," he called.

Several other couples joined them.

Wasn't this supposed to be fun? That had been his intention when he planned this and now all he could think of was Louisa and the triplets. He'd hated leaving her to manage on her own. How did she get the three of them ready for bed and settled for the night? Would she continue to let them sleep on the floor beside her? That sofa didn't look very comfortable.

Irene gripped his hand hard. "You're not here in your thoughts, are you?"

He jerked his attention to her. "I'm sorry. It's been a long day. And if Mr. Farmington has led you to think I'm looking for a wife, I'm sorry. I'm not."

Her expression softened. "Tell me about the girl who has your heart."

He stumbled. "Sorry. There is no such person."

"Oh, so that's the way it is. You still haven't realized how you feel or you aren't prepared to admit it."

He looked past her into the darkness beyond the tent.

"Let me tell you something," Irene continued. "I was once in your position. I'm not sure of your circumstances but mine were that I'd had an abusive father and wasn't prepared to ever trust a man to treat me right."

He stared at her, surprised at how similar their reasons were. Except he didn't trust himself.

Irene got a faraway look in her eyes as if seeing the past. "There was a man…" Her voice shook. "He loved me. I was afraid to trust him. I kept putting him off, telling him he didn't know his own mind. One day he wearied of it and left for the Cripple Creek mine to look for gold. I've not heard a word since he left. That was two years ago." She shuddered. "I made a mistake. Several, actually. I shouldn't have let my fear push him away. I should have told him how I felt. Most of all, I should have trusted him. He wasn't my father and I knew that. But I couldn't let go of my fears from the past."

The song ended and the band members wrapped up their instruments and marched away.

Irene still held Bo's hand. "Don't make the same mistake. Thank you for the dance."

"Maybe your beau will come back."

She shook her head. "I expect he's found someone else. Someone ready to trust him." She paused. "I should have trusted him. And maybe trust that I am worthy of being loved." She slipped away.

CJ Thorn signaled him over to count the cash. He grinned from ear to ear. "We already took the day money to the bank, but I think there is as much here as we took in all day."

Bo knew a sense of satisfaction that went a long way to easing his sore feet but nothing at all to drive away Irene's warning. It was different with him. He had good reason to steer away from love and marriage.

Forcing his mind to the task of counting money and nothing else, he, along with CJ and Edmund McKay, counted, checking and rechecking the amount. Bo finally sat back, a sincere grin on his face. "The fair is over and we raised more funds than I thought possible when we started this."

"There are so many needs. How will we decide which ones get priority?" Edmund asked.

Bo knew Edmund wished for more equipment for working with the young people in the Young Ranchers program he helped run. So far the ranchers had lent things like wagons, buggies, harnesses, hay forks and Bo couldn't remember what else he'd been called on for. Edmund's brother David wanted to start an orphan's home. Bo wanted to provide for the care of the triplets. There were destitute families in the area all of them wanted to assist. "We need to have a meeting."

"Let's do it tomorrow after church. That will save us all another trip to town," CJ said.

Bo knew what CJ didn't say. They'd been away from their ranches plenty with the fair.

"Fine by me," he agreed although his plans included keeping his promise to help Louisa with the triplets. But he could still do that after the meeting.

Edmund straightened. "Let's get this money safely

tucked away for the night so we can all go home to our families." He gave Bo an apologetic look.

Bo shrugged. "I need to get home and make sure my ranch is still there." His laugh lacked the amusement he'd aimed for.

Edmund, CJ and Sheriff Jeb's horses waited.

"I'll get Cash and catch up to you."

The others mounted up and headed for town and the bank's safe.

Bo jogged over to the pen where the horses and various wagons and buggies had been hitched. Cash was the last animal there. He swung into the saddle and trotted after the others.

He turned down the side street toward the bank even though he longed to go up the street that would take him past the doctor's house. He made another right up Main Street. The three mounted horses were almost at the bank. The riders swung to the ground.

A fourth figure emerged from the shadows. Three pairs of arms headed for the sky.

Bo had been right about that thief. He'd waited until the last day to attempt a robbery. If only Bo had brought a gun, but who brought firearms to a dance?

He pulled Cash to a halt and left him beside the train depot. He looked about for a weapon and saw a chunk of wood that must have fallen off someone's load of firewood. It was small. He picked it up and slapped it into his palm. It might work.

Ignoring how much his feet hurt, he trotted as quietly as his cowboy boots allowed toward the bank. Time was of the essence.

He skirted Mercy's café and slunk over to the shad-

ows the walls of the bank provided. From there he tiptoed toward the front, where he'd last seen his friends.
He eased around the corner. They still stood with their
arms in the air.

CJ was trying to reason with the thief. "You won't
get away with this. We'll hunt you down and put you
in jail."

Keep talking. Keep his attention on you. Bo gathered
up his strength and leaped across the space between
him and the robber. He jabbed his stick into the man's
back. "Drop your gun or I'll shoot." *Please, God, let
him believe this is a pistol.*

The man lowered his gun to the ground and lifted
his arms over his head. As Bo had suspected, it was
the thieving boy's father. He saw no sign of the young
lad and wondered what had become of him. Jeb sprang
into action, taking the gun and putting it in his waist-
band. He took the rope from his saddle and tied the
man securely. Only when he was done did he turn to
Bo. "That was either really stupid or really brave." He
marched the prisoner away to the jail.

CJ and Edmund burst into laughter. Edmund grabbed
the stick from Bo and pointed it at him. "Stick 'em up."
At the play on words, the three of them hooted with
laughter.

They sobered quickly and Edmund clapped Bo on
the back. "If he'd suspected what you really jabbed into
his back, we might not be all standing here. Glad it
worked out."

The three of them looked around. "Where is Mr.
Henley? Wasn't he supposed to be here to open the
bank for us?"

They clattered up the steps and banged on the door. Bo tipped his ear to the door. "I hear thumping." He tried the door. Locked. They hurried around to the back door and found it unlocked.

"Now let's be a little cautious," CJ warned. "There might be more than one thief in our midst."

"There was a young lad with that man." Bo wondered if the father would abandon the boy to deal with the consequences on his own. "I'll go," Bo volunteered. After all, as had been pointed out to him several times in the last few hours, he was unmarried. No family to leave behind should he be walking into a trap. The thumping sounded again and he tiptoed inside, keeping to the edges of the room as he made his way toward the sound. It seemed to come from the office area and he eased silently in that direction, trying to remember the room as he made his way in the dark.

He found the open door and paused, listening for clues. More thumping. He found the desk and eased around it. The sound was so close he tensed, half expecting someone to tackle him. Instead, someone or something kicked him. He jerked back, every muscle coiled to respond to an attack.

Instead more thumping and—was someone mumbling?

He listened to the noise for several seconds, his heart pounding loud in his ears.

When nothing happened, he squatted and reached out a tentative hand and touched a body, a living, squirming body. What was going on?

He felt around on the desktop for the lamp and matches to light it with. As soon as the wick caught, he lifted the light to see what lay before him. "Mr. Henley." The banker lay trussed up and gagged. "I found Mr. Henley," he called to the others who trooped in as Bo untied him.

George rubbed at his wrists. "Someone came from behind me as I entered the bank. When I refused to open the safe, the culprit tied me up. Thank goodness you came along. Did he rob you?"

They told him how Bo stopped the intended robbery and Jeb had taken the man to jail.

CJ turned the money over to Mr. Henley, who locked it in the safe.

"Didn't you have men posted here during the dance?" Bo asked. Every time he'd checked, there were two men guarding the bank.

"I did. I wonder what happened to them."

Borrowing the lamp from the bank, they started a search and soon found the two men tied up and gagged. "Someone tricked us." Their stories were almost identical. Someone had called for help, and when they went to see what was needed, they were ambushed.

As soon as they were sure the two men weren't hurt in any way, Jeb sent them home.

With a burst of guilt, Bo realized he had been hoping one of them had sustained a minor injury that would require seeing the doctor. Bo would be the one to assist the hurt party to the doctor's office. It would have provided the perfect excuse for checking on Louisa.

The money safely locked up, the robber behind bars and everyone safe and accounted for, there remained no reason for any of them to linger. CJ and Edmund hurried away. CJ said he would find the boy and make sure he was taken care of.

Bo made his way back to Cash. But rather than swing into the saddle, he led the horse back the direction he had come and then up the next street. He passed the new church and parsonage. A lamp burned in the parsonage. Brandon studying.

Bo paused outside the doctor's house. The doctor had left the fair as soon as the dance ended. Bo hoped he would still be up but the house was dark. At least that meant the babies were asleep. His heart filled with a gentle feeling. A feeling that included concern. *God, keep the people within those walls safe. Send them restful sleep. And help us find the babies' mother.*

He needed to get home. But still he stood in the silent street, unwilling to leave Louisa on her own.

The light went out in Brandon's quarters, and with a deep sigh, Bo mounted up and rode home.

It wasn't like he had anything to offer Louisa except his prayers. But Irene's warning wouldn't leave him. Her circumstances were different. Or were they? He wasn't sure what he believed anymore.

A fretful cry pulled Louisa from her exhausted sleep. The babies had had too much sun and excitement at the fair and had been difficult to get to sleep. Yawning, she stumbled to the lamp and lit it, knowing she didn't have a hope of getting to the fussing baby before he woke his brothers.

Jasper sat up, looking so miserable every vestige of Louisa's fatigue fled. She scooped him up. "What's wrong, little one?"

For answer, he leaned his face into her shoulder and sobbed.

Theo and Eli wakened. Their bottom lips quivered and tears pooled in their eyes.

She sank to the floor so she could pull the other two close, cradling them all. She sang softly, not wanting to disturb Father. He'd had so little sleep the last few days with the fair and other needs.

They settled, two across her legs and one in her arms. She tossed a cushion to the floor and eased over to lie down.

She had waited up last night hoping Bo would come by. He hadn't. And she had no reason to think he would. He'd been more than kind in escorting her to the fair. Dancing with all those beautiful ladies last night would emphasize to him her plainness. Not that it mattered. There was no room in her life for any kind of romance.

The only reason she wished he'd knock on her door was to help with the babies.

But no knock came. And she knew he wouldn't come. The fair was over and he would be back at his ranch.

She didn't know how long she slept before Jasper cried again and set off the other two. The lamp still burned but early morning sunshine peeked through the kitchen window. "Who would like some breakfast?" But how was she to make breakfast, get dressed and soothe three babies at the same time?

Father shuffled out of his room and headed for the stove. Realizing it was cold and the coffee not started, he grunted and started the fire, ground the coffee beans and put water in the coffeepot.

"If you watch the babies long enough for me to get dressed, I'll prepare breakfast."

"Of course." He sat on the sofa and she parked the babies at his feet, ignoring their protests as she dashed into her room and pulled on the first dress she laid hands on. An old maroon-colored one that had seen plenty of wear. A faint stain halfway down the skirt reminded her of a time she'd helped Father when a family had the grippe.

She hesitated half a second. Maybe she should choose something more fetching but the babies were fussing and Father called, "Are you about done in there?"

It didn't matter what she wore, so she pulled the dress on, settled for pinning her hair back. The comb Mrs. Longfeather gave her mocked her from the top of her bureau. That was yesterday. A time of make-believe. Today was back to normal.

She dashed from the room. The wood box by the stove was empty. She'd have to run out to the wood-shed for more, but when she flung the back door open, there in front of her was a large pile of wood, nicely stacked. Had Bo been there and thought to do this little kindness? She glanced up and down the alley but she saw no one, nothing.

She heaved a heavy sigh. He might have at least said hello.

With no time to worry about such matters, she took wood into the kitchen, pulled aside the coffeepot that now boiled and poured Father a cupful. She gave the triplets a drink of milk to tide them over until she could prepare breakfast. She flew from one task to the next, preparing food, feeding the babies and setting out a plate for Father. After being fed, the triplets were content for the space of about fifteen minutes.

Leaving the dishes half-washed, she again sat on the floor…the only place she could gather all three of them to her lap…and held them. Singing was the one thing that seemed to calm them and so she sang.

Father had gone to the office to make sure it was ready should anyone need him and returned after a bit. "Are you going to church?" he asked.

She glanced at the clock. Even if the little ones settled down, she didn't have time to prepare herself and them. "I don't think I'll make it today. You go ahead without me."

"Seems best. I checked them and there doesn't appear to be any sign of earache or fever."

"I think they had too much sun yesterday." She'd been selfish to keep them out all day. Perhaps taking their happy state for granted. "Maybe they'll sleep this morning."

A few minutes later, Father left. Louisa hummed to the babies and patted their backs. To her relief all three fell asleep. She sat with them against her until she felt certain they were well and truly in a deep sleep, and very slowly and cautiously shifted them to the floor, hardly daring to breathe as she waited to see if they would stay settled. When they did, she tiptoed away and as silently as possible finished cleaning the kitchen. A job that would have taken a minute or two consumed half an hour as she moved slowly. The same with the soup she prepared for dinner.

The babies continued to sleep, and with nothing else to do that couldn't wait, she sat at the table with her

Bible. She opened it but her gaze drifted away from the pages. The window allowed her to see a number of conveyances and horses tied up. The church was next door, close enough she'd heard the hum of the congregants singing. Despite the activities of the last three days, there seemed to be a goodly crowd. Or maybe because of the fair the people had come to give thanks for the money raised.

Was Bo there? Though with his twin brother as the preacher, she wondered if he ever missed a Sunday. Would Brandon take him to task if he did? She smiled to think of how they would argue. Wouldn't it be like arguing with yourself?

She bent her head to the scriptures but after a few minutes realized she had no awareness of what she read. Restless, she moved to the window to look out. So quiet. But peace did not fill her heart. Why had she let herself be lulled into spending the day with Bo? Enjoying herself so much that she was finding it hard to get back to normal?

A man and his family climbed aboard a wagon and drove away. Others drifted into the yard.

Church must be over. She watched, waiting, she reluctantly admitted, for a glimpse of Bo. Realizing she strained toward the glass, she forced herself to take a step backward. Tried to tell herself to stop staring, stop having impossible hopes. But remained rooted where she could see.

Lula May approached and tapped gently on the door. Louisa opened with her finger pressed to her mouth to signal quiet.

"Is everything okay here?" Lula May whispered. "I worried when you weren't in church."

Louisa explained that the babies had been irritable. "They're sleeping now."

"I'll pass the word around so no one else comes to the door. If you'd like help I can send one of the Bachmeier girls over."

Louisa managed not to shudder at the thought of one of those silly girls helping. "Thanks but I'm doing okay."

Lula May hurried away.

Louisa watched her speak to several others. She knew any one of them would help her but they all had their own families to take care of.

One of the babies fussed then stopped. Still Louisa held her position. Several families left. Half a dozen cowboys rode away on horses.

A couple of wagons and a handful of horses remained. She hadn't seen Bo. Did that mean he was still at the church? Perhaps he meant to spend the afternoon with his brother.

Accepting her disappointment, admitting she deserved it for dreaming of things that could not be, she returned to the table. Her Bible lay open before her but she couldn't read. *God, forgive me. I thought I had accepted my lot in life but one day at a county fair with a tall, handsome cowboy and I feel like I've lost my direction. Guide me to the truth. Your truth.* She turned her gaze to the scriptures and read, "What time I am afraid, I will trust in Thee." And a little farther down in the same chapter, "Wilt not Thou deliver my feet from falling?"

Her insides smoothed.

Theo let out a wail, and Louisa, smiling, went to tend the babies. Would God not enable her to cheerfully follow the path laid out before her?

Chapter Ten

Bo had no choice but to attend the meeting of the Lone Star Cowboy League as they discussed the best way to disperse the funds raised at the fair. But his mind was not on the matter. Louisa had not come to church. Yes, he'd expected her to and had been looking forward to seeing her there. In retrospect, he could see he hadn't given much thought to the logistics of getting the triplets ready. But he worried it might be more than that. Was everything all right? Were the babies sick again? Or was Louisa reluctant to see him again? Had she correctly read his desire to kiss her last night and found the thought unappealing? Not that she needed to worry. He'd had a little talk with himself and set himself straight. No more acting like a lovesick cowboy.

Lula May called the meeting to order and Bo did his best to pull his attention back to the present need. Brandon would be some offended if he learned Bo hadn't been able to concentrate on his sermon, either. Maybe he should apologize to his brother. But for what? Being distracted by the flitting images of Louisa and the babies…how she'd blushed when Mrs. Longfeather rearranged her hair and placed that comb, how she'd flushed with victory when she won the clothes-hanging contest, or the feel of her pressed to his side at the horse bucking event. He couldn't pretend he hadn't enjoyed their time at the fair any more than he could say he hadn't wanted to kiss her. If anyone deserved an apology it would be Louisa, but anything he said would only make both of them more awkward around each other.

"What do you think, Bo?" Lula May asked.

"What?" He'd missed the discussion. Quickly he gathered his thoughts. "So long as we provide for the triplets, I'm okay with whatever the majority wants."

Brandon shifted closer and whispered loudly enough for all to hear. "I think your thoughts were elsewhere." He rolled his eyes in the general direction of next door.

Brandon's remarks brought some good-natured laughter and teasing.

Bo ignored them. Let them think what they wanted. He and Brandon knew the truth about his feelings regarding anything serious between himself and a woman, especially a fine, beautiful woman like Louisa. He again pictured her all shy and rosy cheeked.

Somehow he managed to give the discussion enough attention to understand the majority agreed with providing funds to help care for the triplets until the mother could be found and also accepting applications for specific needs by local ranches. They were all aware of the struggles many were facing with the ongoing drought. The league would help purchase feed, supplies or whatever specific need individuals reported. They promised Edmund McKay more resources for his Young Ranchers program. "That's it for now," Lula May said. Bo was on his feet before she finished.

Brandon chuckled. "Something urgent on your mind?"

"Did it ever cross your mind to think Miss Clark might have her hands more than full tending three babies?"

Brandon pushed lazily to his feet. "I've thought of it but she appeared to have all the help she needed yesterday." The look he gave Bo said exactly who he thought provided that help.

Bo might have denied it but what was the point? The whole town and most of the county had seen him. Instead, he headed for the exit.

Brandon followed. "Maybe I should come and help. After all, there are three babies." No missing the teasing tone in his voice. He knew Bo wanted to see Louisa on his own. Acknowledging that brought him to a standstill. Hadn't he been clear to himself that yesterday was to be his one and only day to—?

Brandon's company would be a good thing.

"By all means." It gave him a good deal of satisfaction to see Brandon's surprise.

"Very well. But we better eat before we go over there." Bidding the last of the league members goodbye, they retired to Brandon's quarters.

Bo looked around. He'd been there before but something was different. "What is with all the cushions and pretty little knickknacks? The place looks like a gift shop."

"You're not the only good-looking, unmarried Stillwater, you know."

They looked at each other and laughed. Being with

his twin settled Bo's confusion. Brandon understood like no one else why Bo had vowed to never marry.

Brandon opened his icebox. "What will you have? Roast beef, soup, veggies."

Bo peered over his shoulder. "You've taken up cooking?"

"Nope. This is all part of the campaign to convince me some young lady is worthy of my undivided attention." He pulled out the roast beef and set it on the table along with bread, butter and plates. He carved off thick slices for each of them.

"You interested in any of them?" Bo knew Brandon saw things a little differently than did he. After all, Brandon had gone into the ministry and Bo into ranching. As if his twin thought he could erase the past by serving others.

Brandon shrugged. "I haven't changed my mind."

"Too bad." Brandon had been hurt by a girl he'd loved.

They chewed on thick sandwiches for several minutes before Bo continued the conversation. "I'm not open to the idea at all."

Brandon studied him a full thirty seconds. "In all fairness, you better make sure Louisa knows your views."

"She does and she understands. She doesn't plan to marry."

"Really. Why is that?"

He tried to recall exactly what she had told him. He tried to reconcile what she'd said about only having one suitor who'd been unwilling to wait for her.

The man didn't realize what a mistake he'd made. "I don't really know."

"Hmm. It might be informative to find out."

"She might not be willing to tell me."

Brandon chuckled. "What do you talk about when you're with her? And don't say you only talk about the triplets."

Bo grinned, unabashedly pleased to know they had discussed many other things.

He ate the last of his sandwich and Brandon offered him cake.

"From another prospect?"

Brandon nodded. "Someone who wishes to be considered should I be in the market for a wife, which everyone thinks I am."

They both ate generous portions of the cake, then without needing to consult each other, rose, put on their hats and side by side, steps perfectly matched, left the parsonage and went to the doctor's residence. Brandon stepped aside to let Bo knock.

They waited, hearing the sound of babies fussing. Bo was about to knock again when Louisa opened the door.

His tentative smile widened at the sight of her. Her dark red dress was rumpled, her hair in disarray. Tension showed in the little crease in her forehead. She looked perfectly delightful, but from the way her mouth drew down, he guessed she might not be feeling that way and he stopped smiling.

"We've come to help."

She threw the door wider. "That's an offer I'm not about to refuse. The babies are fussy as can be today."

She added that Annie had been unable to come as her mother wasn't feeling well and needed her.

Bo and Brandon went to the babies and each lifted one.

Louisa followed and took the third.

"What seems to be the matter? Are they sick?" Bo asked.

"Not that I can tell. I wonder if they had too much excitement yesterday. I shouldn't have kept them out so long. It was neglectful of me."

Bo heard a note in her voice that he wished to erase. "They seemed to enjoy the outing." Despite his intention of putting the day behind him in his thoughts, he smiled. "I know I enjoyed it."

Brandon rolled his eyes.

Louisa blushed.

Rather pleased with himself, he sat on the sofa with little Eli on his knee. Brandon pulled up a kitchen chair and sat beside him with Jasper perched on his leg. The two babies looked at each other and chortled. Theo half leaned out of Louisa's arms as he strained toward the others.

Bo understood instantly what the baby wanted. "He needs to be closer to his brothers."

Louisa hesitated long enough for Bo to wonder if she didn't care for the idea of sitting close to him. Then she parked herself beside him on the sofa. Theo reached for Eli and gave a teary smile. As Louisa held the baby, her arm pressed to his side, and he acknowledged that life was rather pleasant.

Brandon watched him, his eyes knowing. Bo gave a barely there shrug. What was wrong with enjoying a temporary situation? It wasn't as if it meant anything more than that. Both he and Louisa were clear on that matter.

Jasper bounced up and down on Brandon's knee, rumbling his lips, droplets spraying over his brothers. Eli looked surprised at the moisture on his face and Theo did his own rumbling and giggling.

Bo laughed at the babies' antics. "They seem happy enough now."

"I'm glad." Beside him, Louisa's shoulders slumped slightly, as if a load had been removed.

Bo experienced an incredible urge to pull her close and offer words of comfort. He couldn't decide if he wanted to thank Brandon for his presence that forced Bo to resist the urge, or resent that he didn't feel free to follow his instincts. He had to believe it was the former.

The babies bounced and cooed at each other. Eli squirmed to be put down and Bo lowered him to the floor. Of course, the two others followed suit and the three played contentedly at the feet of the three adults.

"I think they wanted more attention than I could give them." Louisa sounded regretful.

"I expect they are a little out of sorts. Not because of yesterday's outing but because they miss their mama."

At the mention of their mother, the babies looked up at Bo, tears puddling on each bottom eyelid.

"See, that proves it," Bo said.

"Poor little guys." He and Brandon spoke at the same time.

Louisa laughed. "It's fun to watch you two together and see how you mirror each other."

The men grinned. "It's fun to have a twin."

Again they said it as one voice and Louisa laughed, her eye flashing with amusement as she said, "I wonder if the triplets will be like that."

Bo knew he detected a note of sadness in her tone. Dr. Clark came from the room off the kitchen, yawning. He headed for the stove and shook the coffeepot. Lifted the lid and peered into the contents, then emptied thick black sludge into the slop pail and proceeded to grind beans and refill the pot. Only after it was back on the stove did he look around and see that Bo and Brandon had joined his daughter and the triplets.

"Good afternoon. Would you care to join us for coffee?"

Brandon answered for them both. "Sounds good. Let me run next door and get a cake." He was out the door before anyone could say yes or no.

Louisa stared after him. "Your brother bakes?"

Bo laughed then told of the fancy cushions, the breakable knickknacks, the icebox full of food. "And an array of baked goods in the cupboard. You'd think he was conducting his own baking contest in his kitchen."

"Well, you know what they say—the way to a man's heart is through his stomach."

"If this keeps up, Brandon will have a stomach to rival Casper Magnuson's."

Picturing the large-bellied man, they both laughed. Their gazes melded together in that sweet moment and a tenderness—not unlike fondness—flooded his heart, threatening his carefully constructed barriers.

Brandon rushed in carrying a tall cake, with fluffy white icing, and decorated with pink sugar flowers.

Had he not arrived at that precise moment, Bo's

walls might have crumbled, but he was able to tear his attention away from Louisa just in time.

Brandon took the cake to the kitchen. Doc poured out four cups of coffee. Louisa hurried to the cupboard and took down plates and cut slices of dark chocolate cake for everyone. Bo sat where he was, unsure if his heart was secure enough to join them in the other room, but the doc called for him to come. He scooped up Eli as Louisa took Jasper. They straightened at the same time, their eyes again seeking and finding the other with an urgency that made Bo's heart wobble. Again Brandon saved him from himself by taking the third baby. Bo hung back to let Louisa and then Brandon go ahead of him. He needed as much space as he could find.

Louisa gave Jasper a taste of cake and they laughed when the baby's eyes widened with delight. Both Bo and Brandon offered a taste to the babies they held and were rewarded with matching looks.

The adults lingered over their coffee and cake, reviewing the events of the fair. Brandon and Dr. Clark mentioned the awards given out and the many competitions held, but Bo could only think of a few special moments shared with Louisa.

"How did the dance go?" she asked, driving his thoughts back to last evening.

"It raised a lot of money." That was all that mattered. "Enough to prove too much temptation for a certain scoundrel." Pleased to have a story that drew everyone's attention away from the dance, he told of the attempted robbery.

"You pretended a stick was a gun?" Brandon chuck-led. "Good job."

Bo watched Louisa's reaction. Her eyes widened and darkened. Her lips parted and she looked at him with what he thought might be concern. Then she shuddered and lowered her gaze. "You might have been hurt."

"I can't say it didn't cross my mind. But I wasn't about to let him take away our hard-earned money. We worked far too hard to allow that."

Brandon's grin was exceedingly teasing. "Work? Looked to me like you were having the time of your life."

"My feet still hurt." He didn't even try to keep the injured tone from his voice. He wanted them all to re-alize dancing with all those ladies required a degree of sacrifice on his part. From the look on Brandon's face, he knew his brother was unconvinced. Louisa developed a sudden interest in cleaning every trace of cake from her plate.

The triplets grew tired of sitting at the table and they took them back to the living room and let them get down to move around.

"By the way," Louisa said. "Thank you for stack-ing the wood on the back step for me. Very conve-nient, especially as the little ones fuss whenever I'm out of sight."

"But I didn't. Brandon?"

"Not me."

They looked round at each other.

"Strange," Bo and Brandon said together.

"Could it be the same person or persons who left

the toys and the blankets?" Louisa showed Brandon the items.

"I'll keep a watch for whoever is doing this," Brandon said. "Discovering the responsible party might lead us to the mother."

They each rubbed the back of the baby before them, offering them what comfort they could at the disappearance of their mother.

Doc set up a checkerboard on the kitchen table. "There's nothing like a relaxing game to pass a Sunday afternoon." He rubbed his hands and looked expectantly at the three in the living room.

Brandon got up. "I'll play a game."

Bo's gaze followed his brother to the kitchen, then slowly made its way back to Louisa. Their looks met. He jerked away. Hadn't he already discovered how difficult it was to keep his wits about him when he looked into those warm brown eyes?

She dropped the stuffed animals in the midst of the babies and they reached for them. Eli and Jasper grabbed the same one and had a little tug-of-war. Eli won and Jasper fell to his back, the toy immediately forgotten as he set about pulling off his bootees.

Theo took one of the remaining toys and banged it on the floor, managing to hit poor little Jasper with every bang.

Bo pulled the baby out of reach of his brother's play and Jasper chuckled.

Had he ever heard a more pleasing sound than that? His head came up and he looked directly at Louisa, knowing her laughter was even more pleasing. She watched the babies, allowing him time to study her. What could he do to bring out more laughter?

"Brandon and I slept together until we couldn't both fit into the same bed."

Brandon snorted. "I seem to recall you crawling in beside me long after we were too big."

It was true. After their mother died, they had often shared the same bed. "At least I didn't kick like a mule."

"No, but you swung your arms like a lumberjack chopping down a tree." Brandon made swinging motions to illustrate.

Louisa chortled, trying unsuccessfully to cover the sound with her hand.

Bo and Brandon grinned at each other. Brandon might be teasing him but Bo didn't mind.

Not if it amused Louisa.

She sprang to her feet. Had it embarrassed her to laugh at them? "Goodness, look at the time." She turned to Bo. "Do you mind watching the triplets while I make supper?"

"Not at all." That sounded awfully much like an invite to stay and he wasn't about to turn it down.

He sat on the floor and tossed the teddy bear to Theo, who rewarded his efforts with one of those sweet baby belly laughs.

The other two, not wanting to be left out, crawled into Bo's lap.

He sat with his back to the sofa, content to play with the babies and watch Louisa hurry about the kitchen. This was what life as a married man would be like.

His heart filled with ice.

This was the ideal. He knew the reality would fall far short of that.

Jasper pulled at the buttons on Bo's shirt and Bo let reality slip to the side for the moment.

As Louisa prepared hash from leftover potatoes and roast beef, she told herself not to get too caught up in the pleasure of sharing the afternoon with Bo and his brother, but watching Bo with the triplets did something strange in the secret depths of her heart. It hollowed out a little nest. One that might have always been there…perfectly suited for a husband and children.

A pain so sharp it weakened her knees pierced her. She would never be free to enjoy that privilege. Or at least she would be a withered-up old maid before that time came. And it meant losing her mother. She instantly repented of her thoughts.

God, keep my mother well for years to come. Help me be faithful to my calling.

Her resolve firmly back in place, she finished supper preparations, taking it for granted that Bo and Brandon would join them. After all, without Bo's help she might never have gotten a meal ready.

She stole a glance at him with the three babies playing at his knees. He was so good with them. She could not picture him ever being cruel or unkind.

"I'd like to feed the babies first," she said to no one in particular.

"I'll help," Bo said, as if he knew the words were meant for him. He sat the three up facing him and she took in two bowls of food and sat beside him. It really didn't take two to feed them. They were used to being fed together, though she'd discovered Theo didn't like waiting, so she always tried to start with him.

She relayed the information to Bo and he parked Theo at the left end.

"You know these little guys well considering how few days you've known them. We had friends and even relatives that could never tell Brandon and me apart."

She shook her head in sadness. "That's terrible, especially when you are so vastly different. I simply cannot understand why there would ever be a problem."

He stared at her. She hoped her expression gave nothing away. But she felt the flicker in her eyes.

Bo realized she teased him and laughed. Brandon and Father joined him.

"You'll soon learn that my daughter has a wry sense of humor," Father said. "She still manages to catch me off guard from time to time." The smile he gave Louisa warmed her heart…at least a portion of it. Not the part that she'd only moments ago grown aware of.

The babies ate like hungry birds, mouths popping open and straining toward the spoon as they waited their turn. "They are such good babies," she said, again to no one in particular but again, Bo answered.

"It's obvious they've been well loved." For a moment he grew serious.

She wondered if he thought of his mother. Or did he recall Mrs. Longfeather's words. *You have love to give.* He had admitted the first, denied the second, even as Louisa had denied it when the Native woman said she had love to give a man.

Still aware of the emptiness in the depths of her heart, she allowed that it might be true. But what difference did it make? Her mother would need her for a good long time yet. A fact she didn't regret.

"I wonder how long Mother and Amy will rest before they continue the trip."

Father looked up from another game of checkers with Brandon. They were evenly matched, first one and then the other winning. "I hope Amy will keep in close contact. Perhaps there will be another letter on Tuesday." That was when the next delivery was expected.

The triplets finished, drank their milk and lay back contentedly, playing with their stuffed toys.

Louisa dished up supper for the adults. "Bo, join us. The babies will be okay there. We can see them and they can see us." She allowed them as much freedom as was safe.

He pushed to his feet and edged past the triplets. She pointed out a chair across the table from her. Brandon already sat across from Father.

They bowed their heads as Father thanked God for the food. "And give my wife, daughter and her husband good health and journeying mercies."

For a moment, they were busy passing the serving bowls from hand to hand.

Bo tasted the hash. "This is good."

"Thank you." She should be able to prepare a decent meal. She'd been doing it more than half her life. She'd learned the difference between ordinary hash and great hash was a little bit of onion grated rather than chopped.

The cream sauce on the peas was flawless and she was pleased to have fresh baby carrots right from someone's garden and bread baked from her own oven to round out the simple meal.

They ate at a leisurely fashion, perhaps everyone as content as Louisa to have nothing else demanding their attention. A quiet Sunday was a rare treat for her father. From living next door to the church, she knew people came to visit Brandon whenever they felt the need. As to Bo…she realized how little she knew about ranch life. It was something she wouldn't mind remedying.

The men each ate another piece of cake but Louisa said she'd had enough sweets.

Bo looked askance when she sat down without cake. "You don't like sweets?"

"Only moderately."

Bo and Brandon looked at each other and shook their heads sadly.

"It's a character flaw," Bo said, sadness dripping from each syllable.

"I'll pray for you," Brandon offered.

Their reaction tickled Louisa's funny bone and she chuckled. "It sounds like you two have a sweet tooth."

"Oh, several of them," Bo said airily. "And please don't pray that we lose them."

She grinned, feeling her eyes warm. "You keep eating sweets and you'll soon enough be begging my father to pull them out."

The twins gobbled up the last of their cake and covered their mouths. "I'll keep my teeth, thank you very much." Bo's words were muffled by his hand.

"And I'll keep eating sweets," Brandon answered, winking at Bo.

The meal ended with more joking and teasing than

Louisa had known in a very long time. Perhaps never. Her home life with an ill mother and a weak sister had been one of quietness and tiptoeing around so as not to disturb them. "I suspect you two had many a boisterous day growing up."

The look they gave each other informed her even before Bo answered that there had been days quite the opposite.

"I'm sorry. I should have thought before I spoke."

Bo shrugged, a smile returning. "We learned to have our fun when we could. The last four years we've enjoyed each other's company as never before."

The look he and Brandon exchanged made Louisa realize how lonely she was. Amy had been her best friend and depended greatly on her. Then she'd met Lawrence and no longer confided so much in Louisa. No longer needed her as before. She was happy to have achieved her goal of seeing Amy grow strong and self-sufficient but she missed their time together. Even as she missed Mother.

Though how she'd manage if they showed up tomorrow, she couldn't imagine. The triplets occupied every minute of her day and a good portion of her nights. Except now, they played on the floor close enough to be able to see the adults.

Brandon glanced at the clock. "I must leave. I'm expecting someone in a few minutes." He sent Bo a warning look. "And it isn't a young woman. It's an older man who wanted to talk about his faith…or lack of it." He turned to Louisa. "Thank you for the lovely afternoon and the great supper." Then to Father. "Thank you for the challenging games of checkers. You're a more worthy opponent than my brother."

Bo sputtered. "We're evenly matched and you know it."

"Yes, but I can almost predict your moves the same way you can predict mine. It's fun playing with someone else. You should try it."

"Maybe I will."

Brandon slipped away.

"No time like the present." Father shoved aside the dishes and set up the board again.

Bo hesitated. "I insist on helping with the dishes."

She held his gaze, sensing something fragile hovering between them. "Did your mother teach you to do so?"

"My good sense tells me you shouldn't be stuck with all the work."

His comment struck a tender nerve. When had anyone ever commented on her responsibilities? Had actually noticed how much she did? Why, she herself gave it little heed except for the occasional time she felt overwhelmed. Perhaps having a cruel father made him more keenly aware of what others did. Whatever the reason, she was deeply touched and found it difficult to get a word up her tight throat.

"You've helped with the triplets," she finally managed, providing him with a reason to ease out of his offer if it had only been made out of politeness.

"They are no more your responsibility than mine, so that hardly counts." He pushed from the table. "I'll take you on in a game as soon as I've helped Louisa," he said to Father.

Father looked from Bo to Louisa and back again, a thoughtful look on his face.

Bo gathered the used dishes and carried them to the dishpan to immerse them in the hot soapy water. He rolled up his sleeves and began to wash them. "You know where everything belongs, so you can dry and put away."

Louisa decided at that moment that a man could wear nothing more appealing than soap sudsy hands.

How was she to keep her heart safely moored if he continued to be so sweet?

Chapter Eleven

Monday morning yawned like an empty cavern. After the busy, company-filled previous day, Louisa had nothing to look forward to but caring for the babies and trying to get a few chores done. Bo would not return. He had no reason to come to town…no fair, no Sunday service, no meeting of the Lone Star Cowboy League. He had a ranch to run.

She hugged Jasper. "How can I be lonely with three handsome young men to keep me company?"

Bo had stayed long enough Sunday to help prepare the triplets for bed. He'd rocked a restless Theo as Louisa sang softly until all three were asleep. She and Bo had remained together in the room with the sleeping babies, talking quietly. She ached to ask him about the ranch but feared he might guess how much she longed to be invited to visit his home and misinterpret her interest.

He'd finally pushed to his feet, somewhat reluctantly, she allowed herself to think, though a good portion of her brain knew he lingered only because he felt responsible for the triplets, having been the one who brought them to her.

She didn't expect to see him again for any reason other than discussing arrangements for the babies.

A knock came to the back door and her heart leaped with a burst of joy. He'd come. She rushed to throw back the door. "Annie. I wasn't sure you'd come today." They'd made no arrangement for when the girl would return to help.

"I expect you could use some help." She handed Louisa a battered tin gallon can full of bits of wood. "Someone left you kindling."

Louisa peeked out the door, looking up and down the alley. She drew back. Such strange things. Was there someone with a special interest in the babies? Or in her as their temporary mama? *Mama?* Why had she even thought the word? The triplets were with her only because they'd been ill and needed nursing care. Now they were well. Far too soon, the powers that be would make a decision as to what would happen to them next. The idea of them moving filled her with despair. She had grown so fond of them. But it could not be anything more than temporary. Her mother would soon arrive and Louisa would be busy caring for her.

Annie hung her bonnet on the hook by the door. "How are the little ones doing?"

"Their colds are better. For the most part they are happy, contented babies but they do get fussy at times. I imagine it's because they miss their mother." She was careful not to say "mama" and remind the triplets of their missing parent.

Annie squatted down to face the trio. "How do you tell them apart?"

"Mostly by how they act and their expressions." She pointed out the subtle differences.

Annie studied each of them. "I suppose I'll learn which is which." She stayed on the floor, letting the babies get used to her.

Louisa sank to the sofa. She was weary. Seemed the nights were too short. Or at least the times that she was able to sleep far too small. She looked about the living room, seeing how untidy it had become with a quilt laid out for the babies to sleep on, a pillow and quilt she'd used as she slept on the sofa, an array of items she'd given them to play with.

"They can't keep sleeping in the living room. They get disturbed too easily." She looked about. Her gaze coming to the door to her mother's room. Mother didn't need it yet. "We'll fix up that room for them."

Annie played with the babies as she talked. "What about your mother?"

Louisa explained about the delay in travel plans. "I'm sure we'll have plenty of time to get the room in order after we hear they are on their way."

"Where will the babies go?"

"I pray it will be back to their mother."

Annie's eyes said what Louisa thought. What if their mother wasn't located?

Not wanting to dwell on such a possibility, she hurried over to the bedroom. "We'll scrub the place really well and put a mattress on the floor for them to sleep on. They like to be able to touch each other or even hold hands when they're sleeping."

"Isn't that precious?" Annie cocked her head and studied Louisa.

"What?"

"You spent a lot of time with Bo Stillwater. What's it like to be with someone who has a brother who looks exactly like him?"

Louisa eased out a sigh of relief. At least Annie hadn't asked if they were courting. "They look alike but they are different in so many ways. Like the triplets."

"If you say so. I don't see it myself."

Louisa turned back to the room. "How are we going to work with three crawling babies underfoot?"

"Why not put them in that cart thing?"

"I suppose we'll have to, though I hate to keep them penned up like that." She and Annie gathered together their supplies. Once they had basins of hot soapy water, a stack of rags, and a broom and dustpan ready, Louisa settled the babies in the cart and parked it in the room where they could watch the activity. It would be easy to move them about to work around them. "I'm sorry. I'll make it up to you later."

She and Annie worked steadily through the morning and by noon the room was clean and a mattress on the floor awaited the babies. The bed was set up for Louisa so she could sleep nearby.

They prepared dinner and fed the babies, then put them down in their new quarters. Eli had a good look around, taking in every detail. When he was satisfied he liked the place, he took Theo's hand and curled up beside him. Jasper cuddled close to his brothers and they were soon asleep.

Louisa and Annie tiptoed out and closed the door behind them.

"If you don't need me right now, I have something to do uptown." Annie blushed furiously.

Louisa hesitated. Had Annie made arrangements to meet Jamie against their parents' wishes? She shrugged. They were both of age; they'd have to deal with the outcome of their actions. "Go ahead. I'll keep busy while the little ones sleep." Many household tasks needed her attention.

Annie hurried away and Louisa set about tidying the living room. She'd prepare vegetables and set the meat to cook as soon as that was done.

A knock on the door set her heart to fluttering and she hurried to admit the visitor. "Mrs. McKay."

"Betsy, please." The wife of Josiah, the eldest of the McKay brothers, stood before her with her baby, Andrew, on her hip and three-year-old Eddie at her side. "I brought you something for supper." She handed Louisa a towel-wrapped pot that she clutched in one hand.

Louisa took the pot. "It smells good. Would you like to come in?"

Betsy entered. "It's stewed chicken with rivels. They're pea-sized dumplings. It's how my mother always served chicken soup or stew. I hope you'll like them. You can keep the meal warm on the back of the stove until supper time."

"Would you care for a cup of tea?" Louisa asked, unwrapping the pot and setting it on the back of the stove as instructed. "You don't know how much I appreciate this. It seems I don't have enough hands and enough hours in the day for everything that needs doing."

"I'll only stay a minute." Betsy sat at the table, her little boy content on her knee.

"Where's Adam?" Their twelve-year-old son.

"He stayed with his father. Little Eddie here is too young to follow him around."

The kettle soon boiled and Louisa prepared tea. Brandon had left the chocolate cake, so she could offer Betsy something to eat.

Betsy talked more than she ate cake or sipped her tea. "The ladies know how much work three babies are, so we've gotten together a plan. Someone will bring you supper every night so you don't need to worry about that."

"That's most generous." To her embarrassment, her throat clogged with tears.

Betsy patted her hand. "I understand how weepy a woman can get from lack of sleep and the constant demands of a baby. And you have three to care for. How are they doing?"

She again reported on the triplets. "The men are trying to find their mother. I wonder if she's still around." She told about the little things left or done.

"But surely someone would have noticed her, especially now that there aren't any strangers around for the fair."

"I thought the same thing," Louisa said. "But someone is doing it."

"I'll pass the word along so people can be watching for any strangers in the area. Wouldn't it be wonderful if we could find their mother?"

Louisa tipped her head toward the bedroom. "I hear them stirring. Excuse me while I get them."

Betsy followed her. "I'll lend a hand."

Louisa didn't argue. In fact, she quite welcomed the extra hands to change diapers and then to amuse them while she prepared a snack. Once they had the triplets fed and settled, little Andrew started to fuss and Betsy put the baby to her breast. "He's at such a good age," she said, smiling at her son. "Still not getting into mischief and yet sleeping through the night." She stayed and visited until Andrew was done nursing. "I need to get home."

"Thank you so much for the supper. You have no idea how much help it will be."

Betsy chuckled. "I might have a bit of understanding."

They said their goodbyes. Louisa turned back to the triplets watching her from the floor, where they sat together. "Now, how am I going to amuse you three?" Bo seemed to know how to play with them. How to keep them happy. But Bo wasn't there.

She sat on the floor and took turns tossing the stuffed animals to the triplets, finding their laughter as pleasing as any music.

Someone knocked. Would she ever convince herself not to hope Bo would drop by? Certainly she understood it would be for no other reason than to see the triplets.

Before she could get to her feet, Annie entered. A pretty blonde with fair skin, she didn't have any hope of hiding her heightened color. Louisa didn't need to ask to know she'd indeed been with Jamie.

"Something smells good in here," Annie commented.

Louisa explained about the meal Betsy had brought and the plan to provide supper. "I don't know how long they will do it but I surely appreciate it."

Annie looked around. "You didn't do laundry today?"

"I thought of it but how was I to do so with babies about my feet?"

"I tell you what. I'll get everything set up and I'll do it tomorrow morning." She looked about the room. "It seems to me you need to fix this room so the babies can play without getting into anything they shouldn't. If I tip this small table on its side and put it across the door, it will confine them to the living room when you're working in the kitchen."

"Excellent idea. That way they'll be safe."

As they moved every breakable thing out of reach and prepared the room to accommodate three babies moving about and exploring, Annie provided colorful details about the Saturday night dance. Louisa paused to look out the window. She'd heard the music and wished she'd been brave enough to purchase one dance with Bo. With a shake of her head, she turned back to the room. Even if it hadn't been necessary to stay with the babies, she would not have gone to the dance. Her place was right here.

"There'll be a dance on July Fourth," Annie continued with her happy chatter. "You'll have to go to that one. It won't be quite the affair this past one was but still, it will be nice." Her voice grew dreamy.

Nice, Louisa thought, for a young woman with a head full of dreams and possibilities.

A little later Annie filled the tub of water and left

it on the stove to heat. "I'll be back bright and early tomorrow."

And then Louisa was all alone. Except for three babies busy exploring the living room.

This was her life. Caring for the home. Tending her mother's needs. In the interim taking care of the triplets.

She fed the babies and set the table to wait for Father, who had been away all day at one of the nearby ranches, where a young lad had been injured. If he didn't come soon, she would eat without him and then prepare the little boys for bed.

She was about to dish up a plate of the chicken stew, whose aroma had been tugging at her taste buds for the past hour, when Father trudged in. "You've had a long day. How is the boy?"

"He's fine. He'll be laid up awhile. But I saw their baby wasn't thriving. The woman didn't have enough milk. I suggested she give him some cow's milk. The woman took offense. I wish you'd been there to help explain that the baby wasn't an easy baby but was actually too weak to fuss."

Louisa smiled at her father's approval of her usual assistance. "I hope you were able to make her understand."

"I believe I was in the end. And as always I had a feeding bottle in my bag."

Louisa studied the babies in the other room as she sat down with Father to eat. Their mother had felt she must leave them. The mother Father referred to wasn't able to provide for her baby. Being a mother required terrible sacrifices. And yet she couldn't find it in her heart to be grateful she would in all likelihood never know the experience.

Father finished and headed for his big chair to read a book. The triplets clustered about his feet but he ignored them as if wearied of babies. Or perhaps, just weary. He'd been working hard and she knew he missed his wife.

She'd noticed how Betsy fashioned a toy for Andrew out of a rolled-up sock and she made one for each of the triplets, showing them how to roll the sock like a ball. They played with the simple toys while she cleaned up from the meal, grateful to see there was enough chicken stew left for dinner tomorrow.

Father closed his book. "I need to check on things in the office."

She wandered from window to window. It had been a good day. Annie had helped her. Betsy had visited. No one had needed her father while he was away, so she hadn't needed to tend to any emergencies. She had no reason to feel out of sorts. Yet she did. For purely selfish and unacceptable reasons that she wouldn't dignify by acknowledging.

Bo passed the boulder signaling the boundary of his ranch. "Cash, old boy. I think someone must have chipped bits from that rock and filled my head with them. Otherwise why am I riding into town to see how a young lady is faring with the triplets? It ain't like I can do much to help her." Mrs. Jamieson had been some surprised when Bo informed her he'd like his supper early. Normally this time of year, he worked until dark. To her credit, his housekeeper had said nothing but her eyebrows had gone halfway to her hairline.

The horse's ears twitched as Bo relayed the information to him.

"I know you must wonder about me. We've spent so much time in Little Horn lately. But I'll give you an extra feed of oats tonight when we get home." He didn't tell his horse that it would likely be after dark.

He moseyed down the street at a leisurely pace. After all, he had no deadline and he didn't want anyone to see him and think he was in a pressing hurry. He passed the church and parsonage. No sign of Brandon. Wouldn't he have lots to say if he saw Bo heading for the doctor's house again after being there yesterday? Though he supposed there was no way of hiding Cash, and Brandon would recognize the horse immediately.

So be it.

He dismounted and made his way to the door. Suddenly he wasn't sure he should knock. This was plum foolish. But his hand came up and rapped on the door. Oh, well, now he was there he might as well assure himself everyone inside was doing all right.

Louisa opened the door. Her eyes widened in surprise and well they should. Likely he was the last person she expected or even wanted to have visit.

"Thought I'd help put the babies to bed," he said, as much an explanation for himself as for her.

"I appreciate that." She opened the door wider and he stepped in. At least she hadn't hesitated. He took that as a good sign.

The three babies recognized him and gurgled a greeting. Jasper crawled toward him.

Louisa chuckled. "They're happy to see you. I'm beginning to think they like lots of activity around them."

He scooped up Jasper and swung him overhead, letting the happy laughter erase all his arguments about why he shouldn't have come to town.

He shifted Jasper to one arm, sat on the floor and pulled the other two to his lap to play with them.

"You boys been cooped up inside all day?"

"Yes, they have," Louisa said.

"Let's take them out for a walk before they go to bed. It will help them sleep." He added the latter to explain to both of them why he would march around town with three babies and a woman. Him, the man who vowed never to have a family, who gently but firmly let all the eager young ladies and their mothers know he wasn't interested in a match.

"That sounds like a wonderful idea." She sounded every bit as eager as he. And he wasn't about to try to understand her reasons.

They set the triplets in the cart and rolled it to the street. Brandon stood at the church doorway. He waved, his grin mocking enough for Bo to know he thought the same as Bo…coming to town again so soon after his last visit seemed a little odd.

He tilted his head slightly to indicate he wasn't prepared to offer an explanation.

Brandon's smile widened and he watched them as they passed onward, leaving the main area of town and trundling down the dusty streets of the residential areas. There was something satisfying about seeing children chasing each other in the backyards, women weeding their gardens in the cool of the day, fathers tossing a ball for the older children and grandparents sitting on the porches in their rocking chairs. He knew most of the people and they called out a greeting. Many hurried over to look at the triplets, who seemed to thrive on the attention.

It gave him pause to wonder something. "Seeing how happy they are to see people makes me think they've been raised in town where they saw lots of people regularly."

"I agree," she said. "They seem happiest when surrounded by others."

"I'll ask Jeb if he's sent telegrams to all the nearby towns. Or perhaps not so nearby. But how would she manage to get here on her own and without anyone noticing her?"

They continued walking along the street as they talked.

"I've wondered about that," Louisa said. "But so many people were coming and going before the fair opened and lots of wagons and buggies. I suppose she could have easily been mistaken for someone carrying goods to display."

"That's possible but we can't go twenty feet without someone spotting the triplets."

"She must have covered them with a blanket or somehow kept them out of sight."

They reached the edge of town where a struggling pecan tree grew to the side of the pathway that led to the fairgrounds. They paused there under the shade of the branches. Neither seemed inclined to return to the doctor's house and the triplets played with the dancing shadows of the leaves against their skin.

"How was your day?" he asked.

She told him about Betsy and the arrangement for meals to be delivered each day.

"Perhaps if someone had offered that kind of help to the mother, she might not have grown ill," he ventured.

"It's hard to say. From her note, it sounds like she thought she was dying." She grabbed his arm. "I can't bear the thought of her doing so, leaving these little ones orphaned. Who will take in three babies? Will they end up in an orphanage?"

Right then and there, he silently promised he would do everything he could to ensure they did not suffer such a fate. "I wouldn't want to see them in one of those big institutions in the city."

"David McKay seems in favor of an orphan home." She sounded as if the idea didn't appeal.

"I think he has something different in mind than the big city orphanages. A real home where the children are raised by stand-in parents. There are several groups of children in the area whose parents are gone and they are living with relatives or neighbors. It isn't always the best solution, especially if the friends are desperately poor or already overburdened with children. I can think of one pair I really worry about. The Satler children. Friends of their parents have taken them in but they are struggling to provide for their large family." He wouldn't say so but it seemed to him that they didn't have time or room in their family for the Satler pair.

"I've seen them. They appear to run about freely without supervision. I feel sorry for them."

Her hand slipped down his arm and he captured her fingers in his and squeezed. "Sadly life is not always kind." At the moment he found it difficult to recall any sadness in his own life, though there had been much. Somehow, being here in this peaceful place pushed such memories into the distance, covering them with a gossamer veil.

She chuckled. "Annie came to help today but I don't think that was the biggest reason for her trip to town. I think she and Jamie Coleman had arranged to meet secretly."

"I'm afraid that will lead to even more problems between the families."

"Or—" Her voice was gentle as if full of dreams. "It might be the way they come to reconciliation."

"You think love can overcome any obstacle in its path?" At one time he might have spoken sarcastically but the words came out soft, perhaps indicating he wanted to be convinced it was possible.

She stared past him, searching for the answer in the distance. After a moment, she brought her gaze back to his, her eyes full of determination and conviction. "Love comes in many ways. It is not always romantic love. There is a mother's love for her child. A child's for her mother. Even the love people have for children not their own. I think—" Her words came slowly. "Love provides the power to accept what God lays in our path. Sometimes love calls for sacrifices."

He dropped her hand and crossed his arms over his chest. That wasn't the answer he wanted to hear. It reminded him of the decision made years ago to never marry. A decision he still believed was the best for him.

"You don't agree?"

He shrugged. "I suppose I wanted you to say you believed love conquers all."

"My answer is practical and realistic."

"It is that." Why did he wish for more? The answer came clearly and instantly. "I see you as happily married with a bunch of babies and your answer says to me that you don't see romance in your life."

He caught a flash of pain in her eyes before she gave a sad little smile. "I don't believe romance will come to me."

A thousand little details flashed through his mind. How she'd blushed to be called beautiful. How her one and only beau said she wasn't worth waiting for. Yet how she gave herself freely to others. She was a woman made for love and yet she didn't see it. The pain lingered in her eyes. He wanted nothing more than to erase it and caught her by her shoulders. He gently eased her close, pressed her to his chest and stroked her hair back from her face. She looked up at him questioningly. But he had no words to explain his actions. He simply wanted her to know she was so much more than a servant to the needs of others. He lowered his head, letting her see his intention and giving her plenty of opportunity to withdraw.

Something flickered through her eyes, a warning, perhaps a denial, but she didn't pull away, and he continued his descent until his lips brushed hers in the gentlest of kisses.

She reared back, fleeing from his arms. "Bo Stillwater, what do you mean by…by doing that?"

"Kissing you?" he supplied with a hint of amusement in his voice.

"Yes. That. You have no intention of marrying. So it seems to me you shouldn't be kissing a girl."

"You're right." He shouldn't have kissed her. Someone might have seen them and it could ruin her reputation. "Please forgive me." He meant it sincerely and she seemed to understand that.

"Of course. Perhaps I shouldn't have reacted so vigorously."

Her comment made him wonder. Had her reaction been out of proportion because he struck a tender nerve? One that revealed the truth about how she felt? If only he could find a way to make her open up to all her possibilities. As he sought for something more to say, something to ease the tension crackling in the air, he heard the scream of a hawk and pointed the distant dot out to Louisa.

"Where? I don't see it."

He leaned over her shoulder and pointed in the right direction. "See there?" He had to restrain himself from turning the helpful gesture into an emotion-filled hug.

"Yes. Oh, it must be nice to soar like that." Her voice carried such longing that he pressed his hands to her shoulders, hoping she wouldn't object but take it as a sign of understanding or sympathy. Whichever she chose. His heart swelled with something he couldn't name when she leaned into his hands.

The hawk soared and then swooped to the ground, looking as if it meant to crash.

Louisa caught her breath and reached up to grip his hands.

The hawk caught something, flapped its wings and flew away with its prey.

Louisa and Bo stood as they were. He couldn't imagine what she thought but he didn't want to break away from this feeling of peace.

But the triplets bounced and Theo sputtered a cry. It was time to return.

Return to the house. Return to normalcy. Return to his convictions.

It was time to remember why he had chosen the path he meant to follow. Never before had he known such burning regret over how he'd been raised.

God, help me not forget.

Chapter Twelve

That day formed the pattern of the next few days. Louisa continually told herself she should tell Bo to stop calling. After that innocent kiss on Monday night, her feelings warred with her decisions. Hadn't her heart soared and swooped every bit as wildly as that hawk they'd watched? When it dived after its prey, she'd feared the bird would crash to the ground. Even as she feared her heart would crash with disappointment if she let herself care for him more than wisdom allowed.

Why had he kissed her? Not only was he clear that he didn't intend to marry, she knew she would not be the one he'd choose if he changed his mind. He was far too good-looking to settle for the leftover spinster. There were plenty of younger, more beautiful women who would welcome being courted by him. Not only in this area. She had only to look at the mail-order brides who had been brought in. They seemed to provide a selection that would leave her bringing up a distant rear.

And yet, her wayward side argued, he wasn't courting any of them. Instead he came to town every evening to help her take the triplets for a walk and then he stayed to help get them settled for the night. Yes, she reminded her foolish heart, he left as soon as the babies were safely tucked in bed.

She couldn't deny the truth that was as plain as her face. It was only for them that he came.

Not that it would matter whether or not he saw her as worthy of his attention. She was not free to encourage a man's interest. Not for a good long time to come, God willing.

They received a letter from Amy informing them that Mother was improving and would soon be fit to travel. So Louisa was given a reprieve to continue enjoying the triplets.

And Bo. But she refused to acknowledge there existed a fragment of truth in those two words.

Saturday rolled around and he showed up earlier in the afternoon than he normally did.

"I thought you might need to do a little shopping, so I came to help with the babies."

She didn't tell him that Annie had watched them while she went to the store earlier. Besides, she could always use another spool of thread. So they took the babies for a stroll around town, enjoying the busyness of a Saturday afternoon. Young men lingered about the doors of the stores, waiting for the pretty maidens to come by blushing and excited by the attention.

"I don't see Annie," she murmured to Bo.

"Perhaps her mother put a stop to her seeing Jamie."

She thought it was a shame but could tell from Bo's voice he thought it a good thing and had no wish to upset the peace between them. They stopped at the general store and she purchased her thread while Bo remained outside as the courting-aged boys and girls clustered around asking about the triplets. They were so young. It made her feel positively ancient. One of the gals looked at her and whispered behind her hand to her friend.

Louisa didn't need to hear to know they speculated about the old maid.

What did it matter? She stiffened her spine and went to the cart. "Every day, someone fills a tin with kindling and leaves it on the step for me to use." Every day she set the empty tin outside, and every morning it was full. "I can't help thinking it's because of the babies. Someone has a special interest in them. Perhaps you could all keep your eyes open and see if you can discover who it is. We'd like to find their mother and reunite them."

The boys pushed out their chests. One of them spoke for them all, it seemed, when he said, "We'll find the person for you."

"Thank you."

Bo pushed the cart down the street with Louisa at his side. Yes, she might be an old maid, but she was the one walking with Bo.

For today. There might not be a tomorrow. Especially if the mother was found.

But sufficient to the day is the joy thereof. She misquoted a Bible verse.

They reached the house and Bo helped carry in the babies. Louisa had left water heating on the stove. "I want to bathe them tonight."

"You'll need help for that." He rolled up his sleeves even as he talked.

And silly old maid that she was, heat stole up her neck and burned her cheeks. She hurried to fetch the washtub before he noticed, set it in the middle of the kitchen floor and prepared the water.

Satisfied it was the right temperature, she turned to the babies. Theo sat unclothed and ready to be first.

She blinked. "You undressed him."

"You needn't sound so surprised. Shirts come off one sleeve at a time same for babies as grown-ups. Likewise for pants."

True, but little arms and legs had a tendency to squirm and go the wrong direction at the wrong time. She did her best to hide her confusion about this man. A confirmed bachelor and yet so good with the babies. And so sweet to her? She turned away, her mind whirling with memories of the time they'd spent together over the last few days. She refused to acknowledge that she knew exactly how many days since he brought the babies to her doorstep.

She plunked Theo in the water and soaped him up. Jasper and Eli tried to climb in with him. Bo, laughing, held them back. Louisa scrubbed Theo, then grabbed a towel and lifted him from the water.

"I'll take him." Bo took the dripping baby and set about drying him while she bathed Eli. Jasper again tried to climb in. Both Bo and Louisa were occupied with a baby, but seeing Jasper's intent, they reached for him at the same time. They ended up with their arms pressed together across the baby's back.

A jolt raced through Louisa's body. An awareness

she tried in vain to pretend didn't exist. She knew she'd failed to hide her reaction when he stiffened. She met his eyes, hoping she hadn't offended him. His gaze burned through her thoughts, leaving them exposed should he care to look deeper.

Eli slapped the water, spraying her face and, thankfully, pulling her back to sound reasoning. Relieved, and at the same time disappointed, she jerked her gaze free of Bo's, struggling a little to even out her breathing as she bathed Eli and handed him to Bo. Their hands collided and her breathing again grew ragged.

Why was she acting like a silly schoolgirl? Like those blushing young ladies outside the store?

She bathed Jasper, and by the time she was finished, Bo had Theo in his diaper and nightshirt. He took Jasper while she dressed Eli. Then while she put the night wear on Jasper, he carried out the tub of water and emptied it on the garden.

He returned with the can full of kindling.

They looked at each other with a mixture of frustration and resignation. Neither of them bothered to look outside for the responsible person. Whoever did this was far too wily to be caught.

Between them, they gave the triplets a drink of warm milk and then put them side by side on the mattress in the bedroom, covering them with the thin worn blankets that had been left on the doorstep. Louisa reasoned they might be objects the babies were familiar with and would be comforted by.

They yawned, looked about to make sure their brothers were there. Theo stuck his thumb in his mouth and the three nodded off without a fuss.

Bo and Louisa tiptoed from the room, leaving the door open a crack so they could hear if any of them wakened.

She stood awkwardly in the living room. Would Bo leave now? Should she invite him to stay? Would it be improper now that the triplets were in bed?

Father entered through the back door. "Oh, good. I'm home in time to challenge you to a game of checkers."

Bo rubbed his hands in glee. Several times the two men had played the game, each commenting on the other being a worthy opponent.

She was half-glad that decision about whether or not to ask Bo to stay had been taken out of her hands and equally annoyed that it was only to play checkers with her father.

Nevertheless, she served a simple supper then sat watching them play. Or more truthfully, she watched Bo.

The men finished another game. They were tied in wins. Bo stretched and yawned. "I need to go home. I told Cash I wouldn't keep him out late."

Louisa chuckled at the idea of making a promise to a horse.

Father put away the checkerboard and pieces. "Thanks for the games. Will I see you tomorrow?"

Louisa's eyes narrowed before she could even decide what she thought of Father's question. Was Bo coming to see the triplets and her father, in that order? And herself at the bottom of the list. Did she really expect she would be at the top?

"I'll likely come to help with the triplets." Bo pushed to his feet and turned to her. "Walk me out?"

She wanted to be annoyed. Wanted to pretend she didn't care, but at the way his eyes shone with invitation and something beyond that, she could only think of stealing a few more minutes of his company and escorted him to the door.

They stood outside in the evening shadows. Enough light remained that she could see across the street. Lamplight glowed in the boardinghouse room windows but for the most part the town lay in grayness. She guessed she and Bo were hidden in the shelter of the dark wall and it gave her a delicious sense of being alone with him.

"Tomorrow is Sunday," he said.

"It is."

"Will you take the little guys to church?"

"I thought they would enjoy seeing everyone, and if someone knows who the mother is, their conscience might require that they acknowledge it."

"You'll need help."

"I can't deny it."

"I'll come by early and we'll take them together."

"Like a real family," she couldn't help but murmur.

He made a derisive sound. "A temporary arrangement only."

"I know." And she accepted it.

He turned to her. She could barely make out his features in the growing darkness. But she heard the urgency and eagerness in his voice.

"Why don't you and the babies come out to the ranch with me after church? I could show you around. I think you'd all like it."

"That would be very nice." Very nice? It would be a gift to cherish in the lonely years ahead of her.

"Good. I'll bring a wagon so we can take the cart." He swung his hat to his head. "I'll see you tomorrow." He half turned to leave, then stopped and faced her. He touched her chin. "I'm looking forward to it. Good night." He rushed to his horse, swung to the saddle and trotted away.

She stared down the street long after he was out of sight, long after she could no longer hear the thud of Cash's hooves. Her excitement carried a note of sadness.

As he'd pointed out, this was all temporary.

"I've invited a guest for dinner tomorrow," Bo informed Mrs. Jamieson when he arrived home. "I hope you don't mind."

"Mind? Why, my boy, I can't think of anything I'd enjoy more than to see company in this house. Oh, I know Brandon comes by often enough. But that's not what I have in mind. Tell me, is your guest male or female?"

He chuckled at her obvious matchmaking intent. "Both."

Her eager expression faded. "Please explain."

"I've invited Miss Clark. We'll bring the triplets out. I think they'll enjoy the outing." Let her think he meant the babies.

Her smile widened again. "Excellent. I'll prepare a meal fit for royalty. You know what they say. The way to a man's heart is through his stomach. Perhaps the way to a woman's heart is through being treated like she's special."

He held up a protesting hand. "I'm not looking to win her heart."

His housekeeper gave an unbelieving sniff. "Sounds like you need a good tonic to help straighten you out."

He laughed despite himself. "I'd be content with a meal I can bring her home to."

At the contemplative gleam in the woman's eyes, he resisted an urge to roll his eyes. What had he been thinking to word it like that? As if he wanted to make this her home.

He glanced around. What would she think of his place? It was small but sturdy. Comfortable, at least in his mind. The kitchen was roomy and the small living room cozy. He'd built three bedrooms, thinking one for himself, one for Brandon on his frequent visits and one for a housekeeper.

"I'll put a venison roast on to stew overnight and add vegetables before we go to church. And my prizewinning chocolate cake is already in the pantry."

"That sounds fine." Before he finished the sentence she pulled the meat from the icebox and hummed as she banged a heavy pot to the stove top. "I'll go talk to Clint." He went to the barn to take care of Cash.

Clint wandered over. "Cows need to be moved to fresh grass."

"We'll do that Monday." They discussed plans for the coming week.

"Night, boss." Clint sauntered toward the bunkhouse.

Bo bade his foreman good-night, fed Cash the extra

ration of oats he'd promised him every evening as they rode to town and then wandered outside. The moon had been full two days ago and was still round and bright, highlighting the landscape with silver. He went as far as the nearest fence and leaned on the top rail. Why had he asked her here? What did he expect from the visit?

He straightened and rolled his shoulders. His only goal was to show her the ranch and give her an outing. After all, she'd been looking after those babies for close to two weeks now. She deserved a break.

And with that reason fixed firmly in his mind, he made his way back to the house.

Mrs. Jamieson had retired for the night, and true to her word, a pot sat on the back of the stove, the delicious aroma of cooking meat teasing his nostrils.

Sunday morning, Bo was up before the first streaks of dawn broke across the indigo sky. He had to take care of the chores and get into town in time to help Louisa get the babies ready for church. He slipped into his work clothes, grabbed the water buckets and hurried out to pump water for the house. The full buckets on the cupboard ready for use, he trotted to the barn. He fed the horses and chickens. Pumped water for all the animals and then returned to his bedroom to gather up clean clothes. His Sunday best.

Mrs. Jamieson greeted him as he sped through the kitchen. "Breakfast will be ready shortly."

"Be right back. I'm headed down to the stream to have a bath."

"Now, that's an excellent idea." She eyed him up and down. "Nothing sweeter to a woman than a fresh-smelling man with his hair sleeked back and a crisp white shirt. You know what they say—clothes make the man."

She loved her little sayings and he loved teasing her about their lack of logic. "Shouldn't it be a man is known by his deeds whether they be kind and noble?"

Her hands stilled and she considered the idea. "Well, true as that might be, it never hurts to look your best."

"Can't argue with that." He headed on outdoors, but before the door closed, he heard her murmured addition.

"Especially if you want to win a woman's heart."

He broke his stride, intending to go back and correct her. He was not courting Louisa. Both he and Louisa understood that. But rather than trying to convince Mrs. Jamieson, he continued on his way to a place where overhanging rocks and bushes provided a private place and, in the cool water of the stream, scrubbed off any remnant of horse smell.

Minutes later he returned to the kitchen, crisp white shirt, clean dark trousers, a finely tooled leather belt, scrubbed and polished boots and, to complete the outfit, a black bolo tie with silver tips and a slide with a bit of turquoise. Mrs. Longfeather had crafted the tie.

Thinking of the Native woman, he wondered if Louisa would wear the fancy comb given to her by the same lady. Somehow it pleased him to think they both had something made by Mrs. Longfeather.

"Now, don't you look good?" Mrs. Jamieson practically glowed with approval.

"You think Brandon will agree?" He made it sound like it mattered what his twin thought.

The good woman tsked. "I expect he will have his

mind on nobler things, what with a sermon to deliver today. You know what they say—as a man thinketh in his heart, so he is. Brandon, God bless him, has his mind on heavenly things."

"Oh, yes." Sarcasm dripped from every word. Yes, Brandon was the preacher and a fine one at that, but Bo knew he was also a man with human longings and desires. And that included wanting a family of his own. But although Brandon said he was open to the idea of marriage, he was no closer to it than Bo. What would Bo do if Brandon married? It wasn't a question he wanted to dwell on.

Mrs. Jamieson served up breakfast, and after saying grace, they ate. He hoped she'd excuse him if he gobbled the food, but he knew how much work it was to get the triplets ready for the day and wanted to be there to help Louisa.

Clint had offered to harness the horses to the wagon, and when Bo left the house, the wagon stood ready. Mrs. Jamieson had her own little buggy and would follow later, as would the cowboys.

He arrived in time to help get the boys dressed for church. Louisa wore a pretty light green dress that shimmered as she moved. She wore the fancy comb in the side of her hair. He helped dress the boys, who seemed eager for the outing. But when they were about to leave, he was disappointed to see Louisa hide her hair and comb beneath a bonnet. He knew it was only proper for a lady to cover her head, but he wished she didn't have to hide the comb or her hair.

The triplets rode happily in their cart to the church next door. Dr. Clark accompanied them. Annie, seeing them approach, offered to sit with them and hold one of the babies.

Bo settled back in the pew with Jasper on his knees and Louisa beside him, holding Theo. Annie sat on her other side, holding Eli. Louisa's father nodded his satisfaction that the babies were well taken care of and sat beside Annie.

Brandon rose in front, and his gaze settled on Bo momentarily. No words were necessary for Bo to understand Brandon's thoughts. *Are you trying to make a statement by accompanying Louisa to church?*

Silently he informed Brandon that he hadn't changed his mind about anything. This was only to help out a woman with three babies to care for.

Be careful of her feelings.

Bo nodded. She understood what it meant.

The babies were well behaved, yet holding a little boy on his knee, a pretty woman at his side, joining him as they sang, proved a distraction. He heard only a portion of what Brandon said, caught the words *love*, *trust* and *commitment*, but his mind went its own way. How could he let himself trust love…trust his own heart?

The service ended with a final song, the piano pounded vigorously by Mrs. Hickey. Brandon gave the benediction. People gathered around the babies. He noted that Jamie Coleman seemed especially interested in Eli, though Bo wasn't fooled any more than the parents of the two young people into thinking it was the baby he wanted to be near. It was Annie. Tug and Dorothy edged forward. Tug pulled his son away.

Dorothy glowered at Tug, then turned her disapproving look toward her daughter.

Bo wondered if he would have to rescue little Eli, but Dorothy's look softened at the sight of the baby in Annie's arms.

The babies were carried out to their cart. Mrs. Jamieson caught Louisa's arm to speak to her.

"I'm so glad Bo has invited you to join him for dinner. 'Twill be my privilege to have you there but I hope you don't mind. You know what they say—two's company, three's a crowd."

Louisa's cheeks pinkened as half the congregation turned to listen to Mrs. Jamieson's announcement. Not that her visit was meant to be a secret and three being a crowd was...

"Mrs. Jamieson will be our chaperone." He spoke quietly yet firmly, wanting to protect Louisa's reputation.

"Oh, of course, I wouldn't think of not being there. What was I thinking to say such a thing? You know what they say—"

Thankfully Brandon joined them at that point, saving them from learning what people said.

"Do you care to join us at the ranch?" Bo asked his twin.

Brandon's eyebrows quirked. "I don't think so, thanks. If three's a crowd, four must be a mob." He turned to the doctor. "Would you care to join me for some soup?"

Everyone seemed to have plans, which left Bo free to follow his own. He loaded the cart in the back of the wagon so they could take the triplets around the ranch. He handed Jasper to Brandon, leaving his hands free to help Louisa to the seat, being careful not to let his hand linger a second too long...not with a crowd of interested people watching his every move. Once she was settled, he lifted Jasper to her knee to sit next to Theo, and then he took Eli and climbed up to sit beside her.

Mrs. Jamieson, seeing they were on their way, hurried to her buggy. Clint and the cowboys from the ranch mounted up. Others from the same direction followed suit so that there was a cavalcade headed the same direction.

Bo didn't mind. It let Louisa see that he had neighbors and that although he lived a half hour from town, his ranch wasn't isolated. And why it should matter, he would not confess.

The babies waved their hands and gurgled at the passing scenery.

Louisa chuckled. "They sure like outings."

"Perhaps they're glad of something new to look at." He watched her from the corner of his eye, seeing how she looked from one side to the other, trying to take in everything. Was she liking what she saw?

"Look—horses." She pointed for the sake of the triplets, who bounced hard enough she had to hold tight to the two she held and Bo grabbed Eli more firmly. She glanced at Bo, her eyes dancing with enjoyment.

He grinned as something from the depths of his heart edged close to the surface.

They reached the boulder and he drew to a halt. "This marks the boundary of my property. It's why I've called it Big Rock Ranch."

"It's a good name signifying the strength of individuals who live out here."

Her answer pleased him. "Do you miss the city?"

She looked into the distance, then pulled her gaze

back to his, a warm light in her eyes. "You know, I don't. I was in total agreement with Father's decision to move here. The city air wasn't doing Mother's health any good, and when Lawrence expressed an interest in going to California, we had no reason to stay in Cleveland. Then Father heard about this town needing a doctor. It was like the Lord opened all the doors for us to make this move."

"So it's good for your family. What about you? Can you find everything you need and want in Texas?"

Again her gaze went to the distance and this time lingered longer.

He watched a play of emotions cross her face—contemplation, questioning and then a hint of sadness that made him want to pull her to his chest as he had done on another occasion. And he might have done so but his hands were full. The moment he thought he might halt the wagon and park little Eli between his feet so as to free up his hands, her expression changed. It filled with determination and then a mix of joy and what he could only think was trust.

She faced him. "I have made it my aim to be like the Apostle Paul, who said he had learned to be content in whatever circumstance he found himself."

The ranch buildings came into sight and she leaned forward. "That's your place?"

He slowed the wagon. "It is." Pride filled his voice. "There's the barn, beside it, the bunkhouse and cookhouse. I don't have a large crew and sometimes one of the cowboys doubles as the cook. There are storage sheds, the corrals where we train the horses." He let her take in the setup. "And last but not least, that's the house."

She studied it several seconds then let out a sigh. "It looks cozy with that covered porch along the front."

He released his breath. "A covered porch serves two purposes. It gives a person a place to stand out of the rain and provides shade from the sun."

"I can imagine two chairs there and two people enjoying a cold drink together after a hard day's work."

"I thought the same thing." A man and a wife with the children asleep in their beds. Whoa. That wasn't what he'd thought at all. He'd pictured himself and Brandon sitting out there. In fact, they had done exactly that a number of times, carrying out kitchen chairs and tipping them back to watch the sun set.

Mrs. Jamieson drew up beside them. "You take your time. I'll have dinner on when you get there." She drove on by, twin tails of dust kicking up at her passage.

Bo would have lingered but the triplets grew restless, so they drove on, as well. He pointed out the trees and bushes he had planted and the garden Mrs. Jamieson tended.

The good lady handed her horse and buggy over to one of the cowboys, lifted her skirts and hustled into the house. He could almost hear her words, *you know what they say*, and then coming out with some folksy homily.

He pulled up to the front of the house. Clint strode over, his weathered face beaming at the sight of three matching babies. "I'll take that little fella while you climb down."

Bo jumped to the ground. "I'll get the cart. It's the

easiest way to keep them all corralled." With the help of another cowboy he lifted the cart down and was about to take Eli, but the baby and Clint were studying each other with such interest that Bo, grinning, took Jasper and then Theo from Louisa and put them in the cart before he reached up for Louisa. He held her at his side. "Little Eli is making friends with Clint." A hardened old cowpoke who kept mostly to himself. If Bo wasn't mistaken, tears glistened in the foreman's eyes.

"You ain't found their mother yet?"

"Sheriff Fuller is sending messages far and wide but no sign of her yet."

"Now, that's a shame. A real shame. Young fellas need their mama." Clint's voice grew hoarse. The man had never shared any details of his former life and Bo respected his wish for privacy, but he sensed a painful past in the man's reaction to the abandoned babies. One he identified with, though he had not known abandonment.

"Clint, would you like to join us for dinner?" He thought the man might enjoy seeing more of the babies.

"No, thanks, boss. I'll eat with the boys. That young fella you hired is a mighty fine cook." He handed Eli to Bo and rushed away with a bowlegged trot.

Bo realized he still stood shoulder to shoulder with Louisa and shifted away to put the baby with his brothers. "I expect these little guys are hungry. Shall we go inside?"

He pushed the cart to the door. Mrs. Jamieson opened it wide. "Welcome, welcome. It's such a joy to have you here. A house without children is no better'n a barn."

Bo bit back the response that sprang to his lips that

he'd slept in a barn a few times and his house was far superior to that situation even without children.

"Thank you," Louisa said.

They entered the kitchen and she looked around.

Bo watched her, hoping she'd like what she saw. "Such a roomy kitchen."

His breath eased out. He showed her the living room. "It's small."

"It's cozy. I like it. Do you spend much time here?"

He chuckled. "Now that you mention it, no. During the winter I read a bit, and if Brandon comes out, we play checkers. I'm outside most of the time."

Mrs. Jamieson watched from the kitchen. "A man needs a warm welcome to draw him to the hearth."

"And thank you for providing that."

Mrs. Jamieson made a disapproving noise, then took the babies to the kitchen, offering to feed them.

Louisa spied his guitar. "I've heard you play a time or two at community events. You're very good."

"Why, thank you."

"Where did you learn? Or are you one of those people who can pick up any instrument and play it?" The smile she gave him made him feel several inches taller. Or as Ma would say, made his head swell.

"Do you remember me mentioning Russell Maynard?"

"The man who took you under his wing and treated you like a son. Did he also teach you about being a man who controlled his passions?"

He stared at her. "I don't believe I said any of those things."

Her eyes twinkled. "Am I wrong?"

"I truly never thought of it that way. But yes, I suppose you're right." To some degree. Russell had taught him how to rope and ride, how to size up the conformity of a cow or horse and how to do business with other men. But to be a man of controlled passions? That was expecting a bit much. He realized Louisa studied him, probably read his confusion. He dismissed the questions. "Russell taught me how to play the guitar." He'd said Bo had natural talent for the instrument.

"No one taught you how to sing. That was something you were born with. Did you inherit the talent from your mother or your father?"

The truth of which parent was the singer raced through him with the force of a rifle bullet. His sweet mother's voice had been weak and uncertain. "It was my father." Each word ached from him. He did not want anything from his father. But he loved to sing. Knew he had a rich, deep voice. "I sing like my father."

She seemed to sense that this knowledge had shaken him, and touched his arm, anchoring him in the present. "Is it not good to have something from him you can be glad about?"

"I don't know what to think." It seemed wrong to rejoice about any sort of legacy his father had left him. He'd always seen it as something to deny.

She gave a soft, gentle laugh. "I think I speak for many—perhaps most—in the community when I say we are grateful for your inheritance."

Inheritance? One people appreciated. He could not decide how he now felt about singing. He'd tried so hard to not be like his father, and the one thing he enjoyed like no other was now suddenly stained with the ugly behavior of that man.

"I'd love to hear you play and sing while I'm here if you'd be so kind as to indulge me." Her gentle voice drove away the demons of his past.

"Sure." His answer came too quickly, without thought. And he couldn't change his mind when she smiled at him like that.

How was he to stick to his convictions when she made him feel like he was a man with controlled passions, a man with a grateful gift from the father he wanted so much not to be like?

Chapter Thirteen

Louisa reminded herself over and over that Bo had invited her there solely because of the triplets. He was part of the community that was sheltering the babies and took his responsibilities seriously. But her fickle heart kept seeing the room as perfect for a married couple, kept picturing herself in a role there. Of course her determination wasn't helped by Mrs. Jamieson's constant remarks about how right it was to have a woman and children in the home.

The kindly housekeeper had fed the boys while Bo showed Louisa around the house and while they discussed his musical talent. He had been shocked, dismayed even, to realize something he plainly loved came from his father.

As they shared the lovely meal prepared by Mrs. Jamieson, Louisa vowed she would help Bo see that it was fine to take what was good from his parent. Perhaps it would help him begin to see himself as someone unlike his father in other ways.

They finished the meal with Mrs. Jamieson's fine chocolate cake.

"I heard you made the best cake in the county and now I can add my praise."

Mrs. Jamieson fluttered her hands, mildly protesting while glowing with pleasure over the compliment.

Louisa might have been tempted to linger over coffee and listen to Bo talk about his plans for the ranch but the housekeeper gathered up the dishes. Louisa sprang to her feet and carried the cutlery to the basin of hot water.

Mrs. Jamieson waved her away. "'Tis such a pleasure to have you here that I will gladly do the dishes by myself." She lowered her voice to speak in a conspiratorial whisper. "Besides, I think you should get Bo to entertain us with his music. The man has a look about him like someone snatched the floor from under his feet."

Louisa nodded and whispered back. "He's upset to realize he inherited his musical talent from his father."

Mrs. Jamieson patted Louisa's hands. "Then it's up to you to make him see it as a good gift. You know what they say—music reveals the soul of a man. And Bo has the soul of a fine man."

Louisa could not find any argument to the contrary.

"Go convince him." The housekeeper pushed her toward the table.

It seemed wrong to leave the good woman with all the cleanup, but perhaps it was more important to help Bo cherish and honor his musical gift. She wondered what she could do and she whispered a little prayer for wisdom.

The babies had been chewing on a dry crust of bread but Theo grew restless. It was only a matter of time before he would fuss. "The little guys are tired," she said.

Bo had been staring into space and now pulled his attention to the triplets.

Louisa hurried on with her suggestion before he could offer one of his own. "They love to hear music. It lulls them to sleep. Now would be a fine time for you to play your guitar and sing."

He'd already promised her but even so, might have found excuses not to sing, but he couldn't deny the babies. Still, he didn't immediately get to his feet.

She sensed his inner struggle.

Then he sucked in air and grabbed the handle of the cart. "Come along, then."

Louisa followed them into the living room and sat close to the cart to keep the boys safe as Bo picked up his guitar and tuned the strings.

He turned to Louisa. "Anything special you'd like to hear?"

"My mother's favorite song is 'My Faith Looks Up to Thee.'" Her throat tightened with yearning to see her mother and know she was doing okay. As soon as Bo started to sing in his deep melodious voice, she forgot all else but the pleasure of listening to him.

The triplets' eyes drooped.

"I remember you singing this." And he played and sang "Safe in the Arms of Jesus."

The babies slept even though they were too crowded in the cart. Not that they seemed to mind. It likely served them well when they were smaller but it no longer provided enough room for them to stretch out and so they curled together, a tangle of arms and legs.

"Tell me your favorite song," he asked.

She considered it a moment. "I suppose 'Tell Me the Old, Old Story.'"

"I thought you might say 'Work, for the Night is Coming.'" He waggled his eyebrows to indicate he teased.

Was that how he saw her? A woman with nothing more on her mind than work? Or perhaps he only saw her as useful. Nothing more. Perhaps it was time to go back to town. But before she could voice the suggestion, he started to play and sing the hymn she'd asked for and then broke into a lively tune that drew her thoughts away from everything troubling.

"I believe I've heard that tune before but I don't know the name of it."

"It's 'Turkey in the Straw.'" He put away his guitar. "I think that's enough music for today. I wanted to show you around the ranch before I take you back to town."

"But the babies are sleeping. I hate to disturb them."

Mrs. Jamieson heard her protest. "I'll watch the little darlings. You two go and enjoy yourselves."

Still Louisa hesitated. She'd never gone with Bo without the babies along, her excuse for allowing herself that pleasure. And she'd always considered it his reason. To go without them completely upset that rationale and she wasn't sure she was ready to do that.

But Bo had risen and waited. "They'll be fine with Mrs. Jamieson. She knows how to care for babies."

To refuse now would make it look like she didn't

trust the good woman, so she graciously followed Bo outside. Besides, she could not deny a yearning to see Bo's ranch.

And spend some time with him for no other reason than she wanted to?

No. She would deny that possibility to her last breath.

They walked side by side. She couldn't say if it was her or Bo who made certain to keep several inches between them. And although she told herself she would have done so even if he didn't, she had to grip her hands together in front of her to keep from reaching for him. After all, she thought with a touch of vinegar, shouldn't a gentleman offer his arm to steady her?

They walked through the barn, Bo telling her about the horses. They stepped back into the sunshine and Cash trotted up to the fence to greet them. Bo rubbed his nose and murmured to him.

Louisa jerked back a resentful thought that the horse earned more of his attention than she did. How uncharitable of her. Bo had been nothing but kind and thoughtful, going out of his way to help her with the babies. She had no reason to be so critical. None whatsoever.

Except a wish for something completely beyond her reach.

She brought her turmoil under control. "Why did you name your horse Cash?"

He chuckled and brought his gaze to her, his eyes bright under the summer sun. "Because he cost me all the cash I had with me." He leaned against the fence, the picture of a perfectly content man, one foot angled across the other boot, a horse at his shoulder. "I saw him at an auction and there was something about him that I liked." He reached back to rub Cash's muzzle. "He wasn't well broken and had obviously been mistreated. He was what you might call 'standoffish.'" His low chuckle made Cash whinny. "Brandon thought I was wasting my money. Said the horse was ruined by mishandling."

"But he wasn't?" She couldn't look away from the humor and something deeper, stronger in his gaze.

"Oh, he was all right. It took a lot of patience and kindness to win him over. And now he's as gentle as a pet."

Louisa digested the information. Did Bo not see that he had told her a story that might have been his own? But before she could point it out, he straightened.

"Come along. There's something I want to show you." They wandered by the other buildings. Four cowboys leaned back in their chairs on the veranda of the bunkhouse and greeted Bo as they passed.

She heard respect and affection in their voices. Not the guarded tone she would expect if Bo was a harsh boss. More proof of the sort of man he was. She'd tell him her observations but they again moved on, with him pointing out the significance of each detail she saw, and her attention was diverted. They left the buildings behind, passed a muddy little stream and began a climb.

"It gets rough. Better let me help you." He reached for her hand and she didn't protest. How could she when it was the very thing she'd been wishing for the past half hour? Nor would she try to convince herself otherwise.

In a few minutes she was grateful for his hand for more practical reasons as they climbed a rocky red hill. Several times her foot slipped and she might have fallen if not for his tight grip on her.

They reached the top and sought the shade of the lone tree.

"Let's sit." He nodded toward the dry grassy spot beneath the tree and she gladly did his bidding, eager to escape the blazing hot sun. Their shoulders pressed together as they leaned against the trunk of the tree.

"We could sure use a good rain." Everyone knew it but she hoped saying it showed her genuine concern.

"I've been praying for it as I'm sure most of the believing folk have been." His gaze sought the distance and she followed the direction of his look.

"It's beautiful," she whispered. The red rocks tumbled down the slope to stunted-looking bushes, and then the view opened up to a wide vista that seemed to have no beginning and no end. Streaks of clouds crossed the sky. "I can see forever."

"I know. Makes a person feel small and insignificant, doesn't it?"

It did that but something else, as well. "It makes me feel wild and free."

Neither of them spoke for several seconds. She couldn't say what he thought but she wanted only to drink in the scene, fill her heart and mind with the sensation. "A person could forget everything else up here."

"I often come here for that very reason."

She fought to remember who she was, why she was here, but both seemed like some long-ago, half-forgotten ideas.

They spoke in hushed tones as if the place was to be respected.

Respected? That brought a thought to her mind. "Your men respect you."

"I'm their boss."

"It's more than that. Their tone indicates that they think you are a good man. I don't have to speculate to know you treat them fairly and kindly."

"I try to." He sounded as if it went without saying.

"Bo."

The use of his name brought his gaze to her, his odd-colored eyes pewter in the shade of the tree.

"I don't believe you are like your father. You show patience and kindness in everything you do from how you treat your men, to how you gentle a frightened horse, to how you help with three babies."

His gaze went on and on as if he wanted to believe her, and then a hard, cold look filled his eyes and he turned away. "Need I remind you that half the blood flowing through my veins is from him?"

"You talk like the blood carries your decision-making ability. It doesn't, you know. You use your heart and mind to choose who you are and what you'll be."

He shifted away as if thinking upon her words. Then slowly turned back to face her. "Wasn't it you who said we should trust God to help us find contentment in our choices? Or something like that? That's my goal. Be content with my decision."

She couldn't bear to think of him shutting himself off to all the possibilities before him. "I see you with the triplets and know you'd make a good father. It seems a shame to—"

He sprang to his feet. "You don't know what it was like to live with the kind of uncertainty Brandon and I lived with. Never knowing what would trigger an outburst from our father, not knowing how to prevent one of them. I would never subject a child to that sort of life." He threw the words out like bitter seeds of a bitter fruit.

She started to her feet and he extended a hand to help her. She took it, pulled herself up and held on to his hand as she faced him. "But you do know how to prevent it. You practice it every day of your life— kindness, gentleness and self-control. I believe those are gifts our Heavenly Father bestows and you have allowed yourself to receive them."

His eyes brightened and she knew he wanted to believe her, but then they dulled and he shook his head. "Your faith in me is heartening but misguided." He withdrew his hand and turned to look out over the landscape.

She moved to his side and spoke gently. "Is the God who made this vast land too small to rule in your heart?"

Beside her, he stiffened, but she said no more, knowing there was a time to speak and a time to be silent and this was the latter.

He let out a long sigh, whether acceptance or discouragement, she couldn't say. He studied the position of the sun. "It's time we got back to the house." He reached for her hand and guided her down the path without uttering a word about what she'd said. To her relief, she sensed no anger or discord. She would pray that he would begin to see the promise of his future.

They paused at the bottom of the hill, the ranch buildings before them. He still held her hand but neither spoke nor moved forward. She waited quietly at his side, content to let him think.

He came round to face her. "Louisa, are we very different? You too closed your life to marriage and family."

"On the contrary. My family is of prime importance to me."

His gaze went on and on, peeling back layer after layer from her heart until her longing for a future that included marriage and children lay open and exposed like a raw wound. Still he continued to search for truth from her.

She wet her lips and drew in a breath, searching for words to explain herself. "My mother needs me." Were those brittle sounds from her mouth? "I couldn't live with myself if a selfish act of mine caused her further misery. Or her death." A sob choked off the last of her little speech.

He wrapped his arms around her and held her to his chest. "Louisa, it seems we both must do what we feel is necessary."

She nodded against his shirt, her cheek against the warm fabric, the beat of his heart steadying her own heartbeat. If only she could stay there, safe and sheltered. But as he said, they had to do what was necessary, and right now that meant taking care of three babies.

She straightened. "I'm sorry. I don't usually bemoan my responsibilities. It isn't even that I resent them. I consider it a privilege to be able to make my mother more comfortable and meet her needs."

He took her hand. "I know you do."

They continued down the path. As they approached the bunkhouse, he dropped her hand. Or did she pull away? She liked to think it was the latter, but was it?

They heard the triplets babbling as they stepped to the veranda. Mrs. Jamieson looked up at their approach. "They've just wakened. I'm preparing them a little snack. They are darling babies. You'll have to join us." She pointed them toward the table, and without consulting each other, they sat. They each took a baby and let Mrs. Jamieson take the third. The babies ate bread and jam, getting a great deal of jam on their faces.

As they ate, Mrs. Jamieson turned to Louisa. "I've been thinking while you were out. I know you missed most of the activities at the fair because you so sweetly took over the care of these three. It hardly seems fair, so I've come up with an idea. I will take care of the triplets and Bo can take you to the Fourth of July dance on Saturday."

"I couldn't—" A thousand excuses came to mind but Mrs. Jamieson raised her hand and cut off Louisa's protests.

"I won't take no for an answer and I venture to say that every woman in the area will back me on this. We can only begin to guess how you manage three babies."

"Bo—" She meant to say Bo helped, but again Mrs. Jamieson cut off her explanation.

"Bo will take you to the dance or he will find himself without a housekeeper. You know what they say—

all work and no play." She gave Bo a hard look. "You've no objection to taking her, do you?"

"None whatsoever."

Even though the poor man had little choice in the matter, Louisa admitted to a little thrill of anticipation. He might have little to say about whether or not he wanted to escort her, but she knew he would be a kind, considerate, attentive escort. And for one night, she would allow herself to pretend it was real.

Bo watched the play of emotions on Louisa's face. She'd been railroaded into agreeing to accompany him, but if he wasn't mistaken, she might like the idea a tiny bit. He knew he did. Much more than a tiny bit. Though he felt it could not amount to anything, he still meant to make the most of the one evening given to him.

And then what?

There was only one acceptable answer. He'd take her to the dance. Help with the babies as long as she had them. Only, he explained rather vigorously to himself, because she needed help. And then he'd return to his neglected ranch and bury himself in work. Maybe he'd find another horse like Cash. One that would keep him busy teaching it to trust him.

He ignored the echo of Louisa's words. *You show patience and kindness in everything you do.* What she didn't understand was all those things she mentioned were on the periphery of his heart. Letting himself love and marry and have children would throw his heart wide-open and he didn't know what would burst forth.

They finished their tea, washed the jam off three sweet little faces and made the return trip to town.

Louisa smiled and commented on the scenery but he sensed she was distracted and not necessarily by the three busy babies.

He needed to clear the air between them. "I hope you don't mind that Mrs. Jamieson pushed you to accompany me to the dance."

She faced him, her eyes wide. "She practically blackmailed you into taking me. You don't have to, you know. I won't be offended."

"Mrs. J. doesn't make me do anything I don't want to."

She studied him long and hard and must have read the honesty of his words. First, her eyes brightened. Then smile lines appeared at their edges. The smile spread across her face and she grinned. "That's good to hear."

He wasn't sure if she meant it was good to know Mrs. Jamieson didn't make him do things against his will or if she meant it was good to know he wanted to take her to the dance. He decided it meant both and he sat back, pleased with the turn of events.

They arrived in town and he helped take the triplets inside, then unloaded the cart and took it indoors.

Doc sat at the table with his customary cup of coffee. "Did you enjoy your day?" he asked Louisa.

"I did. How about you?"

"I had a pleasant afternoon in Brandon's company, then a couple hours of peace and quiet." He yawned and stretched. "It might have been a bit too quiet. I miss your mother and Amy."

"I do too."

The doctor looked at the three babies lined up on the

floor watching him and chuckled. "Though at the moment there is hardly room for anyone else in the house."

His comment reminded Bo that the Lone Star Cowboy League would have to call another meeting soon to discuss the future of the babies as well as to consider the requests coming in from various ranchers.

"Join us for supper?" the good doctor said to Bo.

He was about to say yes though he knew he should say no when booted feet clattered up the steps and fists banged on the door. The caller didn't wait for anyone to respond but threw open the door. "Doc, come quickly. There's been an accident on the tracks. A wagon full of people got hit by the train. It's really bad."

The doctor was on his feet. "Let me get my bag and some supplies. How many would you say are injured?"

"I counted a dozen. The wagon was full of kids on a picnic."

The doctor stopped and turned. "I could sure use your help, Louisa."

She waved helplessly at the babies. "Who will stay with them?"

Doc shifted his gaze to Bo. "You're used to the babies and they're used to you. I'm sorry to ask this, but time is of the essence. Would you stay with them?"

Did the man have any idea what he was asking? Sure, he'd helped Louisa many times, but he'd never been on his own. Could he do it? Did he have a choice?

A wagon rolled up to the front of the house. A man called, "Doc, are you ready?"

The doctor hurried to the door. "Come along, Louisa. There's injured to attend to."

Louisa hesitated as if suspecting Bo's reservations.

"Feed them and they'll be fine. If we're too late, put them to bed." And she was gone. The door shut behind her and Bo stood in the midst of three waiting babies watching him expectantly. Feed them? Did she mean now? They'd recently had a snack at the ranch. Wasn't it too soon for more food? He curled and uncurled his fingers as he looked around.

Jasper crawled toward one of the stuffed toys and Bo sucked in a long breath. He could amuse them for a few minutes and pray the injuries wouldn't require too much time.

But an hour later Louisa and the doctor had not returned. Theo started to fuss. Feed them. What? He picked Theo up and left the other two to watch him as he went to the icebox. He was almost certain they couldn't eat anything that required too much chewing. That left eggs. He struggled to hold Theo and bounce him so he wouldn't cry, and at the same time, he found a fry pan and added some wood to the stove.

"Hush, hush," he murmured over and over as he positioned the pan, added some bacon fat from the cup on the shelf. He'd seen Mrs. J. break eggs with one hand but the ability to do so escaped him. He put Theo down by his brothers and Theo wailed a protest, triggering cries from the other two. "Hush, hush." His soothing sound rose sharply.

Feed them. He broke the eggs, picked out the shells that fell into the pan and stirred it all until he deemed the eggs properly cooked. Feed them. How? *Calm down. You know how to do this.* He parked the crying trio in the cart and filled a bowl with eggs. "Who's hungry?"

Jasper's mouth popped open.

Bo fed him.

The other two saw food and opened their mouths. Good. They were quiet and happy to eat.

He finished. Gobbled down the rest of the eggs as the babies watched him. He should clean the kitchen but Eli tried to pull himself out of the cart and he grabbed him. Wouldn't it be awful if the baby fell? What if they weren't okay when the doctor returned?

Shuddering at the prospect, he lifted them one at a time, carried them to the living room and sat on the floor facing them. He tossed a rolled-up sock to them in turn and earned himself a chuckle from all three. Dare he hope they would be content to play the game until Louisa returned? He tossed the sock ball over and over.

Theo threw himself back on the floor and wailed.

Jasper and Eli looked at him then at Bo, their gazes a mixture of accusation and expectation.

"I don't know what's wrong with him." What would Louisa do? Was it time to put them to bed? He tried to think when Louisa tucked them in. "Are you guys tired?"

Jasper chuckled as if the idea was a joke.

Eli's bottom lip quivered and tears pooled in his eyes.

"Don't cry. Please don't cry." He pulled Theo to one side and Eli to the other. Jasper crawled to Bo's knees.

For reward, Theo threw up on Bo.

Bo shuddered. The sour smell made him want to rush outdoors and empty his own stomach. Instead, he grabbed one of the worn blankets and covered the stain.

Eli rubbed his face on the other side of Bo's shirt, effectively wiping his nose.

Jasper patted Bo's stomach.

Tension built in the depths of his heart. Anxiety clawed at his throat as the fussing continued. It coiled and twisted. It filled him with dread. He recognized the feeling. He'd experienced it many times when his father roared about the house and he and Brandon hovered in the shadows, wondering what form of cruelty their father's rage would take.

Afraid of where the feeling would lead, he did the only thing he could think to calm himself. He pulled the babies close and sang, loudly at first, to drown out their sobs, and then as they quieted, he sang more softly.

The babies' eyes began to droop. If he was Louisa he would prepare them for bed, but he was afraid if he moved they would cry, so he remained where he was, singing quietly, the triplets lounging on him.

The door squeaked open and Louisa tiptoed in. Her eyes widened.

His first instinct was to bolt to his feet but he couldn't move without disturbing the babies. Smiling gently, she lifted Jasper. Ignoring his protests, she wiped him clean, changed his diaper and put on his nightclothes. She did the same for Eli, laying the two of them side by side in the bedroom.

As soon as she was finished with those two, she took Theo. Bo scrambled to his feet and faced her, knowing his expression was likely as bleak as his heart. "I knew I could never be a father and this proves it."

Her eyes widened. "What do you mean? It looks to me like you managed very well."

"I felt like I was going to explode."

She tilted her head to study him. "But you didn't. You managed three fussy babies without getting upset."

"Oh, I was upset." He wiped at the mess on his shirt. "I smell awful."

"Theo did that?"

"How did you know?"

"He tends to throw up a little if he's upset."

"A little?" He shuddered. "I hope I never see a lot. Or worse, wear it."

She chuckled.

"It's not funny."

"Bo Stillwater, stop fussing and look at the situation for what it is. You took care of three babies on your own. Yes, they fussed and threw up on you. Yes, it is frustrating at times, but consider this. You did not act out your frustration. You chose to be patient and gentle instead." She leaned closer, all the while jostling Theo to calm him. "You are not your father."

"I'd like to keep it that way." He grabbed his hat and stalked from the room, intending to throw himself onto Cash's back and race home. Instead, he saw the wagon and rumbled his lips.

He climbed aboard and made the trip home at a slower pace than he wished for. It allowed far too much time to review the events of the day.

You are not your father.

No, but he was his father's son, and wasn't that as bad?

Chapter Fourteen

Louisa stared after Bo for two seconds, then turned her attention to the fussy baby. But as she prepared Theo for bed, she couldn't stop thinking of the picture that greeted her when she returned home. Bo with a baby in each arm and Jasper sprawled across his knees. Bo singing, the babies half-asleep. In that moment, something shifted inside her. Her vague yearnings and secret longings had taken on a clarity she'd not before known.

If she were ever free to consider marriage, this was the sort of man she would want. A man who didn't hesitate to let babies crawl over him, didn't shy away from tending their needs. A man of kindness and strong convictions.

She tucked Theo in next to his brothers and returned to the kitchen to clean up.

Unfortunately, Bo's strong convictions included a fear of his own emotions.

Over the next few days, he didn't come.

Had his experience of caring for the babies alone frightened him that much?

Would he remember that he agreed to take her to the dance?

Somehow, everyone else seemed to know of the agreement.

First, it was Helen Carson. She carried a package. Louisa assumed it was another meal from the generous ladies, but Helen bore something different. She folded back the paper to reveal a beautiful, deep rose, satin fabric. Helen lifted the fabric out and let it unfold to reveal a dress. Insets of contrasting printed fabric formed the center of the bodice and alternating gores of the skirt. The long sleeves were fitted with puffy shoulders and a raised collar sported frilled edging.

Louisa stared at the garment. "It's quite the most beautiful dress I've ever seen. Did you make that?" Why had Helen brought it for Louisa's viewing?

"I made it a few years ago for my daughter Molly but it never fit her right."

"How sad."

Helen draped the dress over the back of the chair and sat down next to it.

Louisa hurriedly made tea and served the lady. Her eyes kept drifting to the beautiful dress.

Helen sipped her tea, then pushed the cup and saucer aside. "I hear you are going to the dance with Bo."

"I am." At least if he didn't change his mind.

"That's why I've brought the dress."

Louisa stared, unable to comprehend what the woman meant. Finally she found her voice. "I'm afraid I don't understand."

"I'm sure it will fit you."

Louisa sat back, her hand pressed to her throat. "Me?"

Helen leaned over the table and took Louisa's other hand and squeezed it. "My dear, we all are so grateful for the way you are taking care of the triplets. It's so good of you. This little gift is my way of showing my gratitude."

"But I couldn't." But oh, wouldn't she feel like royalty in such a fine gown?

"But you must. I will be so disappointed if you don't."

After a bit, Louisa agreed to borrow the dress for the dance. In truth, it didn't take long to convince her. After Mrs. Carson left, she hung the dress in her room and stared at it. She might have tried it on but the triplets needed feeding. Modeling it would have to wait.

The next day, Mercy Green slipped over. "I brought you something for the dance." She presented Louisa with a pair of pearl-studded earbobs.

That afternoon, Molly visited. She brought a hot dish for the Clarks' supper meal, but before she left, she pulled a comb from her pocket. A very fine comb in filigree silver with a pearl in the center. "I want you to wear this at the dance."

Louisa stared at the young woman. "What's going on? First, Mrs. Carson, then Mercy and now you."

Molly gave a merry chuckle. "We're all so grateful for the way you have handled the babies, but I confess it's more than that. You're such a good, kind person. We're all so happy to have you and your father here and your mother, too, when she arrives. Please accept that this is our way of expressing our gratitude."

After that, it would have seemed churlish to refuse. Besides, she'd wondered what she would do with her hair. The comb Mrs. Longfeather had given her was the wrong color.

"We want both you and Bo to have a good time at the dance."

"If he doesn't change his mind." He hadn't been there since Sunday.

"Why would he change his mind?"

Louisa could think of a dozen reasons but mostly because, after fleeing his uncertainty about the triplets, there was no other reason to return. "He was coerced into agreeing to take me."

Molly laughed until she had to wipe her eyes. "No one coerces Bo. If he agreed, it's because he wants to take you. Don't worry—he'll be here on Saturday."

Louisa's relief lasted until Molly left and then her uncertainties returned. Day after day, Bo did not come. How had she grown to expect him every evening? Didn't he realize she needed help putting the babies to bed? Where was he? Would he really take her to the dance? Or would he pretend he forgot?

Her days were full with caring for the triplets and running the house. Thankfully Annie came every second day or she wouldn't have been able to manage.

By Friday, she barely managed to hide the quivering of her insides. Would Bo take her to the dance or would she sit waiting hopelessly alone? Why was she pinning so much on this one event? Neither of them wanted anything more than what they'd had during the few days of taking care of the triplets together.

Except the depth of her wanting was real. Guilt

drove her to the bedroom where the triplets slept. How soon before Mother arrived and all this pretending would end? The last letter they'd received said Mother was improving and they hoped to resume their journey soon.

Mrs. Jamieson drove into town early Saturday afternoon and bundled up the babies and their belongings to take to the Big Rock Ranch. Mary Gillen, along with her ten-year-old son, accompanied her to help get the triplets safely to the ranch.

Louisa tried to calm her insides with the assurance that Bo must be planning to come if his housekeeper was here. But her uncertainty prevented her from asking Mrs. Jamieson for news of her boss.

The kindly housekeeper squeezed Louisa's hands. "You enjoy yourself at the dance and don't give the babies another thought. Between me and Mary, they'll be perfectly fine."

Louisa stopped worrying about her own situation. It was selfish in light of the needs of the triplets. "Still no word of the mother."

Mrs. Jamieson's countenance sagged. "It's sad but I fear they won't locate her. A person can disappear for good if they want to."

What would become of the little boys? But she didn't voice the question aloud and waved goodbye as they drove away.

She glanced up and down the street. People hustled from place to place. She looked in the direction of the fairground, where she'd observed a tent being set up the day before, but she could see nothing of it from the doorstep. Her shoulders rose and fell with a soft sigh and she turned back inside.

She wandered throughout the house, putting things to right. In the bedroom where the babies had slept, she stared at the mattress and then the bed. How long before the mattress would be taken out and Mother would be using the bed?

She paused at the spare room where Amy and Lawrence would sleep until they left to travel west. She tidied Father's room, then finally allowed herself to go to her own small room. She stood in front of the dress that she'd pressed to perfection. The earbobs and hair comb sat on top of her dresser. Was she foolish to think of donning all this fine apparel? The remaining hours until the dance started lay before her like a black cave. What was she to do to distract her thoughts?

Father came from the office. "I'm going to check on those from the train accident." The dozen people injured had suffered broken bones, cuts and various other things. However, nothing really serious, which was amazing considering their wagon had been hit by a train.

"Do you want me to come with you?" It would pass the afternoon and perhaps take long enough she'd have a good excuse for missing the dance.

"There's no need. I will have supper with one of the families, so don't make me anything." With that he left.

Now she really had nothing to do but wonder if Bo would show up or not.

Worrying and fretting was wrong. She would not allow herself to do so and she took her Bible to the table, made tea and sat down to read. The quiet was so pervasive she kept looking up to see what was the matter. But she determinedly stayed there and continued to read even though the words skimmed over her brain without making sense. Then some familiar words caught her attention.

Fear not: for I have redeemed thee, I have called thee by thy name; thou art Mine.
When thou passest through the waters, I will be with thee; and through the rivers, they shall not overflow thee: when thou walkest through the fire, thou shalt not be burned; neither shall the flame kindle upon thee.

She chuckled. A dance was hardly a flood or a fire, but whatever happened tonight, God was with her and that was enough.

Mealtime approached. It seemed strange to have only herself to prepare food for, but she made a sandwich of cheese and leftover roast beef Mercy Green had delivered earlier. Enough to sustain her should she end up dancing the night away. She grinned at her foolishness.

The sandwich was barely gone when someone knocked. She jolted to her feet. It was too early for Bo to have come for her, but if he had, what would she do? She took one step toward the door, then turned and took one toward the bedroom. The knock came again. "Louisa?"

She sagged with relief. That was Molly's voice. Opening the door, she saw the woman in a fine dress in a golden color, her hair fancy. "You're beautiful." Her cheeks burned at being so forward.

Molly grinned. "Thank you. Daisy and I are here to help you get ready."

She noticed Molly's younger sister behind her, also looking beautiful in a rich royal blue gown. "But—" Nothing more came forth. Hadn't she done this very thing for Amy many times? Helped her prepare for an outing? Amy wasn't here but these ladies had offered. She gladly accepted, though she wondered if they would have allowed her to refuse. She'd learned that women out here had very strong opinions about things, and once they made up their minds…well, there wasn't any point in arguing.

The pair hustled her into the bedroom. They helped slip the dress over her head. Then Molly pulled her to the kitchen and told her to sit. Daisy brushed out Louisa's hair, sweeping it up to the top of her head and pinning it in place. Louisa could feel strands falling down to her shoulders. Molly took over, curling the strands with a hot curling iron.

When they were done, they stood in front of Louisa and looked at her from all angles. Seemingly satisfied, Daisy took the fancy comb and put it at the top. Then she led Louisa to a mirror. Louisa stared. Was that really her?

"What if Bo has changed his mind?" This would seem so foolish. So vain.

Both the ladies hugged her. "He'll be here," they assured her.

A knock came at the door. Louisa's heart leaped to her throat. She couldn't move. Couldn't think. Was it really Bo coming to escort her to the dance?

Molly, feeling sorry for her, went to the door and

opened it to let in her husband, CJ. Calvin Barlow followed on his heels, eyes for Daisy only.

Louisa held her breath as the shadow of a third man remained at the door. Molly took CJ's arm, Daisy took Calvin's and they exited.

Bo stepped into the light and Louisa forgot how to breathe.

Bo stared at the vision of loveliness before him. Had she grown more beautiful in the days he'd forced himself to stay away? After the frustration of looking after the babies, he knew he must stop pretending that they could have a future together. That he could allow himself to think of being a family man. He'd argued with himself daily about going to town. Someone should help her with the babies. Annie would. Or maybe Brandon. The idea of Brandon stepping into Bo's place scratched at his insides.

She didn't need Bo. Was better off without him.

He would have avoided going to the dance, but Mrs. Jamieson made sure word of his promise got around, and everywhere he turned, someone mentioned it.

"Taking that gal to the dance," Clint said, his voice low and lazy, "is right fine of you."

Bo grunted a response. He wasn't about to engage in conversation with his foreman about Louisa.

CJ came by to discuss another meeting of the Lone Star Cowboy League. "Molly says Louisa is excited about the dance. Molly's ma took her a dress she'd adjusted to fit Louisa. Molly says Louisa will be like a queen in it."

Bo refrained from pointing out that Louisa looked

fine in a soiled apron with her hair tousled from caring for the triplets. But seeing her now, he realized how wrong he could be. His mouth was dry; he couldn't make his tongue work.

She lowered her gaze. "I'm overdressed, aren't I?"

He swallowed hard, ordered words to leave his mouth. "You're lovely. I will be the envy of every man at the dance."

The pink stealing up her cheeks was his reward.

Doc Clark picked that moment to step from his office. He ground to a halt and stared at his daughter. "Louisa," he said, his voice warm with approval, "you look so much like your mother did at that age."

Louisa again blossomed like a rose.

The doc kissed her on the cheek and shook Bo's hand. "You two go have a good time." He glanced around. "The triplets have gone with your housekeeper?"

Bo answered in the affirmative. "She was thrilled to have them. Said it was far too long since she'd had babies to tend." He didn't add that Mrs. Jamieson had given him a hard look and reminded him the house would never be a home until there were babies in it. Instead, he crooked his arm to Louisa. "Shall we?"

Her cheeks still pink, she placed her palm on his forearm as they left the house. He'd borrowed Mrs. J.'s buggy, at her insistence, and helped Louisa aboard, his hands lingering at her waist, and he suspected she grasped his hand a moment longer than necessary.

He didn't mind in the least. Tonight was for enjoyment.

They arrived at the fairgrounds, where a goodly crowd gathered. He paid admission and led Louisa to one of the tables encircling the dance floor. The band struck up a tune. "May I?" He held out his hand and led her to the dance floor.

The music carried their feet over the wood platform, but his attention dwelled on the woman in his arms. Everything about her picked at the locks on his heart. She lifted brown eyes to him and he forgot everything but the pleasure of this moment. She danced, light as a feather, her rose-colored dress swirling about her ankles.

The silver comb in her hair caught the light like a dull moon. "You look very nice," he murmured, leaning close to whisper in her ear.

"Thank you, kind sir." She tipped her head to speak close to his ear. "You look mighty fine yourself."

He grinned from ear to ear. "Mrs. Jamieson made sure I cleaned up really good. Even checked behind my ears."

She chuckled. "I do the same with the triplets."

At her words, their gazes locked and something sweet and everlasting filled his heart. A voice in the distant recesses of his mind warned him this was not permanent. This was only a dance. The music stopped. They quit dancing, their gazes still locked.

He didn't know how long they stood thus until Brandon nudged him. "Move along, brother."

Bo pulled Louisa's arm through his and led her back to their table.

Brandon followed and asked to dance with Louisa.

She shot a look at Bo that he could only interpret as protest. He knew without a doubt that she wanted to dance this dance and perhaps every dance with him, and while Brandon led her to the dance floor, he leaned back, a satisfied grin on his face.

He made sure he got the next dance.

Out of good manners, he danced with several of the other ladies and allowed her to dance with his friends, but he claimed as many numbers as he could without drawing undue attention to them.

All too soon the last dance was announced and he drew her to the floor, her hand firmly in his. He looked down into her flushed face. She had danced every dance. But not until she was in his arms had he seen heightened color, and he tucked the knowledge into a little corner of his heart right next to his collection of good memories.

The music ended, the musicians packed up and the crowd drifted away. He took his time about leaving, not that he would admit that he hoped they would avoid the crowd and he could have her all to himself. But he made sure to speak to all the members of the Cowboy League, have a word with Clint and seek out Brandon, all with Louisa firmly attached to his arm.

By the time they returned to the buggy, the other conveyances had departed and the last of the cowboys were mounting up to leave.

He came to the side of the buggy to assist Louisa, only neither of them made a move toward climbing to the seat. "Did you have a good time?"

Only the lantern on the side of the buggy provided any light. But it was enough.

She nodded. "I had a wonderful time. Thank you for taking me."

"Any of the men would have been honored to be your escort."

"I'm afraid I find that hard to believe."

He touched the pearls at her ears. "Don't you think it's about time you started believing in yourself?"

Her eyes, dark and unreadable in the low light, met his. Even though he couldn't see clearly, he felt her searching his gaze for his meaning.

He bent closer. "Louisa, you are a beautiful woman, but more than that, you have a beautiful spirit. I am honored to know you." He waited to see how she would respond and rejoiced when she lifted her face to him.

"I want to kiss you." His words sounded husky even to his own ears. Perhaps tonight, after dancing together, it would be appropriate to offer one kiss.

"You may." She leaned toward him.

He wrapped his arms about her and drew her to his chest, forcing her to tip her head back. Her arms slipped about his waist, one palm pressed to his back. He lowered his lips to hers, tasting a sweetness that flooded through him to every cell of his body. She leaned into his kiss.

He eased back and stared at her big eyes. He loved sweets, he had enjoyed deliciously cold water from a spring, but neither compared to the absolute, undeniable pleasure of holding her in his arms and feeling the touch of her lips on his.

"Louisa," he murmured, her name a joy on his tongue.

"That was nice." Her mouth formed an O. "I shouldn't have said that."

Low laughter came from deep inside. "You can't take it back and I'm never going to forget it."

She looked at his chest, then slowly, so very slowly that he caught his breath in anticipation, she brought her head up, her eyes locked with his. She cupped her hand to the back of his head and pulled him down for another kiss, one that again flooded him with the sweetness of roses and candy and honey and everything sugary he'd ever encountered.

She ended the kiss and bent her forehead to his chin.

He would have been content to stay like that forever but a dog barked and someone hollered at it to be quiet. It was late. Time to get Louisa home before her father came looking for her.

He turned her toward the buggy and lifted her to the seat. He stood at her side looking up at her. She met his look, a tiny smile upon her lips.

Feeling rather pleased with himself, he climbed up beside her and drove back to town. He should not have kissed her. But he didn't regret it. He couldn't let himself care for her in a special way. Neither of them wanted it. Might she be persuaded to change her mind? Every turn of the wheel, every beat of the horse hooves beat out an insistent argument that he couldn't ignore nor could he pretend he wished it could be otherwise. It didn't matter if she changed her mind. He couldn't change his. Could he?

He let the horse take his good old time along the trail toward town. Golden fireflies of lights danced from some of the windows in the homes they passed. Others were dark, the residents retired for the night as if they were done with the day. Louisa pressed to his side, her arm around his, her palm on his forearm.

On his part, he didn't want the evening to end. What could he do to extend it?

They reached the street without him finding an excuse to delay taking her home and he turned toward the doctor's house.

Louisa sat forward as the house came into view. "There's a lamp lit in every room. There's been some sort of emergency. I must get home to help Father."

"We're almost there." He flicked the reins to increase the horse's pace. No other conveyance stood before the house, leading him to believe the visitors, whoever they were, had parked in the back. He leaped off as soon as they stopped and lifted her down. He wasn't letting her face this alone, and followed her to the door.

She threw it open. The doctor came from the room where the triplets normally slept, his face drawn.

"Father, what's wrong?"

Chapter Fifteen

One look at her father and Louisa knew to expect the worst sort of news but nothing prepared her for his announcement.

"Your mother is here. Amy and Lawrence too. They are all very sick. I don't know how they managed to get here in their condition." Tension crackled from his voice.

"Mother? Sick?" While Louisa had been out dancing and dreaming. Kissing and wishing.

"Very sick." He shuddered. "I fear the worst."

Louisa pulled the comb from her hair and the earbobs from her ears. She'd return them at first opportunity. She clenched her fingers around them. Fripperies. Symbols of foolishness. The whole evening had been one of foolishness. She should have been home preparing the bedroom for her mother.

"What can I do to help?" Bo asked.

She told herself she'd forgotten he had followed her into the house. But the awful truth remained that she felt his presence keenly and an errant portion of her brain lingered on the pleasures of the outing with him.

Father spoke before she could sort her tangled thoughts. "I fear what they have is contagious. The babies won't be able to stay here even if we had space and time to care for them. Can you see that arrangements are made for them?"

"I'll call an emergency meeting of the Lone Star Cowboy League for tomorrow after church. Mrs. J. will keep them tonight."

Louisa had never had a chance to kiss them goodbye. Hadn't expected they wouldn't be returning. Things were happening too fast. "I'll check on Mother." But she wore a borrowed gown. "I must change first."

She took a step toward her room. Bo caught her arm. She faced him. Saw the concern in his eyes. Lowered her gaze to his mouth. Only a few minutes ago she'd enjoyed kissing him, had even allowed herself to forget her responsibilities. The time for dreaming and forgetting had come crashing to an end. "Thank you for a lovely evening. But now you must go. I have to take care of Mother and Amy."

Father had disappeared into Mother's room, so Louisa could speak from her heart. "Tonight was only pretend. We both know that."

His eyes caught the golden glow of the nearby lamp and reflected it back like moonlight. His eyebrows went up and then settled into place again. "I haven't forgotten. I'll see to the babies. Is there anything I need to take?"

She gathered up the scattered bits of baby clothing, tossed them into the basket and handed it to him. She forced herself to release her hold on the basket.

Father called her name.

No more time for dreaming. No more time for pretending or wishing or wanting. Her responsibilities, her life, her future lay right here. "Coming," she called. She took a step back from Bo. "Goodbye." Not waiting for him to leave, she hurried to Mother's room, her footsteps slowing fractionally when she heard his soft answer.

"Good night."

She took one look at her mother and her heart smote her. Mother lay pale as the sheets, a bruised look around her mouth. The discoloration indicated how hard Mother's heart worked under the strain of her illness. "Mother, I'm sorry I wasn't here when you arrived."

Mother's struggle to breathe made talking almost impossible. She could only flutter her fingers from the bedcovers to indicate she heard. Her eyes were shadowed and wide with fear.

"Stay with her," Father said, "while I get some of her medicine." Years ago, Father had concocted a mixture that eased her breathing, and he hurried to his office to fetch it.

Louisa sang as she wet a cloth in the nearby basin of water and gently sponged Mother's brow.

Father returned and gave Mother a spoonful of medicine. "I'll stay with her. Would you check on Amy and Lawrence?"

She stopped in her own room long enough to exchange the fancy dress for a plain cotton one that she wouldn't have to worry about soiling, then crossed to the other bedroom and sucked in a deep breath. Amy lay curled on her side, every bit as pale as their mother.

Lawrence sat on the mattress that had been in Mother's room, a basin in his hands. He looked slightly greenish.

It was he who spoke. "Sorry to show up in this condition. We thought everyone was well enough to travel, but both Amy and your mother took a turn for the worse yesterday. I could think of nothing but to get here as soon as possible."

"You did the right thing." She sat beside Amy and stroked her head. "Are your lungs tight?"

"No. But I'm weak as a kitten." Even her voice was weak.

"You'll be fine now. I'll take good care of you."

Amy squeezed her hand. "I know."

Louisa hurried away to get warm water to sponge bath her sister and mother. She made a soothing honey-sweetened tea for the three invalids. A little later, Lawrence sprawled on the mattress asleep. Mother dozed with Father at her side. Amy closed her eyes and breathed deeply.

Not knowing how long they would stay that way, Louisa lay on her own bed, fully clothed, ready to jump up at any moment.

Her call came before dawn.

"Louisa." Amy's weak voice barely reached Louisa's room yet she sprang to her feet, instantly alert. She hurried to tend her sister, taking her fresh water, holding her head to help her drink.

Father tiptoed out of Mother's room. "She's resting for now." He shook his head.

Louisa understood he worried that Mother's heart would not hold out. "I'll keep watch. You go rest a bit." They both knew it was only a matter of time before someone outside this house would need his attention. An hour later, the someone came. The doctor was needed at a nearby ranch.

"I'll take care of them," Louisa said, tipping her head to indicate the invalids.

"I know you will. They couldn't be in better hands." Father took his bag and went to the waiting buggy.

They couldn't be in better hands. Her father knew he could trust her to make sure Mother and Amy got well. And Lawrence too, though he had a much stronger constitution than the other two.

She made a thin gruel for them and spoon-fed both her sister and mother. Lawrence took one look at the food and gagged.

"I don't think I'm ready for food yet."

Louisa rushed from one room to the next, afraid to leave either of her patients for more than a few minutes. Her steps took her to the kitchen between the bedrooms to make tea, get fresh water, prepare a basin to sponge one or the other.

She paused in front of the icebox. If she had a chicken she could make soup for them. But she had none. When Father returned, she would slip away to the store and order a chicken.

But wait. It was Sunday. The store wouldn't be open.

She glanced out the window at the sound of a wagon. People were arriving for the worship service. Bo had mentioned a meeting of the Cowboy League after the service. This was the Sunday they held their after-church social hour. Would the league members meet at that time? Who would take the babies? Would anyone let her know? Would Bo come to see how she was?

Shaking her head to clear her senses, she turned back to the task at hand. There'd be no Sunday service for her this day.

And there'd be no more thinking that Bo had any reason to visit her.

She made a light broth of vegetables for the invalids. Mother was so weak she could not feed herself, so Louisa did it patiently and with a tinge of guilt as if she should blame herself for Mother's condition. With part of her brain, she knew she carried no blame, but with another, she feared she would fail in providing good enough care.

Amy would have refused any nourishment if Louisa hadn't fed her. Lawrence continued to turn green at the mention of food.

She glanced out the window after she'd taken care of the noon meal. Wagons, buggies and horses still waited for their owners. The yard behind the church held scattered groups of men, and children raced about after each other. The women must be inside or sitting out of the sun. Her gaze skimmed the gathered people. Neither Bo nor Brandon were among them. She refused to acknowledge an ache to see Bo and turned away from the window.

The hours sped past as she tended the ill. When Amy didn't need something, she stayed at Mother's bedside, afraid to leave her alone lest she was unable to catch her breath.

Busy as she was, she strained toward any sound to indicate a visitor. When the anticipated knock came, she ground to a halt halfway between Mother's room and the kitchen. Her fingers clenched the basin of water in her hands. Her heart jumped, landing halfway up her throat. He had come.

She left the basin on the table and rushed to open the door and stared at the caller. Somehow she pulled herself together. "Mercy." She glanced over her shoulder. Should she invite the woman in?

"I won't stay. I understand you have your hands full with your family, but I wanted to let you know that the triplets have been taken care of."

Louisa nodded. "Who?"

"David McKay has hired a nanny to help for the triplets." She chuckled. "I think he's hoping that helping with the babies will keep Maggie out of trouble."

"I'm glad they're at least staying together." Though she wondered how safe they would be with the mischievous Maggie assisting with their care.

"Mr. McKay insisted on it." Mercy patted Louisa's arm. "I'll leave you now."

Louisa glanced up and down the street. Only a few stragglers lingered about and none of them was Bo. She closed the door. She'd made it clear to him that their time of pretending to be something neither of them wanted to be was over. But she could not deny the thin wedge of disappointment prying into her heart.

Dismissing the foolish futile yearnings, she turned back to her tasks.

Over the next few days, she worked feverishly to see that the ill were fed nourishing broths, to see that Mother—and to a much less extent, Amy—was comfortable. She changed the bedding as it got soiled and scrubbed it, hung it out to dry. It was important that the sheets were clean and dry on a daily basis. The work offered an added bonus. It almost kept her from having time to think of Bo and how much she missed the triplets.

Bo had plenty of things to occupy his time. Big Rock Ranch needed his attention. The Lone Star Cowboy League had decisions to make. There were cows to check on. A horse to work with. And Cash liked to get out and run. Bo took him out for a jaunt every day. It had been a week since he'd seen Louisa and her words still rang in his ears. *We both know it's only pretend.*

He'd been telling himself that for days but to hear it spoken with such firm finality didn't sit well.

He let Cash stretch out, his legs galloping up the miles.

But she was right. He couldn't trust himself to develop a healthy, safe relationship and he'd grown perilously close to thinking it might be possible.

He and his horse crested the hill, the ranch buildings below them, and he slowed the animal to cool him. A horse was tied to the post in front of the house. He recognized it as the one Brandon usually rented from the livery barn and his heart immediately clenched. Had his brother come with bad news?

He let Cash lengthen his pace into a trot and rode directly to the barn. One of the cowhands was nearby and he called to him. "Rub Cash down and take care of him." He crossed the yard in long strides.

Brandon sat on the veranda waiting for him.

"What brings you this way?"

Brandon pointed to the chair beside him. "Can't a man come to visit?"

Bo perched on the chair. "Been missing me, have ya?"

Brandon gave a playful punch to Bo's shoulder. "Thought you might be needing some comfort about now."

"Huh? Me? Why?" He eyed his twin. "You got something you're wanting to say?"

"Maybe." Brandon leaned back, his boots on the nearest post. "I haven't seen you at the doctor's house since last Saturday."

"I haven't been there." He leaned back too, imitating his brother's pose.

"Then I guess you haven't heard."

"I'm guessing you'll get around to telling me when you're good and ready."

Brandon lowered all four chair legs to the wooden floor with a crash. "You got any interest in Louisa?"

Bo stayed where he was, staring into the sky. He wouldn't meet Brandon's gaze, knowing Brandon would read Bo like a page in a book.

"I told her about our father and was clear that I had no intention of ever marrying." Though she'd almost convinced him that he didn't have to turn out to be like his father. "Did you ever stop to think that we inherited our musical ability from our father?"

Brandon didn't respond for a moment. "I guess it's of no interest to you, then, to know Louisa is ill."

Bo's chair crashed to all four feet and he stared at Brandon. "Sick? How sick?"

"Her father came and asked for prayer for her."

Bo clattered to his feet. "Why didn't you tell me sooner?"

"I thought you didn't have any interest in her."

"Well, you thought wrong." He saw the cowhand who had taken care of Cash saunter across the yard and called to him. "Saddle up my horse."

Brandon rose to stand beside Bo. "Where do you think you're going?"

"To see Louisa."

"I doubt the doctor is going to let you into her room."

"Then I'll wait."

The cowhand brought Cash to the house. Brandon followed Bo down the steps and swung into his saddle at the same time as Bo swung to Cash's back. As one, they turned the horses toward town, Brandon staying at Bo's side.

"Brother, it seems to me you aren't being honest with yourself," Brandon observed after a bit.

Bo grunted. He didn't want to discuss it.

"Seems Louisa matters more to you than you care to admit."

Another grunt would have to suffice. Bo was well aware that his actions were at odds with what he wanted to believe. He'd deal with that difference after he'd made sure Louisa was okay.

Brandon badgered him to talk until Bo said with some disgust, "Can't you let me work this out on my own?"

Brandon laughed heartily. "Sure thing. But if you feel the need to talk…"

"Have I given you the impression I want to talk?"

His annoying twin brother laughed again. "I've hardly been able to get a word in edgewise."

They reached town and Brandon turned off at the parsonage. "I'm here if you need me."

Bo went on to the doctor's residence and banged on the door.

Doc Clark opened the door, his eyes narrowing at the look on Bo's face.

"Where is she?" He pushed into the room. A young woman he took to be Louisa's sister, Amy, sat on the sofa holding a book in her lap. She seemed a little pale but other than that seemed well and healthy. A young man lounged beside her. No doubt her husband. In a wheelchair sat a frail, pale older woman.

Bo snatched off his hat. "Mrs. Clark, I presume." He tipped his head toward the others. "I've come to see Louisa."

The sister's eyes, as brown as Louisa's, sparkled.

Doc grabbed Bo's arm and steered him toward the door. "Louisa is too sick for visitors."

Bo dug in his heels. "How sick is she?"

Amy followed her father. "She's worn herself out caring for us. I expect she'll recover in a few days."

"I'll be next door. Will you let me know when she can receive visitors?" He looked at Amy, hoping for an ally.

"We'll send a message." She took her father's elbow and he saw an instant softening in the doctor's countenance. "Won't we, Father."

Doc nodded. "But not before she is much stronger." He closed the door between Bo and those in the house.

Bo stared at the barrier, then ground about and

crossed to the parsonage, where he strode in without knocking. "They won't let me see her."

Brandon glanced up from sewing a button on a shirt. "Warned you they wouldn't."

Bo crossed the floor in long strides, then turned and crossed it the other way. Back and forth he went until Brandon stuck out his leg to stop him. "You're stomping holes in the floor."

Bo threw himself into the nearest wooden kitchen chair. "I need to know she'll be okay."

"Brother, I think what you need to know is what your intentions toward her are."

"I—" He swallowed. "You know—" He rubbed at his neck. "I can't—"

"Seems to me you have. The question is, what are you going to do about it?"

"I'm going to—" He let his hands dangle between his knees. "I don't know what I'm going to do."

"Then I suggest you figure it out before you see her."

He grabbed his hat and strode from the house. In the yard, he looked around. Where was he to go? He looked down the trail to the fairground, now empty and dusty, and strode in that direction.

Every step brought a memory. Louisa with the babies. Louisa flushed and shy. Louisa dancing, her eyes full of stars. The two of them kissing after the dance.

He could no longer deny his feelings for her.

But it didn't erase his fears that he wouldn't make a good husband or a good father. He reached the fairgrounds and stopped beside the lone tree. Her words returned to him.

She thought he had a choice. She believed he practiced kindness, gentleness and self-control in his life.

Is the God who made this vast land too small to rule in your heart?

She had faith in him.

Could he find that same faith in himself?

He covered every inch of the fairgrounds as he wrangled with his thoughts. The sun began its evening descent and he realized how long he'd been away. What if a message had come from next door and he'd not been there to receive it? He raced back to town.

Brandon assured him there had been no message.

"I'm not leaving until I hear something."

Brandon shrugged. "Suit yourself." He pulled food out of the icebox. They shared a simple meal. "The triplets are doing well at the McKay ranch."

"Good to hear." Bo decided he would visit the babies as soon as he knew Louisa was okay.

By bedtime, no word had come from next door, but Bo wouldn't go to bed until every light had gone out in the doctor's house. Sleep did not come easily as he fought an inner war.

Dare he speak of his feelings to Louisa? Was it too great a risk to think of a future with her? Did he have enough faith in himself to consider marriage?

In the darkest part of the night the answer came. It wasn't necessary to trust himself. He had to trust God. Exactly as Louisa had said. Kindness, gentleness and self-control were gifts their Heavenly Father bestowed. He had to believe that they were his.

He fell asleep and didn't stir until pink fingers of dawn traced across the sky. His heart racing with anticipation, he bolted from the bed and rushed to the kitchen, where Brandon had coffee ready and poured Bo a cup.

"No message yet," Brandon said, and Bo plunked down at the table.

"Waiting is hard."

"Yep. It's Sunday. Church this morning."

"I guess it will help pass the time."

Brandon chuckled. "Glad to know what purpose I serve in your life."

Bo leaned back, grinning at his brother. "I'll do my best to listen but I can't promise not to miss a word or two."

"Your thoughts are next door, aren't they? Have you figured things out?"

"I hope so." He told Brandon of his thoughts.

His brother squeezed his shoulder. "God is sufficient even for our past."

He and Brandon went to the church a little later. Bo did his best to keep his mind on Brandon's words, but time and again, his thoughts wandered. Was Louisa getting better? Or worse? How long would he have to wait until he could see her? Talk to her? Tell her of his change of heart?

He waited all that day and into the next before Doc came over. "She's weak but able to be up. She said she'd like to speak with you."

Bo was on his feet and practically pushing the older man out the door before him.

He stepped inside the house and saw her. Pale but as beautiful as ever. He wanted to fall at her knees and confess his love but her mother and sister and brother-in-law were all in attendance. Louisa introduced them. "Would you like tea or something?"

He twisted his hat. "I'd like to talk to you, if I may. Are you up to a little walk?" Doc made a protesting noise.

"Or we could go to the church."

"I'd like that," she said at his last suggestion. She pushed to her feet and he drew her arm through his, holding her firmly lest she feel any weakness.

Neither of them spoke until they reached the church and were settled in a pew. "How are you feeling?" he asked.

"Much better, thank you."

"Your sister says you wore yourself out caring for them."

She studied her fingers, twisting together in her lap. "I did what I had to do."

He leaned back, his shoulder against hers, and gathered his thoughts. "Louisa, I was so worried when I heard you were sick and they wouldn't let me see you."

She shifted to watch him.

He turned to meet her look full on. "It made me think about things." He took her hands and pulled them to his chest. "I realize the most frightening thing was not having my father's blood flowing through me but losing you. I will trust God to help me be the kind of man I should be. Louisa, I love you. Will you marry me?"

She slipped one hand free and stroked his cheek. "I'm so glad you are free of that fear because you are the most gentle and most kind man. You cared for three babies who weren't even yours. I've watched you deal with conflicts with nothing but patience when others are wanting to throw fists. I'm guessing any of those would have sent your father into a fury. But not you." She grasped his chin as if she feared he would turn his gaze from her. "You are not your father."

He nodded, his throat too tight to speak. Hearing those words from her healed a wound that had festered for so many years he had grown used to the pain. Only now that it was gone did he realize the burden it had become. He lowered his head and caught her lips in a teasing kiss. Then, smiling down at her, he repeated his request. "Louisa Clark, I love you. Will you marry me?"

She pulled back, her eyes dark. "Bo, I love you more than words can say but I can't marry you. At least not now. I can't leave my family. I almost lost them with this illness. They need me and I will always be there for them. Amy has her life now but I will take care of Mother as long as she needs me."

He pulled her close and pressed her head to the hollow of his shoulder. "Then I will wait for you. Forever, if I must."

She shuddered and a sob escaped her.

He tilted her head back to stare at her. "Louisa, did I say something wrong? Tell me and I will correct it."

She shook her head and struggled to speak. "Wes said I wasn't worth waiting for."

Her old beau. "He was blind, or stupid, or both. But he was wrong. You are worth waiting for. I will be here to see you every chance I get. I will take you to the ranch when you feel you can leave your family. I will wait and count it a blessing." He kissed her thoroughly to prove his point. She wrapped her arms about his neck and clung to him long after their kiss had ended.

He planted kisses on her hair, breathing in the fresh-air scent of her. He longed to share every moment of every day with her, but until that day arrived, he would spend as much time with her as her circumstances allowed and do his best to make her days pleasant.

Chapter Sixteen

Louisa pressed her head to Bo's shoulder, safe in the circle of his arms. He promised to wait for her. However long it took. His words sang through her heart. A man who loved her enough to stay by her side even though she must tend her family. God had blessed her beyond her greatest dream. She could wait, serving her family faithfully, knowing Bo would stay at her side.

They sat thus quietly talking of various things. Louisa was anxious to hear about the triplets. Bo told her of some of the needs coming before the Cowboy League.

Finally, reluctantly, she shifted forward. "I must get back to my family." Guilt washed up her. "I've been away too long." What if someone had come for Father and she hadn't heard? She bolted to her feet, but before she could run back to her responsibilities, Bo caught her hand and turned her to face him.

"Is there anything I can do to help?"

Her heart turned to warm honey. "Knowing you love me is enough."

He caught her face between his hands and kissed

her so sweetly it brought a sting of tears to her eyes. How could he ever think he would be like his father?

Taking her hand, he led her from the church, across to her home. He paused at the door to kiss her again. She clung to him a moment and then, her eyes lingering to the last possible moment, she opened the door.

He smiled. "I'll be back."

She nodded and closed the door between them. Only then did she turn to face her family.

"Father was called away." Amy hovered over Mother, who seemed even paler than she had been when Louisa left. Amy held the bottle of medicine.

"Mother." Louisa sprang forward.

Amy spared Louisa a quick glance. "She's okay now. I gave her some medicine."

Did Louisa hear accusation in her sister's voice? "I'm sorry. I shouldn't have stayed away so long."

She hustled to the kitchen and began making another pot of soup. After a few minutes, she had to sit down to catch her breath and wait for the pounding of her heart to subside. When she started to rise again, Amy gently pushed at her shoulder.

"I'll look after the soup. You rest."

"You've been ill."

"So have you and you are barely back on your feet."

"I'm fine. I've always been strong." But Louisa reluctantly allowed Amy to finish the soup, only because she was too weak to do it herself. However, she didn't miss the furtive glances between Amy and her husband. Were they annoyed that she had been away so long? She ducked her head to hide her smile. She didn't regret a moment of it. She was loved well enough for someone to wait for her to be free to marry.

"Louisa?" Amy's voice brought her back to the moment. How long had she been smiling so contentedly?

"Yes?"

"Here's some soup. Sit up to the table to eat."

Louisa ate, and she helped with the housework. She tended Mother's needs. All the while, her heart secretly sang with joy. That night, she went to bed, pleasantly tired and beautifully content to know that Mother and Amy were growing stronger every day.

The next morning, she rose, anxious to face the day. She looked out the window at the bright sunshine and chuckled a little. Somehow she had the feeling she could make time pass more quickly by rushing into her work.

She was about to hurry to Mother's room when Father stepped out. "I should have checked on her earlier," she said by way of apology.

"You've been sick. You need your rest. Mother slept well."

Relieved to know no one suffered because of her weakness, Louisa prepared breakfast for everyone.

Mother insisted on joining them at the table. Louisa dished up food for everyone before she sat down.

Amy looked around the table. "Lawrence and I have an announcement to make."

Louisa knew they would be anxious to continue their journey west but she would miss them.

"We've decided we aren't going further."

Louisa stared. Had she heard right? Were they concerned about Amy's health? "You're getting stronger every day." She didn't want her sister to give up her dreams.

"Yes, I am. There's no need to coddle me anymore."

"Coddle?"

"I don't mean in a bad way but I fear I've been guilty of taking advantage of your good nature." She smiled at her husband. "Lawrence has helped me see that I'm capable of so much more than I've allowed myself to believe." She glanced at every member of the family. "We believe it's time for Louisa to follow her heart. Lawrence and I have decided to settle here. He's seen many opportunities. And I am going to look after Mother." She met Louisa's startled gaze. "You and Bo deserve every happiness and you shouldn't have to wait."

Louisa's mouth dropped open. She couldn't find a thing to say.

Amy ducked her eyes a moment. "I'm sorry. I went to the church to tell you Father was leaving and I overheard you and Bo talking. I slipped away immediately but I heard enough to understand you were telling him you couldn't marry because you had to take care of your family."

Mother gasped. "Louisa, I never want to stand between you and your happiness."

She took Mother's hands. "You wouldn't. I love taking care of you, and Bo understands. He will wait."

"You could get married and live here," Mother said.

"No. He's a rancher. That wouldn't work."

Amy held up her hand, "Did you forget what I said? I am going to look after Mother."

Louisa looked at her with some doubt.

Amy drew herself up. "It's time you stopped looking at me like I'm weak and useless. Didn't I help Mother while we traveled?"

"And she did fine," Mother assured them all.

"You got sick." Louisa wondered if they'd all forgotten that fact.

"So did you." Amy gave her a challenging look.

"So I did."

Father lifted a hand. "Amy is right. She's strong enough to care for Mother. Louisa will be close enough to visit and assure herself all is well. If Amy and Lawrence are settled in their own minds then I heartily approve." He gave Louisa a teasing smile. "I've seen you and Bo together."

Louisa sat back, trying to take it all in.

Lawrence grinned at her. "You better let Bo know, don't you think?"

Louisa couldn't think. Then the importance of the discussion hit her. She bolted to her feet.

"Maybe you should eat first," Amy said with a goodly dose of humor.

She nodded, waiting for Father to ask the blessing. She ate, though she couldn't have said what it was she put into her mouth.

"I'll get a buggy for you," Father said when they finished.

A few minutes later, she was on her way to Big Rock Ranch.

He'd been willing to wait.

Would he be willing to marry sooner rather than later?

She saw Bo riding Cash, heading toward the west.

He saw the buggy approach and turned to meet her. He wouldn't know who it was yet. She knew the moment he did. He spurred Cash into a gallop and didn't slow until he drew abreast.

"What's wrong?" He rode beside her.

She pulled the horse to a halt and faced him. "We don't have to wait." She let him digest the information, knew by the way his eyes gleamed that he understood her meaning.

He jumped from his horse, landing solidly on his feet, and reached up for her.

She gladly let him lift her down.

"Tell me what happened."

She relayed the events of the morning to him. As soon as he heard the news, he whooped and tossed his hat in the air, catching it and placing it on the seat of the buggy. He pulled her into his arms. "How soon can we be married?"

Rather than answer a question that would take a time of discussion, she stood on tiptoe and pulled his head down and kissed him thoroughly, her heart free to give and receive love.

They discussed the triplets. Both of them missed the babies. The triplets' mother had still not been found. The future of the babies remained unsettled.

"After we're married, if their mother hasn't been found, we could take them back," he said.

She thought about it. She would gladly give them a home, but she and Bo weren't married yet, and in the meantime… "They're settled in their new home. Would it be fair to move them again?" she asked.

Bo reluctantly agreed it wouldn't. "But we can visit

them often." It was later, her head resting on his chest, that they discussed when to marry and decided they would wait and see how her family felt about having a simple ceremony as soon as possible.

"I've waited a long time for you to come into my life," she murmured.

"No longer than I. Though in my case it wasn't so much waiting as running from the possibility of love and marriage. And all my running led straight to you." They kissed again.

Bo grew serious. "I want to do something. I want to pray and thank God for bringing you to me." He took her hands in his and bowed his head.

She bowed hers too, their foreheads touching.

"Father, God, You have brought us together and we are grateful. Here and now, I vow before You to do my best to trust You in our togetherness that I might be the sort of man Louisa deserves."

Her chest seemed too small to contain her swelling heart, her throat too tight to allow words out, but she managed to speak. She must add her prayer to his. "Heavenly Father, I thank You for a patient, kind man like Bo. One who was prepared to wait until I was free to marry. But oh, how grateful I am that You have worked things out so we don't have to wait. I vow, here and now and in this place, to love and honor this man every day of my life."

"Amen," they said in unison.

They smiled at each other.

"I feel like we've spoken our wedding vows," she whispered.

"Me too." He looked about. "This will be our special place from now on."

"I like that." Perhaps she'd plant a bush and some flowers here to mark the spot.

Epilogue

Louisa and Bo met with her parents in the living room of Louisa's home and presented their request to marry soon.

Mother smiled gently. "You should get married as soon as you want. There is no reason to delay that I can think of."

Father nodded. "You have my blessing."

They discussed options with her parents, then went next door to the parsonage to find Brandon. He placed a playful jab on Bo's shoulders and hugged Louisa.

"You're sure you can put up with this ugly man?"

Louisa chuckled. "Did you forget he looks exactly like you?"

Brandon pretended to look shocked. "Oh, well. So long as you don't mind."

"I don't mind in the least."

Bo pulled Louisa to his side. "How long before you can marry us?"

Brandon grinned. "I could do it tomorrow if you want."

Louisa and Bo looked at each other. She didn't have to say anything because he understood how she felt.

They turned to Brandon. "Can we do it Sunday?"

And so it was agreed.

Word soon got around, and as had happened at the Fourth of July dance, the women of the community immediately took over. A white wedding dress and a veil were delivered to the door. Louisa heard whispers about making the day special.

For her part, nothing could be more special than the event itself.

Sunday morning dawned bright and clear. They had decided to attend church as usual and then to slip away before the final hymn to prepare for the wedding ceremony, which Brandon would perform before the congregation left. Amy insisted on being the one to help Louisa prepare and at Louisa's insistence used the turquoise-and-silver hair comb to hold the veil in place.

She returned to the church on Father's arm. Bo stood at the front looking resplendent in his black suit and white shirt. She guessed he had borrowed the suit from Brandon.

They exchanged the customary vows but Louisa and Bo had earlier decided their private vows were more special.

Brandon hugged his brother and kissed Louisa on both cheeks before he turned to introduce them as Mr. and Mrs. Bo Stillwater.

The ladies had prepared a banquet. Somehow gifts appeared. The celebration lasted until evening and finally Bo and Louisa slipped away.

He drew to a stop before they reached the ranch

house and she saw he had built a little bench—big enough for two—and planted a bush where they had vowed their love for each other.

"It's beautiful," she said.

But nothing could rival the look of promise in his eyes. They were about to start a life of love and joy together.

* * * * *

Don't miss a single installment of
LONE STAR COWBOY LEAGUE:
MULTIPLE BLESSINGS

THE RANCHER'S SURPRISE TRIPLETS
by Linda Ford

THE NANNY'S TEMPORARY TRIPLETS
by Noelle Marchand

THE BRIDE'S MATCHMAKING TRIPLETS
by Regina Scott

Find more great reads at www.LoveInspired.com

Dear Reader,

As I wrote this story, my heart went out to the mother of these baby boys. A widowed mother trying to cope on her own with failing health and the care of three babies. My heart goes out in the same way to single mothers of today as they struggle with parenting alone, facing challenges and crises without a partner and as they live with the pain and disappointment that brought them to this place. My prayer is that each of you will find encouragement in friends and extended family, but most of all, I pray you will let God's love fill in the empty, lonely places of your heart.

You can learn more about my upcoming books and how to contact me at www.lindaford.org. I love to hear from my readers.

Blessings,

Linda Ford

COMING NEXT MONTH FROM
Love Inspired® Historical

Available May 9, 2017

THE NANNY'S TEMPORARY TRIPLETS
Lone Star Cowboy League: Multiple Blessings
by Noelle Marchand

After being jilted at the altar, Caroline Murray becomes the temporary nanny for David McKay's daughter and the orphaned triplet babies he's fostering. But when she starts to fall for the handsome widower, can she trust her heart?

HER CHEROKEE GROOM
by Valerie Hansen

When lovely Annabelle Lang is wrongly accused of murder after rescuing him, Cherokee diplomat Charles McDonald must do something! To save their lives—and their reputations— Charles proposes a marriage of convenience. But will this business proposition turn to one of true love?

AN UNLIKELY MOTHER
by Danica Favorite

When George Baxter, who is working undercover at his family's mine, finds a young boy who's lost his father, he's determined to reunite them. Caring for the boy with the help of Flora Montgomery, his former childhood nemesis, he instead discovers hope for a family of his own.

THE MARSHAL'S MISSION
by Anna Zogg

Hunting a gang of bank robbers, US Marshal Jesse Cole goes undercover as a ranch hand working for Lenora Pritchard. But when he discovers the widowed single mother he's slowly falling for may know something about the crime, can he convince her to tell him her secret?

LOOK FOR THESE AND OTHER LOVE INSPIRED BOOKS WHEREVER BOOKS ARE SOLD, INCLUDING MOST BOOKSTORES, SUPERMARKETS, DISCOUNT STORES AND DRUGSTORES.

LIHCNM0417

Get 2 Free Books,
Plus 2 Free Gifts —

just for trying the Reader Service!

Love Inspired. **HISTORICAL**

SPECIAL EXCERPT FROM

Love Inspired HISTORICAL

After her disastrous wedding that wasn't, Caroline Murray certainly isn't looking for love—but who could help falling for an adorable set of triplet orphan baby boys in need of a nanny? And how can she resist the handsome single dad who has taken the babies in?

Read on for a sneak preview of
THE NANNY'S TEMPORARY TRIPLETS,
the heartwarming continuation of the series
**LONE STAR COWBOY LEAGUE:
MULTIPLE BLESSINGS.**

"Why can't Miss Caroline be our nanny?"

All the grown-ups froze. David's eyebrows lifted. Had his darling daughter just said "our nanny," as in she'd consider herself one of Caroline's charges?

Caroline recovered from her surprise. "I'm sorry, sweetheart. I couldn't."

Maggie's eyes clouded. "Why not?"

"Well, I'm not going to be here very long for one thing. For another, I've never been a nanny before."

"Maybe not," Ida interjected. "But you certainly seemed to have a way with the triplets. I can tell from the quiet in this house that you finally got them to nap. Besides, we wouldn't need you for long. Only until this nanny David's trying to hire can get here."

"Ma, Miss Murray is here to visit her family, not work for ours. It wouldn't be right for us to impose on that."

"Of course we wouldn't want to impose, Caroline, but your family would be welcome to visit here as often as they want."

"Oh, I don't know." Caroline touched a hand to her throat

as she glanced around the kitchen. Her gaze landed on his, soft as a butterfly, filled with questions.

Did he want her to help them? The answer was an irrevocable no. Did he need her help? His mother's meaningful glare said yes. When he remained silent, Ida prompted, "We sure could use your help, Caroline. Couldn't we, David?"

He swallowed hard. "There's no denying that."

Caroline bit her lip. "Well, I'm sure my brother and sister-in-law could spare me now and then."

"We'd need you more than now and then." David offered up the potential difficulties with a little too much enthusiasm. "You'd have to stay here at the ranch. The triplets need to be fed during the night."

Caroline bit her lip. "What about the piano?"

David frowned. "What about it?"

"Would y'all mind ever so much if I played it now and then?"

Ida grinned. "Honey, you can play it as often as you want."

"In that case…" A smile slowly tilted Caroline's mouth. "Yes! I'd be happy to help out."

Maggie let out a whoop and reached for Caroline's hands. Somehow Caroline seemed to know that was her cue to dance the girl around the kitchen in a tight little circle. Ida sank into the nearest chair with pure relief. David opened his mouth to remind everyone that he was the man of the house with the final say on all of this, and he hadn't agreed to anything. Since doing so would likely accomplish nothing, he closed his mouth.

Don't miss
THE NANNY'S TEMPORARY TRIPLETS
by Noelle Marchand, available May 2017 wherever
Love Inspired® Historical books and ebooks are sold.

www.LoveInspired.com

SPECIAL EXCERPT FROM

Love Inspired

As a minister, blacksmith and guardian to two sets of twins,
widower Isaiah Stoltzfus needs help! Hiring Clara Ebersol
as a nanny is his answer—and the matchmakers' solution
to his single-dad life. It'll take four adorable children to
show them that together they'd make the perfect family.

Read on for a sneak preview of
A READY-MADE AMISH FAMILY
by **Jo Ann Brown,**
available May 2017 from Love Inspired!

"What's bothering you, Isaiah?" Clara asked when he
remained silent.

"I assumed you'd talk to me before you made any
decisions for the *kinder*." As soon as the words left his lips,
he realized how petty they sounded.

"I will, if that's what you want. But you hired me to take
care of them. I can't do that if I have to wait to talk to you
about everything."

He nodded. "I know. Forget I said that."

"We're trying to help the twins, and there are bound to be
times when we rub each other the wrong way."

"I appreciate it." He did. She could have quit; then what
would he have done? Finding someone else and disrupting
the *kinder* who were already close to her would be difficult.
"Why don't you tell me about these letters you and the twins
were writing?"

"They are a sort of circle letter with their family. From
what they told me earlier, they don't know any of them well,
and I doubt their *aenti* and grandparents know much about

them. This way, they can get acquainted, so when the *kinder* go to live with whomever will be taking them, they won't feel as if they're living with strangers."

He was astonished at her foresight. He'd been busy trying to get through each day, dealing with his sorrow and trying not to upset the grieving *kinder*. He hadn't given the future much thought. Or maybe he didn't want to admit that one day soon the youngsters would leave Paradise Springs. His last connection to his best friend would be severed. The thought pierced his heart.

Clara said, "If you'd rather I didn't send out the letters—"

"Send them," he interrupted and saw shock widening her eyes. "I'm sorry. I didn't mean to sound upset."

"But you are."

He nodded. "Upset and guilty. I can't help believing that I'm shunting my responsibilities off on someone else. I want to make sure Melvin's faith in me as a substitute *daed* wasn't misplaced. The twins deserve a *gut daed*, but all they have is me."

"You're doing fine under the circumstances."

"You mean when the funeral was such a short time ago?"

"No, I mean when every single woman in the district is determined to be your next wife, and your deacon is egging them on."

In spite of himself, Isaiah chuckled quietly. Clara's teasing was exactly what he needed. Her comments put the silliness into perspective. If he could remember that the next time Marlin or someone else brought up the topic of him marrying, maybe he could stop making a mess of everything. He hoped so.

Don't miss
A READY-MADE FAMILY by Jo Ann Brown,
available May 2017 wherever
Love Inspired® books and ebooks are sold.

www.LoveInspired.com

Turn your love of reading into rewards you'll love with
Harlequin My Rewards